A
Harlequin
Romance

WELCOME

TO THE WONDERFUL WORLD

of Harlequin Romances!

Interesting, informative and entertaining,
each Harlequin Romance portrays an appealing
love story. Harlequin Romances take you
to faraway places —— places with real people
facing real love situations —— and
you become part of their story.

As publishers of Harlequin Romances, we're extremely
proud of our books (we've been publishing
them since 1954). We're proud also that Harlequin
Romances are North America's most-read
paperback romances.

Eight new titles are released every month and are
sold at nearly all book-selling stores across
Canada and the United States.

A free catalogue listing all available Harlequin Romances
can be yours by writing to the

HARLEQUIN READER SERVICE,
M.P.O. Box 707, Niagara Falls, N.Y. 14302.
Canadian address: Stratford, Ontario, Canada.

or use order coupon at back of book.

We sincerely hope you enjoy reading
this Harlequin Romance.

Yours truly,

THE PUBLISHERS
    Harlequin Romances

A SINGING BIRD

by

STELLA FRANCES NEL

HARLEQUIN BOOKS

TORONTO ● WINNIPEG

Original hard cover edition published in 1970
by Mills & Boon Limited, 17-19 Foley Street,
London W1A 1DR, England.

© Stella Frances Nel 1970

Harlequin edition published January, 1972

SBN 373-01559-3

Reprinted May, 1972

Printed in Canada

CHAPTER 1

SAMANTHA MACDONALD flipped the latch, nudged the door with her knee and stepped into the room. Her bag landed squarely on one chair, she on another. Off came her shoes and she sank back with a relieved sigh, brushing back tendrils of windblown hair and closing her eyes.

Presently she opened them, to look directly across the room at the photograph that hung on the wall, and yearned, a deep ache in her breast, for the living presence of her beloved Mary-Gran.

For Grandmother MacDonald, affectionately called Mary-Gran by her niece, was now only a loved memory ... a photograph facing her across the small sitting-room. Mary-Gran, mothering and watching over her since that far, rainy night when a car had skidded on the wet surface of the road, and left six-year-old Samantha MacDonald orphaned. Mary MacDonald aged starkly with the death of her only son and daughter-in-law, but finally came sharply to terms with herself, to provide the love and upbringing that was sorely needed for her small granddaughter.

Now she too had gone ... Samantha had sat with her one dark night, holding two gentle, withered hands in her own warm clasp, and dearest Gran had smiled farewell, peaceful in the knowledge that her granddaughter was secure financially, with a home of her own. Her presence was sorely missed by Sam, who would for ever keep a special corner in her heart for this beloved one.

Samantha moved reluctantly in the old rocker, sighing as she glanced at the clock. It had certainly proved a hectic day at the hospital where she worked in the welfare office and also as relieving nurse. Today had been mostly relieving and her feet ached from trotting along those stone corridors.

With an exclamation she started up. John would arrive any moment now, she had a gorgeous steak waiting to be grilled and no man would be amused at waiting for dinner, especially after a long, tiring drive!

She busied herself in the kitchen while her thoughts dwelt on the Australian, John Lane, owner of a large sheep-station in the south of Australia, his greater love being for books and writing. A business trip in connection with his latest work had brought him to Edinburgh, where Sam had met him while spending a well-earned holiday with her friends, Flora and 'Dobby' Dobson. John attended one of the happy gatherings and she liked his gay humour, while he in turn became very attentive in the days that followed. He called for her as often as possible and they wandered by car and on foot, studying historical castles and places of interest. Picnic hampers appeared magically out of the car boot and Samantha enjoyed herself immensely.

'I do believe our Aussie is smitten badly, lassie,' Flora Dobson had stated when they were retiring after a hilarious party at a mutual friend's home. 'He organised the most romantic records and practically hissed at the other lads who dared to dance with you!'

Samantha, brushing the thick masses of dark hair, had paused in confusion. 'I like him too, Flora, he's fun to be with, charming and so alive and ... well, I like John.'

'Ah, lass, I shan't tease again, except ... I fear we may have to travel down under, Dob and I, when next we hope to see our friend the MacDonald!'

Car tyres crunching on the drive brought Sam back to the present. She whipped off her tiny apron, took a quick peep at her reflection in the small kitchen mirror and managed a sedate walk to answer the front doorbell.

John Lane's greeting seemed restrained, but the gladness in his grey eyes assured delight at seeing her again. Samantha smiled her welcome and opened the door wider. The man hesitated for a moment and turned to look at the garden. 'Mind if we don't go in right away, Sam? I fancy a quick look around your pretty garden before the light vanishes completely ... it looks so lush and colourful, not a bit like the Outback. I'm intrigued.'

She led the way down the slate steps and they ambled down the narrow pathways between flowering shrubs, glowing borders and soft green grass. John seemed disinclined to speak and Samantha did not break the silence, sensing a mood. He stopped to contemplate a cluster of larkspurs and then passed on without comment. Finally they reached the front steps again and only then did John speak. 'It's a sure guess that you love this place, this garden very much. Its peace and charm finds a reflection, glows from within you as well.'

'Well, thank you, John. The peacefulness you feel here is entirely due to Mary-Gran. I feel she's still here, will always be.'

'Don't be sad, Samantha, be happy with the memories you have. She would like that.' John touched her shoulder gently and they turned away.

'I'm sure you must be starving—what a bad hostess I am! I shall give you, as a special favour, a glass of my grandmother's sherry, hoarded for special occasions. Would you like that?' His sudden penetrating gaze shook her slightly. 'Maybe you d-don't care for sherry. I—I don't keep all sorts of drinks and . . .'

His smile was whimsical. 'I'd love some special sherry and am honoured that you consider this an occasion. I also brought a bottle of champagne, in case things turned out . . . very special. So, my very dear Miss MacDonald, would you . . . do you think . . .' John gazed into widening green eyes '. . . you don't think this will make us into a couple of alcoholics?'

Sam's laughter joined his rather shakily. For one panicky moment she thought that he was going to ask . . . well, what special occasion was he referring to?

'Of course not, silly,' she managed at last. 'Shouldn't your bubbly be on ice?'

'Supply the ice and it shall be done. I'm starving, bring on the ox, let's have a bash at it.' He took her hand as they entered the cottage.

'Can you beat that? Besides being a charmer, the lass can also cook!' John Lane looked incredulous as they sat in the cosy sitting-room, sipping coffee out of tiny cups.

'Thank you, sir,' Sam smiled cheekily at him.

His captivated gaze studied her. Tilted green eyes flecked with golden sunlight, framed by sooty eyelashes that were tipped in bronze. High cheekbones and a . . . yes, quite delectable mouth, features not quite patrician, her nose tip-tilted slightly and if one looked closely one discovered a feathery brush of freckles dancing across said nose. One felt impelled to come closer . . .

'First things first,' John reprimanded himself aloud, and

7

Sam's eyes flew to his face. He spoke again hurriedly. 'I want to talk about my family, Sam, if it won't bore you. Once I start on that subject nothing short of a clobber on the head will stop me.'

'I'd love that,' Samantha laughed. 'I don't mean clobber you, but to hear about your family. I've always wanted to be one of a big family, so I'll join yours vicariously, while you tell me all.'

'That's just it, honey,' John's eyes sparked, 'when I've told you all about the Lane clan I hope you'll consider joining us in reality. I want ... well, the thing is ... I mean ...' He started up as she also rose to look at him in startled amazement. 'Oh, dash it, I'm jumping my fences and doing it badly!'

Amusement struggled with astonishment and Sam felt she knew quite well what was coming and she was not ready for it, not sure of her feelings at all! She spoke hurriedly. 'What do you mean ... do sit down, stop dithering and tell me about your grandmother. She lives with you, doesn't she?' Sam sat down and he stood looking at her for a confused moment before returning to his chair.

'Yes, Grandmother Mame, we call her by name, except the small fry. My sister Amanda, Allan her husband and I all live in the original homestead. Mame is a great girl, direct and no-nonsense; she bullies the entire family. Even Mark defers when Mame calls the tune, but we all dote on her.'

Samantha interrupted, 'Mark is the cousin who's running your farm ... er ... station while you're here? Why "even Mark"? Why shouldn't he defer as well?'

'Well, Mark is rather autocratic himself, being nominally the head of our clan, used to having his own way ... iron-hand-in-velvet-glove so to speak. Mame has him well-taped, though,' John grinned at her.

'He sounds like someone I wouldn't include in my choice of relatives,' Samantha said indignantly.

'Don't get me wrong about old Mark, honey. He can be dark and dour sometimes, but has big responsibilities and carries the burden exceptionally well. The family adores him and if we all defer to him it's because he's usually right. Mandy, my sister, four years my senior, is a honey and devoted to her husband Allan and her two small fry ... one daughter named after Mame but commonly known as

8

Twinkles, mad on ballet...'

'I used to be quite mad on ballet as well and had lessons. When I started my job at the hospital, the madness died a natural death for want of time.'

'You could, quite possibly, pass on some tips.' John realised he was getting into deep water again, choked on a puff of smoke, continued hurriedly, 'The other one, Hamilton, Ham to all and sundry, going on seventeen and crazy about horses ... do you ride, Sam?'

'We had two lovely horses. I often went careering round the countryside.' Sam saw the glint in grey eyes and forestalled another misplaced outburst. 'Tell me more, John.'

'Stephen, Mark's half-brother, lives with him and is inclined to wilfulness, fond of visiting the local maidens when he should be attending to his job. Mark and he are constantly doing battle.'

'Living with old "iron hand" probably causes him to play truant so often!'

'Oh, come now, Sam dear, you really will convince yourself that Mark is a tyrant, and he's not that old! Many a girl has set her cap, but that cousin of mine seems immune. I wish he and Sheila ...' He stopped abruptly.

'And who might Sheila be?' Her curiosity was aroused, for John Lane suddenly looked very hot and bothered. 'More family?'

'A rather ... er ... distant branch.' He left his chair, walked to the fireplace to stand with his back to her. Abruptly he turned. 'Sheila is the girl everybody expects me to marry. She lives with her parents a couple of miles from our place. We've grown up together and the family have fondly and mistakenly imagined that we would hitch up some day. Sheila helps me a lot with my books.'

Samantha gravely considered this startling news.

'Well, she does sound like the right person for you, John. Knowing her all your life, and helping you, should be a good start for marriage. Why do you want Mark to have her ...' She trailed off because John had stepped forward to draw her to her feet.

'But that's just it, darling ... I've met you and no one else matters. I'm very fond of Sheila, but this changes everything. You must have guessed my intentions when I wrote to you, to let you know I would be spending a few days here at the

9

local inn?' Grey eyes looked pleadingly into hers.

'Let's sit down, please.' Samantha's legs felt shaky. 'I did have a feeling regarding your intentions, John, but I ... I don't know what to say.'

'Just tell me you love me enough to marry me, my darling.' John leaned down in front of her chair and took her hands. 'Or is there someone else?'

'John, we've known each other such a short while. I'm feelingly slightly bewildered. There's no one else I care for more than you, but is that love? Call me a romantic if you like, but I've always imagined love would come in a blaze of glory!'

John edged closer. 'Don't say any more, love. At least you haven't said an outright "No". I guess I've rushed you, but with no one else in the way, that's good enough for a start. Give me a chance to show you what love is and can be. Think about it, will you?'

Samantha looked at him mutely.

He pulled her up and held her very close for a long moment. 'I'm calling again tomorrow and will be here till the end of the week. By that time you should know. I have high hopes of taking you back with me. Goodnight for now, darling. Sleep well and dream lovely dreams ... let me be in them!' He planted a kiss on the top of her silky hair, released her and was gone.

Samantha stood helplessly in the middle of her sitting-room, listening to the diminishing sound of the car, and her thoughts were hopelessly confused. 'He's forgotten the champagne ... tomorrow is Sunday so I don't have to work ... He'll be here a whole week ... I've heard it's very hot in Australia ... oh dear!'

Now it was Friday and John expected an answer tonight.

He had been perfectly sweet this past week, waiting for her when she came off duty, doing whatever she wished most agreeably, never once speaking of the burning question uppermost in both their minds. He would leave for Edinburgh the next day, coming back for her if her answer was in the affirmative. If not, the chances were he would leave directly for Australia.

'I've decided to accept, so why this stupid dithering?' Samantha wandered restlessly in the garden. She would be leaving this peaceful spot, it would remain hers and old Mr. Willoughby would be only too pleased to live here and mind the place for her. He was dependable, and one day she and John would come on a prolonged holiday and enjoy the sights and smell of her beloved moors again.

But above all, Samantha would have a family to call her own and had an instinctive feeling that she could and would love them all if they were like John Lane ... perhaps with one exception, that imperious cousin! Anyway, she possessed spirit of her own and no one, simply no one, was going to squash her under big boots like a ... an Australian bug!

She would be part of a big family, with all the ties this implied, something she had yearned for all her life. 'Was that all marriage to John meant?' a small voice asked in her ear. 'How stupid, of course I love him too,' she whispered back fiercely.

John stopped the car at the gate and she was there to meet him. Her face was expressive and the man moved fast, coming close to grip her shoulders, to look at her with questioning intensity.

A strange, foreboding, nebulous mist obscured Samantha's vision for a moment and then cleared, leaving her with a dazed impression of distant blue haziness which puzzled her even while she smiled tremulously.

'Your champagne is back on the ice, John!'

Cupping her upturned face in his hands, he kissed her gently. 'My love, may you never regret the decision I can see you've made. Now say very firmly after me ... "Yes, I will marry you, John." '

'Yes, I will marry you, John darling,' she repeated obediently.

'Yoicks!' exclaimed the literary man, and lifted her slight figure in a bear hug.

CHAPTER 2

'HAPPY, Sam?'

'Yes, John, only a few butterflies seem to be imprisoned in the region under my ribs!'

'At the thought of marrying me or because you're leaving

11

your homeland for destinations unknown?' John took her hand under his on the steering wheel and glanced teasingly at her.

'Please Mr. Lane, watch the road!'

They were travelling along the busy highway, on their way to the hotel where they were to spend the night before boarding the trans-continental plane for Australia. Across the seas to Adelaide, and from there by car to the Lane homestead, deep into the heart of the south sheep country. Her future home ... 'down under'. How would the family accept Samantha MacDonald, a complete stranger in their midst? And the girl, Sheila, was she going to be heartbroken or would she fight for what she believed to be hers?

A proud MacDonald head was flung back. She would be worthy of any family and the other girl would just have to accept the circumstances!

Samantha turned to her companion. 'Your grandmother's cable made me feel good, John, accepting me so wholeheartedly, sight unseen.' The cablegram from Mrs. Jonathan Lane nestled in her bag: 'Await in pleasurable anticipation future granddaughter. God's blessings be with you. Love. Mame.'

'Yes, Mame's a dear old thing. I'm so glad you agreed to have our wedding over there, as much as I would like to put that ring on your finger right now. The family wouldn't be pleased if we deprived them of the excitement of attending our wedding, Mame especially, and it stands to reason that they certainly couldn't all come over here. We're not so deep in the wilds, you can have your choice of wedding dress and finery. Adelaide is quite up to date in fashions.'

'I didn't fear you were so backwoodsy for one moment,' Sam commented drily.

John laughed. 'Indeed we're not, honey. Mark sent an airmail letter and I quote: "Hope your *business* trip was not too disrupted. Think deeply and beware the unknown quantity!" Have you brought along your excellent qualifications and pedigree papers, sweetie?'

'Oh, the beastly man! I hope when he falls in love ... I mean if he ever can get a girl to put up with him ... true love knows no levels ... anyway, you're a grown man, not a blind teenager, and surely can do as you please!' Samantha sat up straighter, an indignant flush on her cheeks, her green eyes sparkling.

'Whist! Cool down, you fiery creature. Mark is like that, and you'll soon get used to him. Very family-conscious, like a hawk over his brood. I've upset his plans somewhat—Sheila and all that. But, brother, wait until he sees what I've captured! He'll go green with envy and thereby be more haughtier than ever, wanna bet on it?' John laughed joyously and tooted loudly on the car horn, thereby making a dear old lady emit a startled screech as she shook her ancient umbrella at him!

The old lady reminded Sam of someone and she closed her eyes in silent communion. 'Dearest Mary-Gran, soon I will have other kin of my own, but no one else will ever take your place in my heart.'

'Why so pensive, darling?' He took his glance off the road. 'Homesick already?'

'No—just thinking,' she sighed.

'Sit closer. Buck the stars! This road is long and I do so badly want to take you in my arms, just to make sure you're my girl!'

Warm colour spread across her cheeks and for one fatal moment her companion's eyes strayed to admire moulded lips and satin-smooth hair. John Lane's eyes switched back to the road—a fraction too late to avoid the truck that loomed out of the side street.

The impact sent his car spinning in a double somersault.

Samantha looked at Dr. William Strang and he returned her gaze gravely.

'My dear Samantha, we are truly unable to say at this stage whether John will walk again. The extensive injuries he sustained, damage to nerve centres have caused the paralysis, as you know. He's lucky to be alive.'

'Yes, I know, Bill, and it's due to your wonderful care. I fully realise how you fought to keep him alive and shall be eternally grateful ... even if he never walks again.' Samantha leaned forward earnestly. 'I have a deep conviction that John *will* walk again.'

'Well, he is stronger now and we can only carry on with the treatment that he has been having these last few weeks. I have a very high regard for the Austrian, Hans Getsenberg. He's a brilliant man in his field and at least he didn't dash any hopes when he examined John, although he didn't say much, only promised to see him again within two months. He left orders for strict treatment and therapy. Miracles can still happen, Sam, especially with faith and hope such as you have.'

'I gather it will be a long and painful treatment, and my heart aches for him. To have both legs paralysed ... He always led such an active life, and now ...' She sighed.

Dr. Strang looked reflectively at the girl and felt pity stir in his heart for her. 'My dear, it will not be so painful but a long and slow business, and to tell the truth, more painful for you. You see, you'll have to bear the brunt. The treatment will make John feel an awful sense of helplessness and that's when you will be needed, to cheer him up. His feeling of uselessness, inability ... do you realise what I mean? Are you still determined to go home with him, marry him?'

A slight flush stained her cheeks, but his questioning gaze was returned with a tilt of chin and steady eyes. 'I do and am, Bill. Oh, John has tried very hard to reject me, but I'm determined ... he will get well again!'

'I'm pleased you grasp the implications. You'll need any amount of courage and spirit, and John is a very lucky man, because I think you do possess just what's needed.' Bill smiled encouragingly.

'Thank you. If that will make him happy, so shall it be.'

'How is your ankle? It was a nasty break ... when does the plaster come off?'

'Any time now. Dr. Montrose is quite happy about it. Don't worry about me, I'm fine, thanks.'

Admiration shone in Strang's eyes and then he became briskly businesslike. 'Now, John is in good shape for the journey home. I know Luke Mannering very well, he'll have all the data on future treatment and you can trust him implicitly. He is a fine doctor and the Lanes know him well. Amanda will fly back with you. I believe Grandma wanted to come too and they had quite a battle to stop her, believing the journey and anxiety would be too much for her. Quite a tartar, I gather?'

'Yes, she wrote to me.' Samantha grinned suddenly, impishly. 'I can envisage sparks flying already, but I have a feeling we're going to be good for each other!'

'And Mark?'

'Mark? What of him? You know he came with Mandy and stayed till John was off the danger list. I didn't see him, being laid up in a different hospital, and he spent all his short time with John. I'm convinced he disapproves of me, not good enough for the Lanes . . .'

'Just a minute!' Bill positively glared. 'I happen to know your own MacDonald clan, I come from there. Your dad and I . . . well, be that as it may, just you give Mark Lane what for when you see him! Amanda kept him well informed on your progress, I can assure you.'

'Sure and I will and all.' If the subject of their talk had been present he would surely have disintegrated beneath the withering look in gold-flecked eyes!

Bill showed mock alarm. 'Don't dislike him too much, lass. Actually he can be devilishingly charming.'

'Devilish being the operative word,' she retorted as she rose to leave. 'But he'll find he's not the only one with a two-pronged fork tucked away! I'll be seeing you, Bill, before we leave, and thanks again for being so wonderful with my John.'

For a long while, after he had helped Samantha to the car, William Strang sat at his desk and gazed reflectively out of the window. She's a wonderful girl, he thought, and sighed, God help her . . .

The physical side of marriage and the implication of the accident had not unduly worried Samantha. She had given it thought, but only in so far as it would concern John and his well-being. She was content to wait, for her belief that John would walk again was strong. Her dreams of marriage, a loving husband and babies did not dim. When the time came she would reach out for her rightful heritage as a woman. Samantha was content to wait for that day.

What qualms she felt now were more about the country she would soon be going to—so different—no softly rolling hills, heather and dales nor bubbling trout streams. Her knowing friends had hastened to enlighten her, 'Hot sun, arid wastes, few trees and thorny scrub, scarcity of water and mile upon mile of heat haze, to make one look like a limp rag doll by day and shiver in the cold of night!'

Mandy informed her, rather tartly, that it was not all that bad. But Mandy was used to it, loving her homeland with the blind eyes of love.

Amanda, a neat young matron with acorn hair and grey eyes who had, right away, treated Sam as one of the family— casual, down-to-earth, Amanda Jones had taken the bewildered girl under her wing while the shock of the accident wore off and kept up her spirit during the days when John was still on the danger list. Samantha blessed the way of this one Australian.

Adelaide. A lasting flash of dazzling blue sea against verdant green land and the giant jet-liner was on the runway. Amid orderly fuss and courtesy they went through the Customs, a smiling man in blue uniform wheeled John out to the entrance where the Lanes' Holden awaited them.

Samantha's impressions were vivid, of casual orderliness and the attractive Aussie drawl which was extended and heard again in the soft tones of Allan Jones as he greeted them at the barrier. A tall man with grey eyes and a shock of fair hair, he made no bones about his deep affection for his wife, hugging her for all the world to see. One long arm then went around Sam's shoulders while his other hand gripped John's. A host of emotions mirrored the tanned face.

A second car, ranch-wagon type, waited for their luggage with one of the station hands at the wheel. The man in blue helped to settle John in the spacious car, stepped back with a friendly salute as they moved away. Once out of the city limits they settled down for the long trip ahead. Mandy sat in front with her husband and there ensued a non-stop chatter as they brought each other up to date on events.

Now it seemed that the miles stretched for long weary hours between outcrops of rock and swells of low hills. Far in the distance a haze of darker blue gave promise of majestic mountains, well wooded. Sam stopped her study of the countryside and turned to the man at her side. John had refused an airlift in the mailplane, insisting that he could quite well stand the car trip and wanted to be with Samantha on her first trip through his country.

'Tired, darling?' she smiled encouragingly. 'Still far to go?'

John's smile was strained. 'Not too far by Australian estimates. Blue Hills is at the foot of those ranges.'

Blue Hills! The name conjured up a hazy mist of recollection for the girl and she shivered suddenly. The moment passed.

16

They crossed a dangerous-looking bridge and she looked down at the broad waterway. 'What a lovely river! I thought there wasn't any water except bore-holes and water-holes dotted around for the stock.'

Mandy giggled at her surprised expression. 'Lassie, you have a lot to learn, although I must admit you're nearly right, but this has been a good year for rains. No wonder you've looked so apprehensive for the past hour or two. Didn't you notice it, John?'

'Yes, as a matter of fact I did.' John looked at Sam rather oddly. 'I gathered, from her unease, that she was having second thoughts about coming all this way ... to a very uncertain future.' Sam's mouth opened, but he went on, a strained touch of bitterness evident, 'Sorry for that. I guess I'm a little tired and grumpy.'

A serene hand was placed over his. 'That's all right, John. I do understand how you feel. Just bear in mind everything is going to be fine very soon. Mandy, do let's stop for our hamper lunch and tea. I could do with some Aussie tea, hot and strong, for I swear all Australia's dust has lodged in my throat!'

Allan stopped the car and Sam made a dive for the tea flask. She handed two cups to John while she unscrewed the top of the flask. 'Thanks.' His eyes thanked her for more than the cup of tea. He looked at his watch. 'If we don't dally too long we should be home by sunset.'

John's prediction proved correct and as they drew into the circular drive westering flares of orange and gold suffused the sprawling homestead in a soft welcoming glow, turning the surrounding shrubs and trees a translucent green. Samantha slid out of the car and stood in expressive rapture while John watched conflicting emotions sweep across her face.

Amanda nudged her back. 'Move on, girl. This is old stuff, we crave only a long, cool something to drink. If you stand like that much longer I won't answer for the insect content in your open mouth! Hello, Mike,' this last to the man who had walked up to help the driver of the luggage car remove the wheelchair. He greeted her with a quick side appraisal of the stranger from Scotland, then turned to John with a wide smile and with gentle dexterity the two of them transferred him to the chair.

John took the girl's hand. 'You've met Tad, poor fellow, he's travelled in our dust all the way. This is his buddy, Mike. Two fellers who blindly presume they're indispensable ... Miss MacDonald.'

'Aw, boss!' Tad grimaced, they turned a dusty grin towards Samantha. 'Ma'am, may I make bold to remark that the scenery has become mighty purty all of a sudden in these parts.'

'Well, well, such gallantry, I can't believe it!' Amanda Jones looked at Tad unbelievingly.

'Thank you, Tad. How do you do, Mike.' Samantha ignored Mandy and held out her hand to Mike, who took it in a large calloused grip, blushed and stuttered, 'Howdy, miss, and also welcome.'

'Suffering wombats, what's going on down there, how much longer must I wait? John ... Mandee! Come at once.'

'Heavens! I'd forgotten our Mame could screech like that!' Amanda grabbed Sam's hand. 'Push, boys, in top gear—don't be scared, honey, it's only Grandma making herself heard. She'll drool over you in a minute. Okay, John? Forward march!'

Tad and Mike lifted the chair over the two shallow slate steps, then made off with astonishing alacrity.

Mrs. Jonathan Lane leaned lightly on the cane in her right hand. No cuddly pink and white granny, this one. Tall and spare and upright in trim grey dress with an oversized cameo brooch at the neckline, silky white hair drawn into a bun on the back of her neck. A beaky nose and wide mouth, redeemed by deepest blue, really beautiful eyes. Eyes which rested like homing birds on the man in the wheelchair.

Amanda stepped forward to put her arms around the old lady and was received in a firm embrace and the blue eyes lifted from the man for a swift encirclement of the granddaughter. Mandy was soundly kissed, then pushed firmly aside.

'I've sent your two delinquents to the bathroom. They would choose today to take a spill at the crossing. Better check for bruises.'

Amanda Jones smiled wisely and clutched her husband's hand, to draw him into the house.

'Hi, Mame, my darlin' bell-bird.' John grinned rather crookedly into his grandmother's eyes which had immedi-

18

ately turned back to him. 'This is my girl, Samantha.'

'I can still see quite well, plenty of time. Well, John?' Her voice was strangely gruff.

Sam knew without doubt that infinite love and emotion was being sternly curbed for this moment. She, Samantha MacDonald, had received but a cursory glance, and her heart sank. Mame was not going to like her.

John looked taken aback at this short statement and question and sent Sam an appealing apology with his eyes.

'Look at me, boy! Plenty of time to stare elsewhere later. Now, let me see ... you look pretty fit, at a guess it won't be long before you'll be chasing your treasure all over the place.' Mame stooped and kissed him on his mouth. 'Welcome home, J-Johnny.'

Her voice developed a slight shake on his name and she gave a snort, fumbled for a hanky. 'That damned cold coming on again!' She wiped her eyes, put the cambric back into her pocket and then lifted her eyes to regard, with piercing intentness, the girl standing slightly to the rear of the chair. Her gaze drifted from satiny dark hair, down the slim body, then back to Sam's face and hair.

'Loosen your hair,' came a sharp order.

Samantha looked her astonishment.

'Loosen it, I say!'

With a gasp the girl's hands flew up to draw out the pins, and her hair fell in a cascade around shaking shoulders. The last shimmering sun rays made a soft halo as it touched her head.

'I do declare! Well, there's plenty of it. Mmm, yon body's a bit spare, guess it'll fatten up given some decent tucker. Eyes ... queer combination, green and yellow. How come?' The question aimed sharply at Samantha.

A tiny pulse started a protest in her throat and Sam tried desperately to still the rage that was building inside her. She felt for all the world like a ... a filly, up for inspection! Should she high-step at a quick gallop around the veranda to show her legs, how many hands high was she? No one was more aghast than she as words spilled out of her mouth.

'The better to see with, Mrs. Lane dear. My teeth are also in excellent condition, don't you think? How do you do?'

(What had she done now, who had uttered those wicked words ... surely not Samantha MacDonald? The old dear didn't mean anything, and even if one's rage got the upper hand hadn't Mary-Gran taught one to respect one's elders? So you were going to be good for each other? Poof! there goes my chance of making a good first impression!)

Silence greeted her outburst and, for once in her life, one elderly person became dumbfounded!

John recovered first. 'Gosh, Sam dear——' he began, at a complete loss for words.

'Humph!' Mame had also found voice. 'No need for you to apologise on my behalf, John Lane. My senses are still good enough to realise that I've been a rude old woman. Will you accept my apologies, Samantha MacDonald?'

Did that glint in the blue eyes denote anger or devilment, wondered Sam as she swallowed hard on the thought that if she had to go on bended knees, she would endeavour to wipe out her own rude words, make Mrs. Lane accept her own sincere apology.

'Surely it's I that should ask you to forgive me, Mrs. Lane? I . . . I just don't know what came over me. My manners have entirely deserted me. Mary-Gran did teach me that . . . that . . .' She stopped suddenly, for Mame had reached forward and taken a firm grip on her shaking shoulders.

'That's enough, girl, don't drool so. I like spirit, so don't disappoint me now. We'll all gracious accept apologies. I'm a silly old woman (don't let the family hear that admission!). Welcome to Blue Hills, Samantha MacDonald . . . you may kiss me if you wish.'

'I do wish, most awfully,' Sam breathed, leaned forward to kiss her cheek, but Mame turned her head and the kiss landed on her mouth.

'Always kiss where it's meant to be and kiss only when you mean it.' It was an order.

Mandy and Allan had reappeared with the 'delinquents' in tow and the old lady turned her sharp eyes on to them. 'Has everybody lost their manners? Amanda, show Samantha to her room. Allan, go along with John, and you two scamps stop gawping like a couple of crows. Time enough to get acquainted later. Don't be late for dinner.' She stalked into the house and Sam, nearest to her, distinctly heard the muttered, 'Spirited filly, indeed!'

Later Sam stood out on the veranda and looked at the distant towering mountains, barely visible in the gathering

20

darkness. Her bedroom had two doors, one leading into the house and the other on to this side of the wide encircling veranda—the sleep-out, where she now stood. A swish of wheels and John neatly cornered to join her.

'Hello, sweet. Good, I see you're ready. Enjoyed that shower, I'll bet.' He clasped her hand. 'Lovely view from here. You must meet Mora, he's my aboriginal valet-cum-nurse and his wife Mina is our cook, a dainty lass of plus-minus a hundred-and-ninety · pounds. Cindy, their daughter, is maid of all work. Why, you haven't met the scamps yet, or have you?'

'No ... and all because I couldn't hold my tongue or act as a lady should,' Samantha blurted out. 'I'm almost afraid to face them at dinner ... what are you laughing at, John Lane?'

'Because it's the first time I've ever seen our delectable Mame at a loss for words.' He gave another amused chuckle. 'Oh, her face! And never before have I heard her make a voluntary apology ... you sure took that lady down a wee peg. But forgive her all that, I know she's been very anxious on our account and the gruff manner hides a heart of pure gold.'

'I was a silly ass, and promise I'll do my best to make amends for my impolite actions.'

'For you to be happy here is all I ask. Luke will be here tomorrow ... dear Lord, if everything is going to be all right, make it soon, so that I can help to make you happy.' He brushed a hand across his forehead. 'Say it, Sam, tell me to belt up.'

'Yes, do that small thing, otherwise I promise you I'll create another scene.' She smiled to soften her words. 'I've told you, time and again, to be patient, however difficult it will be. Look, John, there's a light over that way. Is it another homestead?'

John followed her pointing finger. 'That's quite a long way away, the nights are clear and distances deceptive. That's Mark's domain. He must be back from Kingston ... or it could be Stephen.'

Mark's domain—another Lane she had yet to meet. Angrily Sam shrugged off a shiver of apprehension. It wouldn't do at all to start getting complexes at this stage.

'Shivering, darling? You're surely not feeling cold, the

21

night is warm. Fetch a wrap then, and we can join the family.'

Mame lifted an imperious hand. 'Not the usual tonight, Mike. You'll find champagne in the bucket on that side-table. Mind how you draw the cork, I've had it on ice all day.'

Mike Simpson, very spruced up and self-conscious, moved over and Tad Martin walked with him to watch anxiously as he picked up the bottle.

'Champagne! Well now, that's doing it fine.' Allan rubbed his hands gleefully and winked at his wife. 'Watch yourself, old girl, you know what happens to you when bubbly appears on the scene!'

'Allan Jones, behave yourself!' Face crimsoning, Mandy cast a quick look at their offspring.

Those two had other distractions, Samantha being the centre of their interest. Not only because she was good to look at but, wonders never cease, she had actually backchatted Granny Mame before she had even entered the house!

As the glasses were raised, Sam stole a glance at John and surprised a wistful look in his eyes—and knew, instinctively, he was thinking back, thinking of another bottle of champagne—the one she had kept at the cottage. What fun they had then ... it seemed aeons away. Smiling steadily at him, she willed him to smile back at her. Gradually the lost, sad look disappeared. 'It will be like that again, some day,' she promised silently. A queer ache in her breast was firmly tucked away as Allan raised his glass to propose a toast.

After dinner, which was not such an ordeal as she had feared, with Mina bustling around cheerfully (very plump indeed!) and her white-coated husband, Mora, ready with a rebuke at things not done to his liking, the family adjourned to the large sitting-room. It was here, Mandy confided, where they usually gathered for family conferences, heated debates, and when there was company, the carpet would be rolled up to the tune of a good swing-o!

Samantha met the rapt gaze of young Twinkles who promptly seated herself on the couch next to her subject of interest. 'Mom tells me you used to practise ballet, Miss MacDonald. Would you show me some time, please will you?'

She was a thin but graceful child of twelve and her pixie

face glowed as Sam said, 'With pleasure, Twinkles, if I can remember—I'm afraid it's become rather rusty, but we'll polish up as we go along.'

'That will be fab——' The pixie look dropped suddenly. 'Oh, heck, I'll be going back to school in two weeks. We'll have to start right away!' She jumped up hopefully.

John broke in. 'That's out of the question, poppet, Samantha's ankle won't stand the strain just yet. You do know it was broken?'

'Gee, I did forget—does it pain awful bad? Do you think you'll ever dance again?'

Her look was so tragic at this bitter future that Sam bit hard on the smile that threatened, to answer gravely, 'It doesn't hurt at all now, but I'd better rest it until you come back for the holidays. I saw a dinkum summerhouse in the garden. John tells me it's not in use ... maybe we can annex same for our dancing classes?'

'Wow! I'll clean it out tomorrow ... did you hear that, Ham? It will be very private.' A perky chin was lifted.

'Dear Miss Jones, may I join your exclusive dancing studio? I can do a real gone pirouette and my pas de deux are smashing!' Hamilton Jones minced around on his toes, hands daintily on hips.

Laughter broke and Twinkles, after a haughty glare at his antics, subsided into giggles.

The sound of a jeep outside made Ham drop his pose and stomp to the door. 'It's Mark! Mark is back, I'll let him in——'

Sam's stomach literally turned as a fair young man came striding back with the boy. He went straight to Mame and kissed the tip of her nose.

'Stephen! When did you get back?'

Stephen. Her insides settled back in their rightful sphere.

'Word came to me that John was bringing back a smasher, so I naturally hastened back...' Stephen Lane grinned a welcome at John and his voice trailed off as he caught sight of Samantha. He advanced slowly, stopped in front of her and asked in a bemused voice, 'John, are there more where she comes from? What is that Eden called? If, by some heavenly chance, this is not your girl, then my quest is ended.'

He leaned down, took her hand and gently kissed the slim

23

fingers, one by one. A stupefied girl simply sat and allowed him to do so, while an amused gathering looked on, with not one offer of intervention!

Drawing a deep breath, she smiled sweetly and gracefully withdrew her hand. 'Hello, Stephen. I'm Samantha and I'm overwhelmed by your sweet flattery—and gallantry. Thank you, I'm also glad you approve. Where I come from we're a dime a dozen. I guess it's the climate and having Scots grandmothers.'

Mike and Tad started a deep chuckle as they watched the deep flush rise up Stephen's neck, his surprised expression. His eyes left the girl to stare at them and he straightened his shoulders. Turning to John, he spoke softly.

'John, I congratulate you and in all sincerity I say this, if ever I marry, I hope my girl will be as charming as your lady. May she never want to leave us, for then surely the sun will not sparkle on Blue Hills again.' He bowed gravely.

A small silence ensued, as everybody in the room absorbed this—coming from Stephen—startling speech. His lips quirked in a smile and John's shoulder was gripped in affec·tion. 'We're not too bad at that, are we, John? Come, cobbers, you're slipping. A drink ... a toast to beauty!' Turning to Twinkles, Stephen lifted her high. 'Shall we dance, ballerina, heart of my heart?'

What a whirlwind, thought Sam amusedly as he teased Mame and Mandy and ragged the two stockmen unmercifully. Stephen's zest for living sparked off everyone with whom he came in contact.

Mame eventually wanted to go to bed and John looked pale and tired. Sam hastened to his chair, but Stephen forestalled her, gripped the chair and ignoring John's protests steered it gaily with Samantha at his side. Mora was waiting to assist his master to bed. Stephen saluted casually and left them. ' 'Night, Sam, 'night, cobber.'

'Sleep well, dear.' Samantha kissed John and retired to her room, to sleep very soundly through her first night in the Outback.

CHAPTER 3

SHE was up at dawn, had a refreshing shower and decided on a daffodil-yellow sun-frock. She combed her hair with quick, deft strokes and slipped on a green headband to keep it off her face. Low-heeled sandals completed her outfit.

Eager to be outside, she walked out on the veranda. Sounds of activity came from the kitchen, Mina was singing a doleful hymn and a heavenly smell of coffee drifted on the air. Samantha breathed deeply of the fresh air as she walked on grass that was still wet with dew. A sudden chattering in the trees drew her attention ... a magpie or perhaps the galah bird? Trees and shrubs glistened in the clean air ... and she had imagined a thorny scrub, arid earth, drought-stricken lands! Perhaps it was just so further inland, away from the homestead. Having only heard of the mallows, nightshades, tree-tulips and sedges, she could not differentiate between the varieties or species that grew here in the extensive garden. At least she knew what a gum-tree looked like ... the big fellers, John had pointed them out with the remark that there were more than three hundred and sixty different species, being valuable for their oil content and timber.

She had so much to learn! Her walk brought her within sight of a row of bungalows or huts, smoke issuing from some of the chimneys. Standing there wondering about the inhabitants, Sam turned at a clatter of boots as a breathless Ham joined her. He wore washed-out blue denims and shirt, scuffed boots and his hair was wetly slicked back. He seemed tongue-tied, rubbing the toe of one boot against the heel of the other.

Samantha tried putting him at ease. ''Morning, Ham. Tell me, who lives over there in those ... er ... huts?'

'Oh, that's where the abos shack out. You know, Mina, Mora and Cindy. And Jim, Stormy and their lubras and taweenas—piccanins. The men do riding and mustering. Dad is mostly in the office. He's a vet, you know,' Ham finished off proudly.

They watched as two women came out and dumped a couple of tiny, dark tots on the hardened ground. The little

25

ones wore only short sleeveless vests.

'You'll get to know and like them, Miss MacDonald, they're our people. Now and again they get the urge to walkabout and disappear, sometimes for weeks on end, and then suddenly they're back with us. This lot seem quite happy to stay put, they know when they're on to a good wicket.'

'Thanks a lot for all the gen, Ham, and please call me Sam ... you will help me in my behaviour towards them and other things? I know so little of the customs out here and would honestly appreciate your guidance.' Samantha widened her eyes and the youngster drew up importantly.

'Sure I will, you can rely on me. There's another bungalow on the other side, attached to the office. Tad and Mike doss there, and the shearers when it's shearing time. We have the fastest team in all Australia, and it's something to see when they get cracking!'

'That must be exciting. What with the boundary riding, mustering and putting through the race, all that I want to see. The summerhouse I mentioned last night—is it all right if Twinkles and I use it? It looks so cool with the wistaria clinging to it.'

'Mark's sleep-out—he used to sleep there before his shack was completed.'

'Won't he be annoyed if we use it?'

'I don't think so.' Ham scratched his head. 'He only uses it occasionally when we get too much for him, or when he needs a quiet think.'

'Is he very morose, then?'

Ham grinned at her, 'If that means what I think it means, then he certainly isn't! He's a live wire, keeps us on our toes right enough ... when he's around.' His smile was rueful as he rubbed his posterior. 'I have felt the heavy hand when Dad's not here to mete out punishment ... but Mark is still tops and a bit of all right!'

Sam sniffed, ready with a tart retort, but the boy suddenly grabbed her hand. 'Suffering wallabies! I was sent to call you for coffee. Mom's going to hit the roof, it's breakfast-time already.'

Hand in hand they dashed back to the house, arriving breathless just as Mina, with a dark scowl at Ham, started banging vigorously on the length of pipe that hung from the

26

edge of the veranda roof.

Samantha hurried to John's room, but Mora was already wheeling the chair to the dining-room. She bent down for a quick kiss and John smiled at her. 'You're looking fresh and perky, love. Had a good sleep?'

'Oh yes, John, I feel fit as a fiddle. Isn't the air wonderful, did you have a good night?'

'I really did. It's good to be home again, and I'm all set for Doctor Luke, he'll be here with the mailplane some time this morning. Lordy, I'm hungrier than ten horses.'

And what a breakfast!

Mame, seated at the head of the table, chuckled at the girl's expression as she watched large platters of sizzling ham, fried mutton and eggs put on the table by Mina. The home-baked bread, sliced and piled high, looked and smelt delicious. The two stockmen joined them at the table, having been out since before dawn.

'Climb in, girl, you'll be surprised how fast all this tucker disappears when the men start on it. Right now we'll start putting a bit of fat on that skinny frame of yours.'

A protest rose to Sam's lips, but Mame continued with a wicked grin, 'No apologies this time. Help yourself ... no talking while eating, waste of time!'

'Not a bad frame at that,' Allan leered at Samantha across the table, 'now that I've had a good look at same.'

Mandy dug an elbow into his ribs. 'Stop being so personal, you wolf! What will Sam think of us? Never you mind, hon'—she became conspiratorial—'as soon as they're out of sight, then Mame and I will reveal a few things, for a future, handy comeback.'

'Sneak!' Allan hissed at his wife.

John pretended guilty embarrassment while Tad and Mike exclaimed in unison, 'Bless 'em all!' The youngsters were highly intrigued but in no way did this stop their unabated appetites.

The menfolk went off to their duties, Mandy to the kitchen to check the day's supplies and Mame to her room to write letters. Twinkles, busily fortified with mop and brushes, informed Sam that the studio would be ship-shape and ready for inspection by tea-time and skipped off happily.

John and Samantha went out on to the cool side of the long veranda and she settled into a deep old armchair which

27

had belonged to his grandfather. John started to tell her about Jonathan Lane who had started this vast sheep empire, of the two sons, his father and Mark's father, who had both died on the land they loved. Mark's mother had gone back to her homeland, Canada, her son remaining to help his grandmother run the sheep stations that he had inherited jointly with John. John's mother had died shortly after his father, and three years back word had come that Mark's mother too had passed away. Mark had visited her just previous to her death, to plead with her to come back, but she had a thriving dress business of her own and preferred that to a life on a lonely sheep-station that would only revive memories.

'I was always more interested in writing, so Mandy and I agreed to sell half of our land to Mark who is far more pastoral-loving than we two. He's wonderful with horses and cattle and he just has to look at a sick woolly and it gets healthy and sprightly out of sheer shame, I swear!'

'Sheer fright, from the sound of it.'

John laughed and was about to enlarge on the subject when they both heard the drone of an approaching plane.

'Tommy Crawford, airmail pilot, will dash in for his usual quick cuppa. Nice chap, probably dying with curiosity to see you. Luke will be with him, I hope.' John's face looked strained. 'I pray that he'll be optimistic when he sees me. I want to take you in my arms, I want to live again wholly. Bear with me, Samantha?'

Sam studied him tenderly, silently rebuking her heart for not being able to return his love with the same passionate intensity. She loved him dearly. Passion would come, surely, when they were married?

Amanda turned the corner, two men at her heels. Short, stocky Tom Crawford sported a luxurious moustache. He acknowledged the introduction with lively interest, greeted John with the remark, 'Some chaps have all the luck,' remembered the accident and retreated stammeringly, 'Sorry about your prang, old boy, but rely on Luke to fix things. Mandy, where's that cuppa you promised, late on mail schedule today,' he followed Mandy indoors.

Affection shone in John's eyes as he greeted the second man. 'Samantha, meet our doctor-man, Luke Mannering.'

He was tall, with gentle brown eyes. Rather thin, with a slight stoop of shoulders and hands that were long and tapered yet held hers with a steady grip. His eyes twinkled and he had a pronounced drawl. 'Welcome to you, Samantha. I can perceive why our John is so impatient ... what frustration!'

Heavens, everybody out here was certainly frank, outspoken. Thoughts, likes and dislikes were aired with casual blatancy that mocked at modesty and ersatz veneer of polite society. She acknowledged his greeting with a smile, liking this man, this doctor, instantly. John would be in good hands.

Mandy and Tommy came out, laden with tea things, and Mame joined them. Tommy hurriedly gulped two cups of tea in quick succession and left with a wave of his hand. 'Mailbags are in the office. I'll collect the outgoing bag on my way. 'Bye, folks, be seeing you.' Luke would stay for two days, having pressed a locum friend into service at his consulting-rooms.

Samantha was entranced when Allan came in with the mailbag and called them in while he switched on the transceiver set. This was the twice-daily communication between outlying homesteads, doctors, post office and anybody who had anything to report. The morning session was a great favourite among the women, for then gossip, knitting, sewing and cooking recipes were exchanged with great gusto.

The first message was for Luke, from the sister at his surgery. 'Lucy Bennett decided not to wait for him. A fine boy for her, weight eight pounds. Congrats, Doctor, she's naming him after you! All's well, over.' Luke passed some instructions, switched back and another voice came on. 'Doctor Luke, you may have to flee the country soon, too many babies named after you!' A raucous laugh followed.

'Silly old bag, that Donna,' muttered the doctor furiously and looked surprised when the laughter was echoed by present company. More news went to and fro and then Allan switched off.

Mame muttered discontently, 'No news from Mark. That man is the limit! But then he'll suddenly appear out of the blue ... true to form!'

She really misses him ... the thought surprised Samantha.

Luke gripped John's chair. 'Come on, old chap, let's go have our sessions.'

Sam made a movement, but John spoke abruptly. 'We

won't need you.' His face was suddenly white and set as they moved away.

'Come on, honey, it's high time you inspected the house, linen, etc. Future reference and all that jazz.' Mandy dragged Sam by her hand and hummed softly, 'Queen of the House.'

Samantha thought in sudden fright, all this would possibly belong to her one day. Never, ever, could she run such a large homestead as efficiently as Mame and Mandy. 'Mandy dear, please stop a minute. I want to say something and can't while we're galloping along like this ... Please!'

'Okay, chick, out with it.'

'Well, it's ... I can't ... oh, Mandy, I don't know a thing about running a place this size, everything is so well organised. Won't you please carry on as usual? I'll go along with you and you can show me. I'm not shirking and promise to help with everything, share the work. Please, Mandy?'

Amanda Jones gazed reflectively at the ceiling, the walls, everywhere except at the woebegone girl. Moments passed and she felt a pleading hand on her arm. She relented suddenly. 'Shame, for sure I am a tease. We'll definitely carry on as usual, it takes years of practice, but if there's anything you can suggest as an improvement, we have open minds.' She smiled companionably. 'Right now you can help me with an inventory of linen. I'll take a bet there's a mountain of mending piled up.' Amanda wanted to occupy the girl's mind, away from thoughts of John and Luke.

They were busily engaged in the linen room when they heard a screech of brakes outside (dash it, why couldn't Sam's insides behave ... Mark Lane was just another member of the family and *they* were most friendly). Involuntarily she braced herself.

Mandy stopped counting sheets to remark casually, 'Sheila, I recognise that sound ... she'll fly in like a whirlwind, so watch out for the undertow. Treat her warily, Sam, she did expect to annex John, although now he's—oh heavens, there I go, putting my big foot in my mouth again!'

She looked so shocked and Samantha was about to speak when Luke called from the doorway, 'Will you come here, Sam?'

She walked with him to John's room where its occupant, pale and harassed, sat in his chair. Luke sat on the bed indicating that she join him. He pointed at John.

30

'John and I have had a bit of an argument, that's why he looked so ruffled.'

'Now see here, Luke, I'm not going to let Sam——'

'Shut up, boy, let me speak. John needs special treatment every day, Samantha, and I'm unable to stay here all that time. I've suggested that you could do it just as well. I can show you, there's nothing difficult and you have had nursing experience. This exercise is to keep him fit, only until Getsenberg decides the time is right to see him. Now, John insists I send a nurse out here ... what for, I ask you, when everything is quite simple. How do you feel about it, Sam?' Luke stood up and sauntered to the window.

He waited, moments passed, then he turned and faced her. 'If you feel you wouldn't be able to cope, don't be afraid to say so. We'll try to find a nurse. They're so scarce, that's also a problem.'

'Oh, please, Luke, it's not necessary. Of course I'll do the therapy, if you think I'm capable,' Samantha stammered. 'Y-You gave me a shock for the moment, that's why I didn't answer right away.'

'Look, dear, listen to me. I'm aware that it's a simple treatment and easy for you to carry out. Luke has just demonstrated, so I know. But it will be too embarrassing for you ... uh ... and me ...' John flushed and looked away.

Samantha came to stand in front of him, hands on hips. She surveyed him critically. 'So what? I may not be a qualified nurse, but my job at the hospital certainly taught me not to be embarrassed at anything. So must I draw one conclusion? You would prefer a pretty stranger messing you about to a mere fiancée?' She tossed her head and stared out of the window.

'Samantha, that's not true! How can you say such things? It's because you're my fiancée that ... that I ...' John was very heated.

'Well, well, only just back and already the sparks are flying!'

The girl whirled into the room, short dark hair windblown, brown eyes flashing. She bent down over John and kissed him on his mouth. 'Are they messing you around, Johnny? Sheila will annihilate all, just like that!' She snapped slim fingers above her head.

'Hi, Sheila, get off my neck, will you? I can still fight my own battles. But it seems I'm losing this one through the sheer cussedness of a jealous female ... have you met her?'

Sheila straightened slowly and faced Samantha.

'Samantha MacDonald, the welcome mat is at your feet ... quite frankly, I personally would dearly love to write something else on it. After all, you did steal my man from me (sounds like a familiar song?). Anyway, since you're to all intents and purpose in possession, which they say is nine points of the law, I guess I haven't a hope in hell of luring him back. I shall, in my misery, turn to the other cousin!' she finished triumphantly, then added darkly, 'If Mark could ever be comforting. You may speak now.'

While an astonished girl was still trying to dissemble the tenor of this dramatic and impudent dialogue, Mame walked in. Sheila turned with a birdlike movement. 'Mame darlin', I was just saying to these good folks——'

'I heard every word, and if Samantha were to pack her bags right now and declare she never wanted to see any of us ever again, I wouldn't be at all surprised, you ... you ... budding actress! Off with you now, can't you see Luke wants to be alone with John and Samantha? I'll go too—that is, if you don't need me?'

Blue eyes looked so appealingly envious that Sam went straight to her. 'Please stay and hear what Luke advises, Mame.'

Sheila had stopped at the door, but Luke stared at her until, with a shrug of her shoulders, she moved out of sight.

Luke Mannering chose his words carefully. 'I've given John a thorough overhauling. I'm not a specialist in this field, only carrying out the instructions of Bill Strang and Getsenberg, so I wouldn't dare to express an opinion at this stage. But I can safely say that I'm in perfect accord and agreement with them now that I've examined John. My hopes are as high as yours. John must undergo a further few weeks of therapy and then the surgeon wants to see him. I'll show you what to do, Samantha, today and tomorrow, and then you'll be on your own.'

John started a protest, but the doctor stopped him with an upraised hand. 'You settle things with your girl. If we agree she's unable to cope then only will we consider finding a nurse'—as an afterthought—'an ugly one!'

'You've eased my heart considerably, Luke, but what's all

this about a nurse and Samantha being unable to cope? Cope with what?' Mame queried.

In a slightly hysterical tone Sam explained the situation. John stared morosely out of the window and his grandmother wanted to know why he looked so glum.

'Well, you see, Mame, I don't feel it's——' he started to stutter.

'Samantha, come and walk with me ... if I have to listen to all that again I shall blow my top. Come into the garden.' Doctor Mannering tucked the girl's hand firmly under his arm and walked off. Being attached to her hand the rest of Sam perforce followed.

They walked outside, Luke said, 'Don't think I'm being callous with John, my dear. It's the only way, literally speaking, to keep him on his toes. He must not sink into a state of moroseness which would be very bad for him. Both spirit and health must be kept up, for whatever Getsenberg has in mind. We're in touch and I'll keep him informed of John's progress and condition.'

They came upon Sheila, leaning against a tree trunk, methodically pulling a flaming poinsettia blossom to pieces, petal by petal. She heard them but did not look up. Luke walked close and tucked her hand under his other arm.

'Destructive hussy! Come and walk with us.'

'Mandy was so deep in the linen closet, she sounded like a large r-rat, so I left her t-to it.' A noticeable catch in her voice.

'Not to worry, shrimp, John is in good shape. I'm certain you listened in to what I had to say to Mame and Samantha, so all I can add is, entrust to the future with spans of faith and hope.'

They walked on in silence, each one deep in their own thoughts.

Did this girl really love John? Samantha wondered. On the surface she was flippant, but what actually went on under that perky surface? 'I don't want to hurt anyone, please, Lord, don't let her feel too badly about losing John,' she prayed silently.

Luke was also having his own problems, worrying whether he had lifted their hopes too high ... if and when they operated, would it be a complete recovery for John? Let it be, not only for his friend's sake but also for the sake of this

33

girl, who had insisted on coming regardless of the consequences. John had told him of her stubbornness against his pleas ... pleas amounting to downright, rejecting rudeness ... she had ignored them with sweet calm, told John she was his girl, a mere accident was not going to stop her. Instinct told Luke she was that sort of girl, who would remain faithful and devoted, no matter what happened. Was it love or a sense of devotional duty that kept her at John's side? Luke's arm tightened involuntarily on the hand that rested on it.

Sheila pulled at his other arm. 'Stop now, Luke. Are we running a marathon or something? That's for the birds. Give me a horse any day if there's galloping to be done. Miss Mac, let's go to your room. I'm dying to see what exciting things you've brought to ... with you. See you at lunch, Luke, hope you win your race!'

In the bedroom she stood looking around for moments, then moved slowly to the wardrobe and asked, 'May I peep in?' but made no move to do so. With sudden intensity she turned to her companion.

'How much do you love him? Enough to tie yourself for ever to—if he doesn't recover—a cripple? Do you love him that much?'

'I love John enough to put his happiness above all else,' Sam replied quietly.

'But think what that means ... if he can't be a proper husband. Could you be content never to have the love ... physical love ... of a man? You can't be, you don't look the frigid type.'

'My faith in his recovery is so certain that I won't even consider that possibility.'

'Oh, conceded, a very noble outlook. If I were to be his wife, I couldn't stand it, not having that part of marriage. Does that mean I don't love enough or does the fact that you're not concerned with that aspect mean you don't love enough? I'm putting it rather badly. Do you understand what I mean?'

Samantha considered gravely, 'Well, I do follow ... I'm not frigid, I hope, nor as noble as you think. I'll have a charming husband and a home of my own, for which I've always yearned. Marriage vows are for better or worse. I shall face up to them, even if John doesn't recover the use of his limbs ... which I shan't believe for a moment.'

'Now you're being stuffy—sorry about that noble jazz. Tell me'—Sheila spoke impulsively—'if things did turn out that way, wouldn't you feel the need of a—a lover?'

Hysteria threatened again and Samantha swallowed its rising tide. 'I can't be normal, not having thought of that, fully expecting a husband to fulfil my love-life! What were your conclusions?'

The other girl flushed and answered rather defiantly, 'I would wait for the outcome of his operation, and if it was not ... er ... successful, I would probably chicken out. So there you have it!'

'Well, at least you're honest. What of the man's feelings, the hurt to his pride? Have you considered that?'

Suddenly flustered, Sheila laughed shakily. 'You do rub it in ... I haven't really given thought to his view. Rather selfish of me, mmm?' She put a hand on Sam's shoulder. 'I like you, Samantha MacDonald. Funny at that, for I was nurturing a special hate for the lass from Scotland. I think you'll be better for John than I'll ever be. You obviously care a great deal'—she paused dramatically—'but not with the passion of great, all-powerful Love! John adores you, and that alone helps an awful lot.'

'So, after that passionate (you're so fond of that word) outburst, the talented one takes her bow amid thunderous applause.' Sam clapped her hands and moved to the wardrobe. 'Now, I have ze leetle creation, for Modom's eyes only, from our exclusive boutique. It ees exquisite, Modom allows, *non*?' She kissed the tips of her fingers and pulled out a box. Reverently, from layers of tissue, she drew out the frock.

Sheila squeaked in sheer delight. The sheath of shimmering bronze, with an overskirt of billowing green gossamer, a deep yellow rose tucked at the waist was held rapturously in her careful hands.

'Blimey, it's a beaut! There's not much to the top, though. How does it stay up—willpower?'

Samantha laughed. 'I wouldn't dare breathe too heavily!'

'I wouldn't dare to breathe at all. Don't ever let passion strike while you're wearing this, it will surely show!'

'I shall make sure it's a secluded spot, then it won't matter, will it?'

'Rather dangerous, unless you're married to the guy!'

Samantha replaced the creation in its nest of tissue and

they spent the next hour happily immersed in a feminine world. The gong brought them back to earth and they went to lunch in friendly companionship.

CHAPTER 4

THE days slid away as in a dream. Luke left, satisfied that Samantha could manage his patient, promising to return as soon as possible. John had been indignantly shy, but the girl's matter-of-fact efficiency lulled his embarrassment and he was resigned and comforted by her deft hands when she appeared every morning to carry out Dr. Luke's instructions and treatment.

Most mornings Samantha took an early ride, with young Ham a willing partner. Mounted on Champagne, whose colour matched his name and though gentle yet displayed speed and stamina, she was fast finding her seat again. Day by day they ventured further and faster. The fresh, exhilarating air brought her back with rosy cheeks and bright eyes. She ruefully surveyed the freckles that danced across her nose; they by no means detracted from her looks, giving her a piquant glow on which Stephen remarked, 'The Aussie sun has kissed this madonna and left his mark. Delicious, I like it.'

Sam was made to stand in embarrassed silence while the family studied her and passed judgement. Yes, it suited her. 'Only it gives her a split personality—one minute you're looking at a lovely woman made for love, and then, just as one starts feeling amorous—presto!—that freckled gamin grins out at one. So frustrating!' Stephen's grin was wicked.

On this particular morning there had been no time for her usual canter. The men were preparing for muster and that kept everybody busy. Samantha helped in the kitchen. It seemed they were baking enough roasts and vegetables to feed an army! Just before midday Mina shooed her out of the kitchen door for a breather and she found a rickety old chair placed strategically under a red river gum. Whew, it was hot! A vagrant breeze cooled her neck and she closed her eyes to lean back with a grateful sigh.

Feathery clouds were peeping over the distant haze of

mountains and she hoped this was a sign of rain, although summer rains were few and far between. If it ever did rain she would walk in it and not even a shotgun would induce her to step indoors. It would be sheer bliss!

The hills intrigued her and she promised herself a nice long ride this very afternoon, in that direction. Ham was away with the men, but it would be heavenly to be alone for a change—yes, she would take her water-bag and wander away after lunch.

A snack lunch was served to all who remained at home, the men's tucker being packed and sent to them where they were busy at the nearest boundary. Tomorrow they would move further afield, taking packed saddle-bags with them.

Mame suggested a rest after lunch and the women and John retired to their respective rooms. Sam peeped in at Mandy's door to inform her that she was going out later (a sternly enforced rule, when the womenfolk went out alone, someone must be informed of their intentions). Mandy offered to accompany her, but Sam firmly assured her that she knew her way about and would be perfectly safe. A somewhat dubious Mandy hesitated and then reluctantly acquiesced.

Samantha undressed in her room and slipped a mu-mu over her head. It was made of a light material forming a loose shift gathered on a sleeveless yoke, cool and acceptable on hot summer days. She rested for an hour, then made her way to the shower. The water was tepid and did not help much in cooling her body. Back in her room, she stood at the window debating whether she really did want to go for that ride, but the hills drew her gaze compellingly and, almost against her will, she turned away to put on jeans and shirt. Knotting a dark-blue kerchief round her neck, she picked up her cotton sun-hat and went to the kitchen to fill the water-bag.

The horse whinnied as he caught sight of her; he was ready and willing for the outing he had missed that morning. A young aboriginal offspring, lazing in the shadow of the stable, helped Samantha with the saddle. The clouds were thicker over the hills and there was a curious stillness in the air.

It had not rained since she had come out to this land, but she had heard tales of the terrific downpours that occurred.

Not having experienced anything of that sort, Samantha gaily let her chestnut have his way. Those few clouds were far away and she would be back long before the rains came ... if it was going to rain.

She took her time and Champagne was quite content to amble along, to stop when she wanted to examine some plant or tree. Samantha recognised the waratah with its flower heads of dark-red blossoms, wattle tree and kangaroo paw. There were other fleshy-leafed, low-growing plants of which she picked specimens for later identification. Nearing the foothills she glanced at her watch—goodness, the time had flown! She really should turn back ... no, it was not far now, just to linger for a quick look around.

At last she dismounted and there was the most fascinating little brook tickling the feet of the gaunt mountain. Queer-shaped, stunted trees grew out of the crevices in weird and impossible shapes and she noted clumps of green fern where the stream kept their roots cool and damp. The chestnut nickered and Sam looked up as he pawed the ground nervously. The light seemed to have vanished very suddenly and a heavy growl of thunder startled her. She sprang to her feet.

'Lawdy, this is where we make for home, old horse!' Sam soothed and rubbed his neck, for he was moving restlessly. The chestnut hated storms, wanting the safety of his stable as soon as possible. The girl put her foot in the stirrup and as she swung into the saddle a clap of thunder and forked lightning burst across the heavens, splitting the world a-sunder.

Champagne reared up and his rider went flying backwards to land with an almighty crash flat on her back. Stars flamed and she knew no more.

Samantha was dimly conscious of gentle hands touching her forehead, moving over her body in careful exploration. She seemed to be floating in a sea of bubbles ... the hands moved to her head and she winced as hammers clashed and a band of fire threatened to crack her skull. A soothing voice came and went, murmuring over and over insistently, 'Can you hear me, girl, can you hear me? You're all right, honey. Can you move your arms and legs? Don't try to speak—just move your legs and arms if you can.'

The effort of opening her eyes brought a soft moan to her lips and the incredible voice came again. 'You're safe, love, quite safe ... can you hear me?' She lifted her arms, they were leaden, but she moved them and her legs as well.

What had happened to her? A spear of lightning flashed her memory back—and the horse rearing up—she must have fallen, her head ached intolerably. 'Yes, I hear you,' she managed, and the voice encouraged, 'Poor darling, your head is hurting badly, I know. I'm going to bring you to a sitting position. Tell me immediately if it hurts, please.'

At her whispered assent she felt firm arms slip under her shoulders and she was slowly lifted. 'Hurting, girl?'

Samantha gave a negative sigh and the voice became more hearty. 'Good! I'm going to carry you to a better shelter. My slicker helps a little, but you're soaking wet, and we can't have you catching pneumonia.' Strong arms carried her lightly. 'Here's a good overhang of rock, it will be dryer——' She was lowered and found herself sitting most comfortably on someone's lap, her head resting on a firmly broad shoulder.

'Cuddle in and relax. You fell out of the skies and I shan't let you return—you forgot your wings anyway.'

If only her head did not ache so she would be happy to sit here for the rest of her life! The rain stopped, the light grew stronger and Samantha opened her eyes to look into another pair so startlingly blue that she blinked and shut hers again.

'Relax, girl, you've had a nasty bash on the head. Talk only if you feel up to it. How did you get here?'

'Where is he ... my horse?' she whispered anxiously.

'Is that how you came to be here? I rode along the foothills and found you, fallen from the skies apparently. Your horse must have bolted.'

'Yes. Thunder clapped as I was mounting, he reared up and I—I fell off.'

They sat in silence for long moments.

'How does your head feel now, lass?'

'Much better, thanks.'

Samantha made an effort to sit up, but he held her firmly. 'No, don't move yet ... presently we'll try to take you to my house—it's nearest.'

She ventured another peep at him through her lashes. Slightly aquiline nose, a firm generous mouth which looked tender now but showed positive signs of inflexibility as well. A square, jutting chin redeemed by a deep cleft which made it look rather vulnerable, dark wet hair brushed back by impatient fingers and those startling cobalt-blue eyes framed by very black lashes. A strong throat ...

'Satisfied?' he enquired softly, and Samantha flushed and hurriedly dropped her eyes. His house the nearest? The only one she knew of belonged to—no, he couldn't possibly be— not this gentle stranger—that one was old and hard. Her heart began a staccato throb that echoed into her head and almost made her faint. He sensed the change and groaned in sympathy.

'Honey, I'm going to risk taking you on my horse. You need attention, so the sooner we move the better.' Holding her firmly, the man braced himself, a lithe movement brought him to his feet and he began to walk. 'I'll lift you on to my horse, you must hold on for the moment it takes me to mount behind you. Think you can do that?'

'Yes, I think so.'

'Good girl! Here goes—now hold on, I'm coming up. There, lean back against me. Steady on, Frost old boy ... easy now!' They started off, the girl biting hard on her lip as pain thudded through her head.

Mercifully she lost consciousness later, so was unaware of being lifted off again and carried into the house, of the stripping of wet clothes ... to be gently rolled into a large flannel gown and tucked under warm blankets, with hot water bottles at her feet.

Stephen was not at home, so Mark Lane sent for Jix, the abo jackaroo, ordered him to go chop-chop to Missus Mandy with the letter urging her to come immediately by car. He, Mark, had found this girl lying unconscious at the foothills —he had not asked her name—she might have concussion. No other injuries as far as he could make out, but Mandy must come prepared to spend the night. Jix could take Frost as he was ready, saddled.

Mark went back and took the girl's wrist. Her pulse felt quite normal and she was breathing deeply. He surmised that she was not still unconscious but had fallen into a deep sleep. Was this a good sign? He regarded her features intently. Dark lashes tipped in gold fanned her closed eyes and masses of hair, though damp, muddy and matted, showed gleams of copper. Her lips were softly full and pale. Puzzled, he scrutinised her more closely. She seemed strangely familiar—yet he knew that if he had once met her he would not have forgotten.

He turned away and walked to the dining-room, poured a measure of brandy and stood gazing into the glass. A dawning recollection came ... John had written glowing descriptions and they fitted the girl in the bedroom. They would most certainly be here by now, from Scotland. She would be the only stranger without knowledge of the sudden summer storms that could develop in these parts. Why was she alone and what was she doing so far from home? Samantha MacDonald?

Mark Lane downed the brandy, a sudden tightening of fingers on the slender stem brought it near breaking point. His mouth was strangely taut as he waited on the patio, in the rainwashed darkness. The car came to a stop and still the man waited silently while Mandy and Allan alighted. Without a greeting he beckoned them to follow him.

They entered silently and approached the bed. Mark moved to the other side. 'Who is she, Amanda, do you know her?' The question came in a grating whisper and was repeated. 'Who is she?'

Even in her agitation, Mandy registered the fact that he asked 'Who is she?' instead of 'How is she?' It seemed to matter more to him to identify the girl. Because it was too late for that other question? Through a thick mist she leaned over and took a slender wrist in unsteady fingers.

'Mark, it's Sam ... Samantha MacDonald. Oh, she's breathing, she's alive! She's—she's not——' Helplessly Mandy turned to her husband and he put quick protecting arms around her shaking shoulders.

'Of course she's breathing, dear. Did you think ... come now, love, we need you. Mark did write that she might have concussion and no other apparent injuries. Move over and let me see. Being a vet does help. She's breathing quite steadily. Apart from a raging headache, she should do in a couple of days.' Allan straightened up after examining the girl, who stirred and moaned softly at his touch.

'So, as I thought, Samantha MacDonald.' Mark Lane spoke as if to himself. His lips tightened and a fleeting, baffled expression darkened his eyes.

41

Allan looked at his wristwatch. 'Evening session is due any moment now. We'll try to contact Luke for some advice. Come, Mark, switch on your set.' He strode out purposefully and Mark slowly followed.

Mandy gazed at his back, puzzled. What was wrong with him? He was taking this rather badly and had scared the life out of her with that grim look. She was to blame for allowing Sam to ride out on her own, but she really had not noticed the weather, and consequently had not warned the poor dear about sudden storms, nor did she dream that Sam would ride so far on her own. When Sam's horse had arrived riderless they had immediately set out, Allan and two abos, and John was out of his mind, cursing his disability. They had met Jix with the message from Mark and Allan had raced back to pick up Mandy and the car, stopping only to reassure John and Mame. Now they were here and Sam seemed all right, so why was Mark's demeanour so strange, grim? Somebody was in for it, and she had a nasty suspicion that it was yours truly, Amanda Jones!

She leaned forward as Samantha opened her eyes. 'Sam dear, it's me, Mandy. Tell me, for pity's sake, how do you feel?'

'My head's thumping like a drum, otherwise I'm fine, Mandy. Did I scare you? I'm so sorry.' Veiled eyes strayed over the room. 'I've been dreaming of soft voices and strong gentle hands and now ... Where am I—tell me, Mandy, where am I?'

The tremor was so marked in her voice that Mandy hastened to sooth and reassure her. 'You're in Mark's home, darling. He found and brought you here. You've had a nasty fall, just relax and don't worry, you're warm and safe and I shall stay with you.'

That was what the voice had murmured—'warm and safe'. Those firm, tender hands—she was safe in Mark's house. Words spoken tenderly. 'Poor darling, can you hear me?' Mark had said that? Did he know to whom he was speaking —to Samantha MacDonald, of whom he disapproved? And she had nestled in his arms, quite content to stay there indefinitely! Hysteria welled and Samantha struggled to subdue it as she raised her arm across her eyes, to hide her emotion from Mandy's anxious eyes.

'What is it, Sam, please tell me if you're hurting anywhere? Allan and Mark are on the set, getting in touch with John and Luke. Is there anything you want them to know?'

Samantha thought, 'Oh golly, yes, I'm hurting inside, for sure.' Aloud she said, 'Just tell John I'm fine and to send for me as soon as possible, please.'

'Not until tomorrow and then only with Doctor Luke's permission. I'm so sorry about your head, but mighty glad that's all that's wrong with you. Mark looked so desperate when we arrived and scared me out of my wits. I imagined the worst when he met us at the door.'

'I guess it must have been some bind for him to carry me all this way, hence the desperation.' Sam smiled shakily. 'Go and give my message to John.'

'—And call Mandy at once, Allan. Over,' John's voice came over the transceiver as Mandy entered. She sat down and replied, 'I'm here, John. Sam is awake, her head aches like the dickens, otherwise she says she's fine and for you to send for her as soon as possible. I told her only with Luke's permission. Over to Luke?' Allan nodded that they were in touch with the doctor.

'I've told Allan what to do, Mandy. Mark fortunately has the pills that Samantha can take, give them to her and keep her quiet. Tommy will bring me over tomorrow and we shall see if she can be moved safely. I'm darn glad you were there to help her, Mark, otherwise there would have been pneumonia to contend with as well. Over to John.'

'My thanks too, for being on the spot, Mark.' There was a catch in his voice. 'I'll be over tomorrow. Mame refuses to let them bring me now, but I guess a good sleep will do my girl more good than my presence at this stage. See you too, Luke. Watch her, Mandy . . .' His voice faded out and Mame came on. 'Mark, we didn't even know you were back. Look after the girl, and come and see me soon. 'Bye now!'

The operator spoke. 'I'm glad to hear that Miss Mac-Donald isn't seriously injured and recovering, and that goes for all who are listening. Any more messages? Over.' Allan switched off.

Mandy turned to Mark. 'Will you say hello now, Mark? I'm very sorry, it was all my fault. Sam did tell me she was going out and I didn't notice the weather. I would never have allowed her to go on Champagne, knowing how he hates thunder. I didn't think she would ride so far away,' she pleaded with him. 'Don't be angry, please!'

Mark put a hand on her hair and tugged a curl. 'I'm surely not blaming you. The girl was either unaware of or deliberately broke our strict rule of lone riding for the womenfolk. Anyway, hadn't you better say this to John? Miss MacDonald is his girl, not mine. As luck would have it, I saw the storm approaching and decided to ride to the gully, looking for stray sheep. You know how fast that stream can bank up in the gullies. I arrived back this morning.'

'How did the business come off in Kingston?' asked Allan.

'Very well, our grade of wool speaks for itself. I also acquired two smashing bay geldings. They'll be boxed here and should arrive in a day or two.'

'Sam will be wondering what's keeping us. I suggest you two pop in and say goodnight. Give the pills to me, Mark. How many must she take—I presume they're for the headache? Then you can scoot off, Allan, and keep the children quiet, don't let them worry John,' Mandy admonished her husband.

'How is John?' Mark asked her.

Allan answered, 'He's fine, a bit stroppy sometimes, but who can blame him with a lovely fiancée hovering around and nothing he can do about it? Luke is pinning his faith on your friend Hans Getsenberg, and Samantha is quite convinced that John will walk again.'

Abruptly Mark Lane turned and stubbed out his cigarette. 'I'll fetch those pills, Mandy. You go along to her, I'll bring them. She must have two now and more later, if she can't sleep.' He walked out of the room.

Samantha opened her eyes as Mandy and Allan came in. 'Did John get my message, Mandy?'

'Yes, everybody sends their love. Luke will be here tomorrow and Allan will bring John—he insists on coming. Fortunately Mark has the pills Luke prescribes in his medical kit. They're for your aching little head. Allan, say goodnight now and then push off, love.'

Allan kissed her, saluted Samantha and left the room. They heard him calling Mark and shortly after that the car pulled away. 'I'm going to warm some milk while Mark is finding the pills. You must drink it hot ... won't be long!' Mandy hurried off to the kitchen.

Samantha closed her eyes and moved her head slightly ... what a lump there was, it felt the size of a pumpkin! If she kept her head turned it was not so bad. She thought of all the trouble she was causing, disrupting the tenor of the Lane household ... and Mark's. No wonder Mandy said he looked grim. She looked pathetically childish as she lay with closed eyes, her hair a tumbled mass and freckles showing clearly on her pale face. Young and vulnerable.

So thought Mark as he silently entered and regarded her. The picture sent a queer pain feathering under his ribs.

Sensing a presence, her eyes flew open and widened as she stared up at him. Into eyes, glittering pools of blue that seemed to hypnotise, and Samantha strove in vain to tear her gaze away. They were coming closer ... too close ... and then they moved away, casually, to her hair.

'Sorry I couldn't do anything about this.' Mark flicked a strand of hair across her face. 'It might hurt too much. Mandy can fix it later ... here are your pills. Feeling better?' Just as casually he walked to the window, turned and leaned against it. He crossed his feet and, holding one bent elbow in the palm of his hand, cupped the other hand under his chin and regarded her silently.

The girl's hypnotised eyes followed him. This man was tall and his slender hips, in whipcord slacks, moved with flexibility and a resilient grace. No wonder he had carried her so lightly! Those shoulders were broad. She should know—only a short while ago her head had rested very comfortably against them.

He was waiting, a sardonic gleam in his eyes. Samantha flushed, wondering if he could read her thoughts. 'Yes, thank you,' she managed at last. 'I've caused you a lot of trouble, having to carry me all this way, and then——'

'—Having to put you to bed. Wet jeans can be tough, mmm? Anyway, my horse carried you, not I.' His glance wandered from her face to the mound of blankets. 'The gown was the only suitable warm garment I could rustle up.' Mark grinned at the sudden confusion of his victim.

Samantha stiffened—how hateful of him to mention it now and positively rub it in too!

This was not the same man who had treated her so tenderly a few hours ago. Because he knew her identity and wanted to crush that picture out of her mind? Well, she would show there was no need to do so, simply by ignoring it. Sam lifted her chin defiantly and winced as sudden pain lanced through her head.

Mark was at her side in one lithe movement. 'I wouldn't do that again if I were you. Not now anyway. Time for that later, then you can lift that stubborn chin in defiance, without pain.' Without more ado he slid his arm under her shoulders, lifting her slightly, while he fluffed up the pillows with his free hand.

Sam was speechless. She could only stare at him in amazement as he gently manoeuvred her into a more comfortable position. And then he stooped again and kissed the tip of her nose!

'Hello, Samantha MacDonald. We've met very, very informally. Mark Lane at your service ... and you certainly demanded a lot of that commodity!'

She was still looking at him as if mesmerised when Mandy breezed in with the hot milk. 'Here we are!' She looked from one to the other. Mark seemed amused and Samantha was flushed and breathing fast. 'You're not working up a fever now, Sam dear? That mustn't happen. Have you been upsetting her, Mark? She was fine a few moments ago.'

'Now why should I upset her, dear cousin? After battling the elements and risking my very life to bring her back safely, applying first aid and practically breathing new life into a cold body, why should I undo all the good work? I merely introduced myself,' he answered gravely, while his eyes looked positively wicked.

Mrs. Jones studied him accusingly. 'Just meeting you seems to have upset her then, I know you and your ways, Mark Lane! Take your milk with two pills, honey. Who propped you up so nicely—yourself?' At Sam's indignant glance at the man she nodded. 'Hmmm, we'll leave your hair, too painful to do something to it. Let me wipe your face with this cloth, you look so hot.'

'Thanks, Mandy, I feel fine, but please take these hot-water bottles out, they—er—make me too warm.' Sam lowered her lashes to avoid the amused glint in blue eyes.

Mandy slid her hands under the blanket and removed the offending bottles. 'Would you like me to sit with you or would you rather sleep?'

'Those pills will put her to sleep within the next few

minutes. I'll leave now. Stay a while, Mandy. Goodnight, Miss Mac, have a good rest and you'll be fit in the morning.' Mark touched her cheek lightly with the back of his hand.

'Goodnight Mr. Lane, and thank you again. I'm indeed grateful for your superhuman efforts to save my life—at the risk of yours.' She bit her lip too late to stop that barb, but smiled with sweet apology. 'I've learnt my lesson and shan't be so foolish ever again. Goodnight.'

Her smile seemed to shake Mark. He took a hesitant step forward, stopped and glanced at Mandy, ran an impatient hand through his hair and then turned to walk out of the room.

Samantha's lids drooped and Mandy took the glass out of lax fingers. 'I'll leave you now, I'm sleeping in the adjoining room. If you need me, just call out, I'm a light sleeper and will be with you instantly ... promise?'

'Darling Mandy, you're so good to me ...' Drowsiness overcame her and within minutes Samantha was asleep.

Much later, the man on the patio, smoking his pipe and pacing restlessly, heard her moan. He was in the room before Mandy could slip out of bed. She joined him and they stood looking down at the sleeping girl. Mandy turned to him. 'Go to bed now, Mark, she's all right. It's very late.'

Mark Lane left her and went to his room.

CHAPTER 5

THE morning dawned bright and clear, rain-washed earth, trees and shrubs exuded a tangy, fresh scent. It was carried on a soft breeze through the open window and Samantha awakened with the delightful touch across her face and breathed deeply of its fragrance. The sun peeped in at her window and beckoned invitingly. She drew up to a sitting position and found her head did not ache at all, except for a slight heaviness in the nape of her neck.

If only she could have a bath or shower; her hair felt so sticky. She was still debating the risk of getting up and finding the bathroom when she heard a soft tap on the door. At her call it was pushed open and a smiling counterpart of Mina ambled into the room with a tea-tray held aloft.

'Morning, mam.' The dark woman put the tray on the bedside table. 'I'm Danielle, and sure am glad that yo' is looking well. Plurry very sorry dat I'm not here las' night to tend to yo'. 'Twould pleasure greatly if I can do something longa now?'

'Why, thank you, Danielle. I'm pleased to meet you. I would love a bath right now, but I'd better wait, in case I incur Mrs. Mandy's displeasure. Tea is just what I need, thank you.'

'Thank you, mam, I'll take Miz Mandy's tea now.' At the door she stepped aside as Mark strode in.

'Morning,' he said gruffly, and scrutinised the reclining girl intently.

'Morning, Mark—Mr. Lane.' Samantha was thrown into confusion at the sudden intrusion.

'Should you be sitting up? How is the head this morning?'

'Fine, I'm fit as a fiddle and all I crave is a bath.'

'Mandy can give you a sponge-down in bed. I'm not taking any chances until Luke has looked you over.'

'But I'm fine, I've just told you——' she began, but he stopped her with a raised hand. 'Don't argue, please ... morning, Mandy.' Mandy had joined him.'

'Morning, Mark, Sam. Heavens, did I sleep! So much for my boast last night. You're looking better, Sam. Sleep well?'

'She wants to bath, but you'll merely give her a wash in bed, Mandy. That's all Miss Mac is going to have right now.' Mark turned on his heel and left them.

'Well, I'm blessed!' Samantha gazed indignantly at the open doorway, then back at her companion. 'Oh well, bring your tea here, Mandy,' she urged in a more suppressed tone.

Mandy complied and they sipped their tea in savouring silence. Mark Lane certainly took his word and law for granted. One of those masterful men. Sam tried hard to associate this one with that other tender person she had known for a brief time. Did that soft voice, that caressing tone emanate from this same person? That was surely a dreamy figmentation, but real enough to tuck away in the treasure corner of one's heart.

Mandy jumped briskly. 'A quick shower and change, then we'll attend to your needs. Better do as the boss says, settle for a sponge-down. Ructions just might occur if we don't!'

She proved surprisingly adept at the ministrations and when all was done she slipped Samantha's own gown on the girl, having brought it with her. Brushing the tangled hair brought many a wince of pain from Sam, who gritted her teeth and held out until a sympathetic Mandy had taken every snarl out. Danielle magically produced a green ribbon to keep the hair neatly back.

Mandy stripped the bed and put clean crisp linen back while Danielle dusted and tidied the room. Samantha, looking fresh and appealing, settled back to wait for John and Luke. She enjoyed a dainty breakfast and discovered she was ravenously hungry.

Mark walked up from the pens when the car pulled up and Luke alighted with a friendly wave. Tommy Crawford had flown him as far as John's place and, Allan being up to his eyes in book work, Luke had offered to drive with John. They took the chair out and Mark helped to seat John. He felt a raging and wordless pity when he saw how helpless his cousin had become. They had grown up together and there was a very close bond of friendship and affection between them. Mark covered his pity with a casual, 'Hi, Johnny cobber, good to have you back.' They gripped hands in greeting. 'The men are on your south boundary, they should be at gecko bore by tomorrow. How are you, Luke, had any more babies lately?' On that light note they entered the house with a quick lift, by the two men, of the chair up the steps.

Mark put a detaining hand on Luke's shoulder, allowing John to wheel ahead on his own. 'Put me in the picture regarding John. Those two don't want an audience right now.'

'—Not just a ruse to run away from that madhouse, mmm? Don't ever frighten me like that again, my darling.' John was at the side of the bed, both Samantha's hands clasped in his, when the two men paused at the door.

Samantha leaned over and returned his smile, her eyes shining. 'It's good to see you again, John. I feel as if I've been away for ages. Can I go home now?'

'So much for Mark's hospitality!' John teased, his eyes lighting up at her eager query.

Over his shoulder Samantha caught Mark's impenetrable gaze and her pulse jumped suddenly, crazily. She found herself stammering, 'Mark—has been very good to—to me. I'm grateful—but please let me go back with you. I want to see— Mame and the k-kids,' she finished lamely. That cool blue stare unnerved her. Why the devil did she stutter and stammer when he was near? Sam prided herself on her coolness in any given situation and now she was acting like a silly schoolgirl. 'Like a stupid crow,' she chided herself. 'Stop croaking!'

Luke walked forward. 'I'm having a say in this matter, not so? Out, everyone! I'm bursting to turn this young woman upside down and hear the loose bones rattling, callous medico that I am. Of course, if Samantha wants to have an audience, who am I to stop you all watching the performance? Tickets, please!'

John backed his chair to the doorway. 'That sounds too gruesome for my innocent tastes. We decline with thanks, Mark!'

Mark stepped back and waited for John to pass through, paused with his hand on the doorknob. 'I'll leave you too. I don't care much for repeat performances!' He gently closed the door.

Fifteen minutes later Luke smiled at his patient. 'All right, you may get up, you nagging little wombat. I can't find anything wrong with you except for that almighty bump on your head. You're a lucky girl, thanks to Mark's timely arrival and prompt attention. Being drenched could have had quite serious consequences coupled with the shock of your fall. I'll call Mandy.'

'Thanks, Luke, you are a darling, but would you mind not calling Mandy and would you wait in her room while I dress? I want to surprise John, and if you go out now they'll ask questions.' She waited eagerly.

'But who'll help you to dress? Me, I'd love that!'

'You're a naughty doctor-man, and I shall tell all at the next session and then you'll have to flee the country, so there! Sneak out and find Danielle if you think I can't manage on my own.' Samantha pulled a comical face at him.

'Very well, I'll spy her out. Seriously again, Samantha, you'll have to take things easy for the next few days. Quit chasing round the countryside and keep out of the kitchen. I know you'll be tempted to help, with the tally in the offing, but curb it, will you?'

'It's a promise, Luke.'

He stepped out and presently returned with Danielle. When told of the conspiracy, she joined in with gusto. She opened the case that John had brought and laid out the contents. Luke retired through the connecting door, leaving it open. He lay back on Mandy's bed and lit a cigarette.

Samantha felt slightly dizzy when she stood up, but not for worlds would she let on to the lubra, and presently the feeling passed. Danielle helped her, chattering softly. 'Dem's pretty unders, and yo' sure have plurry gorjis figger, beggin' pardon, mam.' Sam blushed as a quiet chuckle came from the other room.

'I'll say!' Clearly Doctor Luke was enjoying himself.

She wriggled into her cinnamon brown shift and on her feet went brown, buckled sandals. A pat of powder over the freckles, a pale lipstick and she was ready. Luke came through at her call and offered his arm. ' "Gorjis" Miss MacDonald, at your service.'

When they suddenly appeared on the patio where the others were sitting, Mandy jumped up in surprise, Mark straightened up from the pillar against which he had been leaning and John gripped the sides of his chair as though he too would stand up. Luke led Sam to his side. 'She's all yours, John.'

Mandy exclaimed, 'This calls for a celebration. I'll fetch the tea—Danielle!' She collided with a beaming lubra.

'I'se jus' come to info'm company dat I help Missy Sam to dress up, not mister flying doc.'

'Well, I should think so? I hope nobody thought otherwise!' Luke was suitably shocked and then spoilt the effect by winking broadly at an embarrassed girl.

Mark removed the pipe from his mouth and Sam knew— she just knew—he was going to say something awful and her palms became sticky with apprehension as he raised a quizzical eyebrow.

'That dress certainly becomes you, my dear. Far more attractive than dirty wet jeans and shirt.'

What a beast of a man, and she was not his 'dear'! She composed herself with difficulty. 'Yes, Mr. Lane, water and sand mixed together usually result in a sorry mess, but it will wash out, don't worry,' she returned pertly, and turned to John with glowing cheeks. 'Tell me, John dear, have you

51

many worrigals—or should I say dingos—worrying your sheep?'

John looked amazed at this sudden change of subject, but Mark burst into hearty laughter. 'Oh, well said, Miss Mac. I'm duly abashed.' He knocked his pipe against an ashtray. 'Lead not the lamb to the slaughter, ye wicked dingo! I shall most contritely remove myself, incidentally, it's session time. Shall I tell Mame you'll be home—when?'

'We'll have tea and then get cracking. I'm going to make this girl rest all afternoon,' John stated firmly.

'Good. I'll probably call in this evening to see her—meaning Mame,' Mark added as he caught a startled expression on the girl's face.

He could be quick on the uptake. Samantha really had thought he meant to call on her. She decided that she must mask her expressions, be more careful in future ... develop a poker face.

Luke evidently had an idea as to the trend of Mark's remark and Samantha's reply concerning the dirty wet clothes, for he was studying her with an amused glint in his eyes.

'What was Mark laughing at?' John was still puzzling.

Luke came to her rescue. 'He was teasing my patient.' John opened his mouth and Luke continued hurriedly, 'What do you know about dingos, honey?'

'A sort of dog or wolf, aren't they?—they don't bark but howl very dismally, especially at night, and cause heavy losses by their wanton destruction of sheep and lambs ... am I right?'

'Yes. Every now and then we hunt them out and destroy as many as possible. They multiply very quickly, we still have trouble with them,' John answered, and went on to talk of other hazards on sheep-stations, forgetting the topic of Mark's laughter. Mandy and Danielle appeared with the tea and Mark followed on their heels.

'All is well, Mame awaits your arrival. When are you going back, Luke?'

'This evening, with the return plane. I gave John his treatment this morning. Sam, you must rest tomorrow, so John can forgo his agony for one day. It won't matter that much.'

'Thanks, Luke, I'm sure I'll manage. I'm not that bad...'

'Listen to your doctor, Mac.'

Mandy spoke before Samantha could think up a suitable reply to Mark's curt order. 'Allan and I will be going off in a couple of days, holidays are over for the scamps.' Hamilton and Mame junior attended school in Adelaide and boarded at a private hostel. Ham would be entering university the following year and was very keen to follow in his father's footsteps, specialising with horses.

Mark offered cigarettes and Samantha accepted one, though she did not smoke often. Mark leaned over with his lighter and again there was the enigmatic look in his eyes as they met hers over the flame. Did he also disapprove of women smoking? Just too bad! She met his gaze steadily and shrugged off a faint feeling of discomfort.

Luke stood up and stretched long arms. 'Shall we go now? Mark, grab that side,' he indicated John's chair.

When they pulled off Mark saluted casually and Sam, looking back through the rear window, watched him walk away with a lithe purposeful stride. He did not look back.

'Oh, Mame, such a fuss!' Sam laughed. 'Just a crack on the head and I'm treated like royalty.' In truth she was very close to tears, the family were so good to her and it was wonderful to know they really cared. She was seated in the old armchair, to which Ham had manfully offered to carry her. When she protested he gravely offered a strong arm for her to lean on and Twinkles had almost knocked her down with a spontaneous, affectionate hug!

Now Mame hovered around. 'Shouldn't she go to bed, her poor head—Mina! Where was that lubra woman—so darn slow with the tea?' 'Please sit down, darling Mame. Mina won't be long and I won't fade away, I promise.' Sam waited while the old lady seated herself. 'I'm deeply sorry for causing all this anxiety and I'm prepared to take what's coming, s-so go ahead.' She looked down at her hands nervously.

Mame scrutinised her with a probing gaze. 'Humph!' she said at last. 'I gather you've learnt your lesson, child, and you're far too pale, so I won't scold you this time. Never go riding on that horse when there's a storm brewing.'

'Yes, Mame,' Samantha said meekly.

'Somebody should have warned you of his hatred of storms.' Mame looked accusingly at Mandy, who was sitting on the steps.

That young matron went scarlet with confusion. 'Oh, now really, Mame——' she began, but Samantha forestalled her. 'Please don't blame Mandy, she didn't realise——'

Mame held up an imperious hand. 'That's enough from both of you. I will not tolerate slackness or lack of observation, so keep both eyes open in future.' She suddenly smiled at them with singular sweetness, 'Pour the tea, Amanda, and lift your backside, lazybones. John and Luke are about to expire.'

'Mame, you're a fraud and a fickle woman!' Luke chimed in.

'How dare you speak to me like that, young man!'

'—and I adore you!' Luke grinned at her frustration.

After tea Mandy and the two men went indoors and the two youngsters sat on the steps discussing the geldings Mark had purchased. Allan had told them and they awaited the arrival of the horses with great excitement. Mame and Samantha remained sitting in drowsy silence.

'Did you like Mark?' The old lady abruptly broke into Sam's reverie.

She did not want to hurt Mame's feelings, knowing how fond she was of her nephew, yet she could not in all honesty answer with a direct affirmative. She compromised. 'He was very good to me, Mame, I appreciate his help and——'

'I asked if you liked him, gal.'

Samantha remained silent.

Mame looked at her intently. 'Mark Lane has evidently rubbed you the wrong way, one way or another.'

'Not at all——'

'Don't lie, my pretty. You'll get to like him, you'll have no option—Mark grows on one.' Thus predicted Mame.

'If you say so, Mame.' The unbelief in her voice belied Samantha's words.

Mame chuckled suddenly. 'I want to be present if and when you two have words. Your cheeky spirit and his fire—well! A bit of spirit and gumption is good for the soul,' she trailed wickedly.

Tommy's plane came in late afternoon and Luke went back with him after extracting another promise from Samantha to take things easy for a few days.

Mark would most likely stay for dinner. Samantha lay on

her bed and thought about that unpleasing likelihood. Mina could bring her dinner on a tray ... no, that would not do. After declaring herself quite fit it would only cause embarrassing questions. No, she would go to dinner looking cool and sophisticated, and if he spoke to her in his cynical manner, she would answer astutely, with aplomb. She stood up and walked to the mirror, tried a laconic pose, then lifted her chin haughtily. Pain shot through her head and she dropped it hurriedly. A suspicion of a smile touched her lips as she remembered another time when she had tried to lift a defiant chin.

If she was going to be sophisticated something must be done about her hair, pain or not. It must be washed and done up in an elegant chignon. Samantha peeped out of her door, found no signs of activity, gathered her toilet bag and towel and sneaked off to the bathroom. The next heavenly hour was spent showering and washing her hair until it sang through her fingers. The swelling on her head had lessened considerably and she ignored the dull pain that still throbbed now and then. The shower refreshed and exhilarated her and she felt ready to meet any new problems.

Choosing a frock was next on her agenda and she studied her wardrobe contemplatively. Before leaving Scotland she had drawn her nest-egg to splurge recklessly on filmy underwear and a few lovely dresses. She finally chose an ivory patterned silk sheath with a neckline high in the front and plunging low down the back ... very sophisticated indeed! The Lane family liked to dress for dinner, so it would not be too obvious, although why she troubled so much to boost her morale she could not fathom, never before having felt this necessity.

Samantha then sat at her window, drying the heavy masses of hair. Mina brought a cup of tea with a message from Mame that she was not to budge from her room till the evening. Mina was pleased to see Miz Sam well and had a few choice words to say about 'that dirty plurry nag dat should be sent to de boneyard'. Sam finally gathered that the reference pointed to Champagne. Mina wanted to send Cindy later, to help Samantha dress, but the girl assured her she was quite capable and did not need help.

Dinner was delayed while they waited for Mark. Time

passed and a huffed Mame decided they would not wait any longer, so the family trooped to the dinner table. They were about to sit down when his car pulled up and a moment later Mark came striding in. He made straight for the white-haired old lady, to lift her in his arms and kiss her before she could voice a protest.

'Sorry to be late, love. I joined the men at the far boundary and we came in late ... how's my sweetheart?' Putting her back on her feet, he turned to greet the rest of the family. The children were delighted to see him, especially after certain information was disclosed about parcels in his car, not to be collected until they had finished dinner. Knowing his way, they immediately sat down and asked their father if they could tuck in—why was everybody so slow!

Mark turned to Samantha with a forthright, probing gaze. 'You've recovered remarkably well and are looking quite beaut, I'll say.' His eyes travelled to her hair, done in a full, low chignon on the nape of her neck. Lithe steps brought him behind her chair and he held it politely as she sat down. Confusion threatened again, but Samantha overpowered it and murmured, 'Thank you, Mark.' He took a seat and the family started their dinner.

Mark said to John, 'We can start your tally tomorrow ... you'll have a good crop this season.'

'Right-ho, Mark, then you can start your own muster. Allan won't be here, he and Mandy are taking the children back to school.'

'Yes, I'd like to stay over for a day or two if Allan can be spared. Shopping, you know,' Mandy broke in.

'Ohhh!' groaned Allan. 'There goes my hard-earned cash!'

'I haven't a rag to wear,' protested his wife. 'How can I compete with all the lovely things that lass brought with her?' She indicated Samantha.

All eyes turned to 'that lass', who suddenly sat upright while scarlet flags unfurled in her cheeks.

'Aw, hon, but you're an old married woman, with your man firmly shackled,' Allan pointed out.

'Yes, shackled to a man with a leering, roving eye. When you look at Sam you positively drool!' Mandy retorted.

Allan lowered pained eyes to his plate and tried, unsuccessfully, to look henpecked. 'Yes, dear. I shall not lift up mine eyes to said vision, I promise—at least not until I've finished dinner.'

'Oh, you——!' His wife made a face at him.

Amidst spirited chatter they finished dinner. Samantha joined in, more composed now. She lost her nervousness, caused by Mark's presence, by studiously ignoring his frequent, level blue gaze. Afterwards they all went out to the cool veranda and the men lit up and smoked with sighs of satisfaction. Electricity was provided by generator and lighting plant. The veranda was enclosed with mosquito netting to keep out the myriads of insects. Samantha sat close to John and his one hand rested on her lap, enclosing both hers in a warm clasp.

Mark's visit, a year back, to Africa was the point of discussion and he answered a query put by Allan. 'The goldmines are quite fabulous and for miles on end, as you approach Johannesburg, there are dumps of wastage and slag. Townships have been built on these. Cities like Capetown, Johannesburg, Durban and Pretoria are modern and beautiful. Overseas people don't realise the culture and industrialism of the Republic and Rhodesia. They still consider that continent wild and untamed.' Mark's cobalt-blue eyes made a startling contrast to the deep tan of his strong face and they were slightly puckered as he recalled, 'Large settlements have been set aside, as we too are doing, for their Bantus, natives, and they're taught their trade in various schools and universities. They also have their water problems, as we have, and becoming aware of the danger of drought and its consequences, their Government has started building dams on a big scale, for the conservation of that precious commodity.'

The company listened with genuine interest, all eyes intent on the tall, sun-tanned man as he continued: 'Along the coast from St. Lucia throughout Natal, sugar cane and pineapples are extensively cultivated in endless plantations.' He paused to light a cigarette and Samantha leaned forward, her interest held by the fascination his deep voice brought into narrative, of that dark continent.

'What about the people—what are they like, Mark?'

Piercingly blue eyes glinted her way. 'Sunny as their skies and open-hearted, Samantha, generous with their friendship; our sort of people. The ladies are up-to-the-minute with the latest fashions and the nightclubs and theatres are every bit

57

as good as one would find in Europe or other continents.'

'No wonder you weren't in a hurry to come back from that trip; more wonder that you came back without a wife in tow!' Mame's smile was sly.

'When I find that girl, if I ever do find her, rest assured I shall take what is mine. And I'll never settle for second best!' A smouldering gaze dropped suddenly, to rest for endless moments on the hands held in John's clasp.

Samantha MacDonald felt a strange compulsion to withdraw her hands from their possessive imprisonment. She did so, lifting them to tuck away a stray strand of hair, covering her impulsive movement with the gesture. Why did his eyes drop to John's hands, and hers? Was he still mad because John had chosen her and not Sheila? His plans for them had gone awry, soured, so that little bit about 'second best' was aimed at her? Sam stifled the pinpoints of anger and deliberately channelled back to a further query on Africa.

'The animals—those lovely wild animals—have they all disappeared, wiped out by indiscriminate hunters?'

Mame's quick eyes had noted the quick withdrawal of the girl's hands and the cover-up gesture, also the spots of colour on smooth cheeks. The old lady felt a sudden constriction in the region of her heart.

'You mean the wild fauna?' Mark seemed to have lost the trend of his narrative; he was silently studying his own hands. 'Almost. Vast parks have been allocated for their protection, in Natal and further north. I took a four-day trip through the Kruger National Park, in the Transvaal, and enjoyed it immensely. We saw herds of elephants, zebra, rhinoceroses and buck. The sable antelope are fantastically beautiful ... monkeys and apes. You're not allowed out of your car while on the road. We took cinés of prides of lions and many others. It would take all evening to describe everything. The rest camps are modern and comfortable. I'll get Stephen to show the movies some other time.'

He stood up and stretched lazily. 'I must push off now, there's a heavy day ahead tomorrow. I'll be here at the crack o' dawn, John. So long, all.' He turned abruptly and swung down the steps. Seconds later the station wagon roared into the night and powerful car lights dwindled, to become obscured by dust and darkness.

When everybody had gone to bed and long after the house

was quiet, Samantha lay wide-eyed, unable to sleep. She fought against the strange longings and thoughts which beset her and eventually fell into troubled sleep. Someone else was also having troubled thoughts; Mame Lane only found rest in the early hours of morning.

CHAPTER 6

THE next morning saw everybody up before dawn. A hasty breakfast for the men and they were off to the pens for the tally. Mandy bustled about, seeing to last minute preparations for the trip to Adelaide. The children were constantly underfoot, very glum at thoughts of back-to-school, disappointed at not being able to see Mark's geldings before they left. Twinkles wandered off to say goodbye to the lubras and tiny taweenas whom she adored. Ham also disappeared and Samantha found him at the stables, whispering earnestly into the ear of his favourite horse.

Twinkles returned and pleaded with Sam not to have any more accidents because it would delay their dancing lessons when she returned from this 'boresome business of education'. Sam duly gave a solemn promise to watch her step and smiled at the anxious pixie face. The Jones family departed amidst boisterous farewells, Allan groaning loudly at his wife's parting shot—'I shall splurge every last cent and then we shall see what my darling roving eye thinks of his old married bag!'

Mina pushed Samantha out of the kitchen and Cindy refused her offer of assistance in the bedrooms, so she finally marched off to John's room. There at least she had a job of work to do that no one else could do! John, poor dear, was definitely not in a good mood this morning, wanting to join in the activities and feeling very frustrated at his inability to do so.

Sam chatted gaily during his treatment, but he would not respond and merely grunted at her efforts to arouse him. Mora waited to wheel him out to the garden where he was then grumpily ordered to be off. 'I'm not a complete nincompoop. I'll push myself. Be off to your other duties and stop hovering like an old hen!'

He finally drew his chair under a fine old myrtle and Samantha, who had walked beside his chair, seated herself on the asbestos bench that leaned against the tree tunk. John looked around in active irritation. 'God, Sam, how long must I carry on like this? So useless ... Why doesn't Luke contact Getsenberg, or vice versa? Maybe that great panjandrum isn't interested in my case ... maybe he knows there's nothing he can do for me! You'll be saddled with a cripple for the rest of your life. You can bet that sweet life I won't let that happen. We can break the engagement, I insist you have your freedom ...' There was bitter desperation in his voice.

'John! Don't you dare speak like that!' Storm signals of genuine anger shook her. 'We haven't faltered in our belief that you'll walk again. Bill Strang, Luke and Mame all share that belief, are you going to give in now? You've been strong and wonderful all this time and now, like a weakling, a silly dolt, you talk about cripples and broken engagements ... I won't have it, do you hear?' Samantha jumped up and stood in front of his chair, her eyes aglow with indignation.

Mark and Mame, unseen by either of them, halted within earshot of her tirade.

'I've been like this for months now, Sam, and they should be able to judge if it's any use—about the operation. The suspense of not knowing——' John flushed and his eyes sparked back at her.

Samantha was actually relieved to see that spark, which she had deliberately invoked. It was far better than the despair she had glimpsed moments ago. 'Luke will keep his promise to let us know the moment Doctor Getsenberg is ready for you, or when you're ready for him. A case like this can't be decided in a—a day. If you're trying, in this silly manner, to get rid of me, just you jolly well say so and I'll vanish like a wisp of smoke. Wanting to jilt me, indeed! Now that we're letting our hair down, what about your writing prowess? It's high time you did something constructive, and you're not too incapable of that, are you? Stop complaining about being useless and stop sulking!' Arms akimbo, she waited.

Mark gave a low angry exclamation and made a move, but Mame stopped him with an admonitory hand on his arm.

'Of course I can write, but my thoughts are only of you. I

love you and—and want you——' John stuttered.

'So? If that's all that worries you—wanting me—well, that can wait, and so can I. I'm not worried one bit. And you can curb your emotions too, my good man. Never having had great emotional or passionate experiences I most probably don't realise what I'm missing, even though——' A discreet cough from Mame, who suddenly felt guilty about eavesdropping, stopped Sam's words in mid-air and she spun round in consternation, saw them and went scarlet as she realised they were close enough to hear every word!

'Sam dear, you mentioned last night that you would like to watch the tally. Mark has come to fetch you if you still want to. John, you're looking well, so much colour in your cheeks.' His grandmother added mischievously, 'Run along, girl, I'll sit with Johnny for a quiet chat.'

Samantha hesitated and stood in hot confusion. Mark greeted John, and waited, his face a tight mask of anger. Resolutely squaring her shoulders, she stepped to his side and they started off in complete silence. The silence became oppressive and Sam was about to break it by explaining her efforts to snap John out of his misery when Mark spoke, softly and sardonically.

'What a dear little innocent you turn out to be ... callous words to a man tied to a chair, unable to reciprocate!'

'I spoke to him like that because he was despondent and I wanted him to be angry and—alive—and don't you call me little innocent!' she flashed back.

'Oh, aren't you? My ears deceive me, then. Just the gentle sweetheart, and loving, I presume, with soft words for her sick beloved? To my inexperienced ears they sounded rather harsh, don't you think?'

Samantha stopped in her tracks. 'Say what you will, Mark Lane. You think John should be treated with soft words and kindness? I agree with the kindness, but not enough to make him feel sorry for himself. That would lower his spirit and consequently his health. He must be fit for the coming ordeal.'

'And being an authority, Doctor Mac, you know best? I won't have you or anyone upsetting John——'

'I shall go on upsetting him if I find it's good for him. I certainly won't tolerate you ordering me the way you do the others—my soul is still my own——' She felt a powerful grip on her shoulders and stopped, startled, to look up into the dark fire that smouldered in blue, penetrating eyes.

'So your soul is still your own and I can't make you do my bidding ... can't I?' He drew her steadily closer. 'Can't I, little innocent? I can see your heart beating now, like a trapped bird against that flimsy blouse, quite fascinating. Maybe your poor little soul already belongs to me. Perchance I'll claim it—one day,' his deep whisper grated.

Samantha was suddenly, burningly aware, alive to the touch of strong brown fingers. Her spine became unaccountably fluid and she was quite inarticulate as she stared into blue pools of fire that lowered to her lips as Mark Lane brought his mouth down ... to be released abruptly as he stepped back.

'It would be most pleasurable and easy to kiss those inviting lips—but work comes before pleasure, I'm sad to say.' His voice was a mocking drawl.

Sam regained the strength that had sapped her spine and senses. 'Why, you—you—is that how, is that your usual manner of attempting to exert authority?' Her cheeks blazed with fury, but sudden hoofbeats behind them stopped her from blasting this monster off the face of Australia!

Sheila reined her horse. 'Hi, Sam, hello, Mark darling. I'm so glad to see you. Missed you most awfully—why were you away when I needed you most? I mean your comforting arms while this lass took away my own true love?' She winked at the tremblingly furious girl and held out her arms to Mark. 'Help me down and kiss me, honey man.'

As the man helped her down. Samantha said, with venomous sweetness, 'Yes, do that, Mark dear. Work comes before pleasure, you know ... I shan't watch the tally—so boring.' She turned on her heel and walked back the way they had come.

Mark stood quite still, his arm resting on the shoulders of a very bewildered girl.

Tears of anger burned Samantha's eyes as she walked away. Anger at the man, his arrogant manner. He was a beastly egotist, that's what he was—presuming that she was easy and would fall into his arms at the slightest provocation. Mostly tears of acid contempt at herself for being so weak. What had happened to her, suddenly so vibrant and aware when he had held her? Sam stopped walking and sank down on the tufts of grass under an acacia bush, to indulge in a wave of active hatred for the man who had aroused the tumultous and unaccustomed emotions in her. Revulsion at herself, for waiting with bated breath his kiss, the dull thud of her heart when he had drawn back. . . ?

She was John's girl and Mark Lane meant nothing to her, yet why did she feel attracted yet repelled, angered yet stimulated by his presence—what was the meaning of the queer rubbery feeling down her spine? She certainly did not care for him, so cynical and autocratic (and tenderly gentle . . . her face burned at the recollection of being cradled in strong, gentle arms and the crooning voice). Samantha stiffened as she remembered his mocking remark about her soul. How dared he, the prying—she had a name for people who deliberately eavesdropped on private conversations! And Mame had stooped with him. Angry and frustrated, she walked back to the garden where John and his grandmother were chatting amiably.

'I didn't feel like going after all. My—my head aches,' she answered their enquiring eyes.

Mame's swift, serious scrutiny circled her face and came to rest on the girl's troubled eyes. 'I'm sorry about overhearing your pep talk with John, dear, and Mark did want to intervene, but I stopped him.'

So she could not hold her anger against the old lady after that quick apology, and it also meant that Mark had not deliberately pried. After all, she and John were right out in the garden where anyone could hear them, not so private, actually.

John was also apologetic. 'I've given thought to our—er—talk, Sam. You're quite right about having patience, and please forget the other things I said. I'll attempt a spot of writing this very afternoon. It will no doubt be difficult to start again——'

'Sheila is here, John, down at the race with Mark. I'm not very good with typing and I'm sure she'll be pleased to help you, as before.'

'Oh good. She's a great help and knows from experience how to treat the vagaries and tantrums of famous writers.' John was really pleased to hear of the other girl's presence. 'You must have a rest, my girl. Your head must still be

63

feeling that bash and you're looking peaked.'

Certainly not because of her head, Samantha thought rue-fully; the day had not begun very auspiciously for her. Had she been too callous with John? No, she would stick to her guns. He was looking better already at the prospect of writing again.

'By the way, John and I are plotting a party for you, when Allan and Mandy get back. It's high time you met the folks around here and they don't mind coming for miles if there's a binge in the offing. Everybody must be dying to meet John's girl. We can discuss the how and when later. I love parties!' Mame was enthusiastic.

John laughed. 'Ever young is my Mame. You'll enjoy it too, love, and Mark can stand in for me where the dancing is concerned. He's far better at it than I anyway.'

Sam thought swiftly and furiously ... that will be the day! That man won't come within ten feet of me and that will be too close, so help her!

She studied her shoe with lowered lashes and John con-tinued, 'Fiona Bennett runs the post office in the village we passed through on our way here, remember? The other familes from the store, garage and resthouse will come, and also those from other sheep-stations. Donna Bennett is Fiona's gran and Luke's pet "old bag"—a dear, but so gar-rulous! You haven't met Sheila's parents. Why have they not visited us lately?'

'Tom hasn't been too well. His gout is plaguing again, and you know how Mary fusses him,' Mame answered his query.

Samantha listened in silence but could not work up any enthusiasm, being more aware of a surging, unreasoning pain in her breast and trying hard to quell it. Sheila cantered up as they went in for lunch, with a request from Mark to send his tucker down to the pens. She was full of high spirits which clashed irritatingly with Sam's mood and highly pleased to hear of the impending party. 'It's about time too, we've been in a groove far too long, what with Mum and Dad such stick-at-homes and all the males haring over the country. They're all back now—John, Mark and Stephen—so let's get cracking!'

She went with Samantha to her room after lunch and flopped on the bed. 'What's cooking with you and Mark, honey?' she asked frankly. 'He was checking the woollies like grim death and nearly blew my head off when I tried a light flirtation with him. I then tackled Stephen, who was reciprocating very sweetly, when Mark bellowed at him and ordered me to remove myself if I had nothing better to do!'

Sam laughed shakily. 'We did have a few words, regarding my treatment of John.'

Sheila regarded her quizzically. 'What do you mean, your treatment of John? I reckoned you were having a spate when I met you two this morning, and that parting crack of yours sounded rather poisonous.'

'Well, John was feeling pretty morose and I merely uttered a few spirited words to liven him up, and got it in the neck from—that man——' Samantha retorted, flushing again as she recalled the consequence of those words. She went on hurriedly, 'John would like you to give him a hand with his writing, Sheila. Will you help him again as you used to? It would help him worlds and stop him from becoming morbid. Please, I would be most grateful.'

'Sure, I'd be delighted. I was practically the only one who could manage him when the writing frenzy took him, and he didn't mind having me around, helping. His spelling is atrocious.' Samantha detected an undercurrent of wistfulness in her voice and wondered again.

Sheila jumped up. 'I'll go right now and assure him of my devotion to continued duty. Not to worry, Sammy; Johnny will be fine again one of these days, just like you knew him in Scotland.' She blinked hard and dashed out hurriedly.

Samantha was too restless to lie on her bed and after wandering aimlessly around the room crossed over to the table to start a long-delayed letter to her friend Flora in faraway Edinburgh. She simply could not concentrate and, leaving it half finished, walked down the passage to John's room and study. The door was half open and she observed John and Sheila, their heads close together, deeply immersed in a large volume which lay open on the desk. She walked away quietly.

In the kitchen Mina was taking huge loaves of bread from the oven and a spicy aroma of cookies filled the air. Mina invited Miz Sam to sample and she promptly ate two—they were delicious. Thanking the lubra, she strolled out and down to the abo huts and sat on her haunches to watch the antics of the small piccanins. There were few aborigines about nowadays, most had moved further north. The stations were fortunate to retain the few who were content to stay put and not keen on walkabout. John said the sight of a full-blooded aborigine near the towns was becoming increasingly rare. He quoted a mere three thousand in South Australia at the present time.

She walked back and entered the summerhouse. It was delightfully cool and the only furnishings were a long couch, small table and two chairs. Sam lay back on the couch. Twinkles had certainly done a good job of cleaning; the air was redolent of disinfectant. A three-foot wall encircled the summerhouse and the upper enclosure consisted of mosquito netting against which wistaria and coral creeper grew in profusion. The sun filtered through in a cool green haze.

Arms under her head, the girl watched the filigree of light and shadows as the sun played on motes of dust. She simply must overcome this feeling of being unwanted, and Luke had insisted that she should take things easy for a few days. Unsuspected emotions had been aroused and the upheaval had left her exhausted in mind and body. A deep yearning flooded her being, for the peaceful little cottage in faraway Scotland ... just to be there with Mary-Gran. If only one could bring back the past ... A strange peace, as if a loved hand had reached out, pervaded her being and her lids drooped. Samantha slept.

Cindy found her there, having found she was not in her room, and reported to Mame that the missy was asleep. Mame decided to let her be; sleep was good for the girl. The old lady was troubled at the tension she sensed between Mark and Samantha and wondered what had happened during the girl's enforced stay at his house. There was something more than dislike of each other ... she, Mame, had sensitive perceptions where her family were concerned and did not want discord among them. She sighed and hoped they would settle their differences soon.

John occupied her thoughts next. He had always been so brimful with vitality and her heart ached for him, but she felt that Samantha had been right in her action. They must not allow him to lapse into low spirits which would be fatal to his health and state of mind. The lass was fond of him, but something was missing. Perhaps the girl was holding check on her feelings because of his disability, wisely waiting for his recovery and their marriage. That Samantha was capable of great loving and giving she did not doubt for one moment and she hoped sincerely that John was the right man for her. Did he love her enough to fulfil her needs when the time came? She would need great tenderness and sensitive loving.

Samantha awakened with a raging headache and a soft voice in her ears. She felt completely disorientated for a few moments. Surely she was back in the hills, but what was her grandmother doing there? She opened her eyes to find Mame smiling down at her.

'It's so cool in here and I'm sorry if I've disturbed you, Samantha, but you really should come in now. Have I brought on a headache, my dear?'

Samantha sat up and put a hand to her throbbing head. 'Is it very late? I sure slept myself into a beaut of a head. It's sweet of you to come, Mame. Sheila still with John?'

'She has just left and will be back tomorrow. You don't look well at all. I advise you to go straight to your bed and Mina can bring a tray. Did Mandy bring the pills? The men aren't back yet. Stephen and Mark will eat with us tonight.'

Sam stilled the protest that rose to her lips about having dinner sent to her room when she heard Mame's remark. Instead, she agreed weakly to the suggestion. Cowardly, but she did not have the strength to fight her weakness. She would yield just this once, but after today, watch out, Mark Lane!

They walked to the house and Sam had a shower, then buttoned up her soft yellow gown over the shortie pyjamas and returned to her room. John was sitting at her window when she entered and he stared at her intently. Nonplussed at the casual way these people had of wandering into each other's rooms, Sam sat on her bed.

'Mame told me you weren't feeling too good. Climb into bed, darling. I'll sit quietly with you. Would you like me to have my dinner here with you?'

'That will be lovely, John. How did you and Sheila fare?'

'It was tough going, always is when I start something new, but we've crossed the first hurdles and will gallop along tomorrow, I hope ... climb in, honey.'

Samantha stood up and looked at him uncertainly.

'What's the matter?' he looked hard at her and a slow grin spread across his face. 'My word, shy, are you—can you beat that?'

'I—I——' she stammered.

'I'm not going to turn my chair, so you may as well get going, I promise my admiration will be purely ascetic. Drop that gown and into bed with you, lass.'

With a swift movement Samantha undid the wrap, allowed it to fall as she turned sideways. A flash of long smooth legs and she was under the sheet!

'My word!' John caught his breath. 'That was the fastest near-striptease I ever did see—or did I see? Would you kindly repeat the performance, you little witch?'

She smiled, although her head was thudding with her swift action. 'Oh no, sir!'

John's eyes sparkled. 'Do you know, I wish I could force a repeat. Now if we were married ... You are lovely, my Samantha. I actually felt a tingle in my toes. Perhaps I don't even need the great Getsenberg ... a bit of striptease every day would serve the same purpose and be so much more interesting. What say you, hon?'

Sam leaned over to the table for her brush and loosening her hair began to brush it very carefully, with long smooth strokes.

John slumped back in his chair. 'Well, I can dream, can't I?' he watched her movements. 'You'd better not do that either, it's just as provocative.'

She downed the brush hastily and pulled the sheet up to her chin.

'That's better. Now we can pass on to decent cultural subjects,' John remarked distastefully.

'Such as—do you know of any?' Sam queried satirically.

'I'll have you know, miss, an intellectual feller like me has a vast amount of knowledge tucked away in his alert, vital——'

'Thickhead?' she enquired ingenuously.

'You'll suffer for that! Genius isn't appreciated.' John sniffed contemptuously and a high giggle escaped from sheet-muffled lips.

Mame peeped in at the door. 'I'm lonely, can I join you? What's wrong with the girl ... hysterical? What an awful squeak ... a good slap usually helps.' She strode towards the bed.

'It's all right, I'm only applauding genius with suitable

laudability.' Sam subsided under the sheet in pretended fright. 'Please tell this man to treat my headache with due gravity.' She felt much better. The pain had lifted from her mind, John was good for her, and she decided firmly to treat any other ... problems ... lightheartedly. That was the only way.

Dusk had fallen, a flush of rosy pink on feathery clouds as the setting sun saluted the day with a farewell kiss. A clatter of hooves and spurts of laughter heralded the return of some of the stockmen. Mame stood up and stretched her arms. 'The men will want a shower before dinner. Would you care for a drink, Johnny? And you, young lady, will have a stiff toddy whether you want it or not ... medicinal!' She walked out.

John started reminiscing on his trip to Scotland and Samantha joined in eagerly, feeling again that pang of longing for her homeland. 'I found some travel brochures among my books today, Sam, it made me think back.' A pensive, backward look started in his eyes and the girl spoke swiftly to dispel any bitter thoughts. 'Oh, do give them to me, John, I'd love to look through them to see if any familiar places are mentioned.'

'I'll fetch them right away. Don't wallop my drink while my back's turned!' The wheels of the chair made a hissing sound as he left the room.

He stayed away a long time and Samantha allowed herself time for a deep wallow into past memories and only surfaced with difficulty as approaching footsteps sounded outside her door. Mame walked in, followed by Mark who carried a tray with filled glasses. He placed the tray on her dressing-table, turned to her, and his very first words almost made Sam forget her resolution to deal lightly with problems.

'Subterfuge ... or real?' He moved back to lean against the window ledge in a familiar stance and raised a quizzical eyebrow.

Samantha battled mightily with a rage that came bubbling to the surface, subdued it and returned his gaze with enforced serenity. 'What do *you* think?' she asked quietly.

Her counter-question seemed to disconcert him for a moment and he regarded her with a probing, intimate stare. 'Sorry, that was rude of me, Samantha. Is it a real humdinger?'

'It was, but improving, thanks.' A tremulous smile touched her lips. At least he had the grace to apologise—her resolution was paying off.

Mame watched them unobtrusively as she handed the girl her drink. 'Here, lass, drink up. Mark agreed with me that it will help. We've taken the liberty of joining you. The other boys aren't ready yet—oh, here you are, John.'

John placed the pamphlets on the bed and took the glass Mame proffered. They sipped in silence and then Mark moved forward, took one of the folders and leafed through the pages. He had changed into an open-necked shirt and his dark hair was damply slicked back. His neck showed brown and strong and a pulse that beat there drew Samantha's eyes as if magnetised.

'Home sick, Samantha?' Mark asked quietly, intercepting her gaze with a deepening blue in his eyes.

She flushed guiltily and her answer was husky. 'Not really. John found these brochures and I asked him to bring them so that I could wallow in memories and contrasts.'

'Contrasts ... are they so great?' He paused to consider this. 'If I could, magically, produce bagpipes and Mame could play them, do you think you could possibly leap out of bed and perform a reel with me and forget the nasty contrasts ... or blot them slightly?' He leaned over very close, mocked pleadingly, 'Would you, could you, hie'land lass?'

A vision of Mame playing the bagpipes overcame Samantha's ready retort to his mocking plea and she burst into laughter, openheartedly and delightedly. The old lady, catching and understanding her glance, began pumping her arms with diligence and puffed her cheeks in perfect imitation of a piper. Mark and John stared at her in amazement and then they too joined in the girl's laughter.

Stephen stuck his head in at the door. 'I'm always barging in on parties to which I'm not invited. Not that I care, I join 'em anyway ... what's the joke?' He came into the room and caught sight of Mame in her queer pose. 'Hold it, let me guess.' He walked round her, studying raptly. Mame expelled the air from her cheeks and he exclaimed triumphantly, 'I know—an elephant having a mud bath!'

Fresh gales of laughter greeted this concept. 'Well, really, I shall never mention contrasts again ... they're too great!' Samantha laughed up at the man standing beside her bed.

He was still standing very close, one knee almost touching her shoulder as she lay up against the pillows. Samantha caught her breath in a gasp as Mark suddenly put the back of his hand against her cheek and then moved it to flick a strand of hair over her eyes. His touch galvanised and shocked her to her fingertips. And Samantha MacDonald had another shocking impulse, to turn her cheek back against that brown hand!

Mina chose to appear at that precise moment, so it was only Mame who noticed the man's gesture and the girl's reaction. Her old heart beat with sudden, oppressive suffocation in her breast . . .

'Am you comin' to dinner or are you ain't? Dat bell's been rung twicet!' Mina admonished them.

Mark abruptly left the bedside and offered his arm to his grandmother. '*Avant-garde!*' he ordered in a sibilant whisper. Stephen followed in a militant stagger. Mina stuck her head back. 'Dinner's acomin' up, Mister John.'

'Thanks, Mina.' He looked at Samantha. 'This was supposed to be a quiet evening for you . . .'

'Oh, John, I just love Mame—isn't she the greatest? Ah, John——' Sam could not talk, for impossible tears were choking her. She held out her hands to the man in the chair. 'John, hold my hands, hold me very tight——' A sobbing breath escaped her.

John took her hands and leaned forward to stroke back the tumbled hair with gentle fingers. 'It's all right, honey, did we make you more homesick than ever? How foolish we are— here's your dressing-gown, darling, you're shivering. We'll sit together. Come, our dinner is coming.'

Comforted by his tone and modesty forgotten, Samantha left the bed and put on her dressing-gown as Mora tapped on the door prior to wheeling in the dinner trolley.

Of course, she must be homesick—that was it. What else?

CHAPTER 7

THE stretch of days passed, melting hotly into bright star-studded nights. At the Lane homestead life moved quietly and methodically. The men were seldom at home, for they were mustering in the far reaches and gullies, getting ready for the wool-clip.

Samantha and Mame mended and cleaned with the diligent help of Mina and Mora. John and Sheila were deeply busy on his new work; most often they had lunch sent to the study. Sam only saw him at breakfast and dinner and when she administered his treatments, noticed that his light burned long after everyone had retired for the night. Sheila eventually brought a holdall of clothes and declared her intention of staying until she had helped John as far as possible.

Mame enticed Samantha out under the shadiest trees at every opportunity and entertained her with anecdotes from her past and gossip about friends. She was tender with the girl and watched her carefully, soon perceiving that the gold-flecked green eyes would stray often to the mountains with a lost yearning expression, as if seeking for that which was hidden and yet unknown ... and then the old lady's heart would be greatly troubled.

When this happened, and it was often, she would send Samantha on an errand, to dispel that heartrending, exploring look from her eyes. Because of her beloved John ... his future needed this girl more than ... all else.

Mandy and Allan returned with hilarious tales of their trip and many groans from Allan when his wife invited Sam to come and view her many purchases.

Doctor Luke kept contact at sessions and one evening he told John that Getsenberg was on his way and they could expect a summons any day. John went quite pale and Samantha felt a constriction in her throat. Mandy took over at the transceiver and started an animated conversation with other listeners, inviting them to a do on the coming Saturday, to get acquainted with Samantha MacDonald. The response was enthusiastic. 'Too right, they would come in uitility, plane, station wagons or hoseback, jackaroos 'n all, what-ho!'

One morning Allan persuaded Samantha to ride with him to watch the tally at Mark's station. It would be a change for her, and though strangely Mame demurred, it was Mandy who sided with her husband and eventually saw the girl off.

Allan drove fast in the utility jeep and the early morning air was exhilarating. Samantha clung to her hat and her eyes watered from the whistle of the wind. The miles were quickly swallowed and soon they passed the homestead to draw up in a cloud of dust at the paddocks and race. The stockmen were busy among the bleating animals and acknowledged the new arrivals with a quick gesture of calloused hands. Samantha and Allan walked to the rails. She had not seen Mark since the night they had gathered in her room and felt slightly breathless as she looked across at him.

The rolled-up sleeves of his khaki shirt revealed arms that were brown and dusty, drill trousers clung to long legs, tightening across his lean hips. A much worn, broad-brimmed hat was pulled low over his forehead. Mark pushed it back rakishly as his quick gaze went to her, and she saw the line of white where the sweatband had pressed against his forehead. A long intent stare from cobalt eyes, a lift of a salutary hand showed he was aware of her presence and then he continued his inspection of the sheep as they passed by.

The woollies were herded through a narrow chute which forced them to come out singly at the other end where a dusty aboriginal, sitting easily on his haunches, notched a stick at every count of one hundred. Another stockman jotted the number into a notebook and the tally was compared and checked for any disparity at intervals during the day.

Samantha was highly amused at the antics of the animals as they passed by, most of them sedately until one would suddenly jump perkily and others follow suit with a spatter of thin legs. The young ones bleated shrilly for the comfort of their anxious mothers. Time passed, the hot sun beat down relentlessly and then Mark called a halt: 'Smoko!'

The waiting abo slammed down the wooden barricade, blocking the entrance to the chute, and he and his mates scuttled off to squat under a tree for the longed-for smoke. The other men sauntered to a long bench, also under a shady tree, where tea in vast quantities awaited them. Mark vaulted the rails with lithe ease and joined Samantha, who had watched the proceedings with great interest. 'Hello there! Allan certainly dragged early. How are the folks at home?' He rested his arms on the top rail, next to her.

'Hello, Mark. The ride was lovely and the folks are fine.' Samantha found her phrases suddenly stilted, but could not think of anything more to say. She felt hotter than ever although the sun had been beating down all morning. She removed her hat and pushed back damp, curling tendrils of hair which had escaped the twisted roll on her neck.

'Shall we move to the shade? I'm sure you could do with a cuppa—I could. Thirstmaking, this job.' They both turned, his arm brushed against hers and Samantha moved as if stung. She hesitated for a split second, then stepped as unobtrusively as possible further away from him as they walked.

'Not bored with the tally?' Colour rose in her face and Mark grinned. 'Don't answer that ... you must be interested, having come all the way to watch and to glue yourself to those rails in the raking sun.'

She felt quick, illogical resentment at his tone, a hot retort rose to her lips, but Mark continued, irrelevantly. 'You mustn't walk or stand in the sun too much, love. Horrible things can happen ... sunburn, sunstroke ...'

Samantha was nonplussed, disarmed at his use of endearment and lost the trend of her sharp retort. 'Yes, Mark.' She was astounded at her own meek answer. Blue eyes studied, circled her flushed face for a quick moment and then withdrew as they joined the men.

Stephen stretched his arms. 'Whew! It's turned out a humdinger—just look at that ball of fire. Don't run away, sprite, stay with us. I'd much rather look at you than at those stupid woollies, so smelly. Now if they all looked like you—stone the crows, counting would be a pleasure!'

Mark laughed. 'The trouble there would be you'd not only want to count 'em——' He left off and Sam was left still more confused at a clearly audible remark from the dusty huddle of men: 'Too plurry right you are!' Mark frowned at a freckle-faced jackaroo, who promptly found that his boot thong had come undone!

'Time, cobbers—push off.' Mark gestured with a hand and turned to Samantha. 'Sit here if you want to stay, it's cooler, then you can walk up to the house, Danielle will give you lunch ... we have ours here. Have a wee shut-eye, you can join us later——' He stopped and considered her gravely. 'I'm not ordering you again; your eyes are very telling. Just a suggestion ... see you later ...' He turned and walked away.

Samantha sat still and looked towards the house. A profusion of shrubs and flowering bushes surrounded it on three sides, at the back a stone cool-room and tall water tanks on stilts were visible. A shower had been improvised under one tank and she guessed the water would be hot in the day as the pipes were exposed. The sheep started a noisy bleating and she sat back to watch the bustling activity.

Noon drew near and, being more curious than hungry, the girl directed her steps towards the house. The patio door stood open, disclosing a buxom, beaming Danielle. 'I heard Missy was here and I'se honoured to give lunch. Dis here patio be cool. Please be seated, tucker come alonga jiffy.' The soft voice rolled and delighted Samantha with the quaint wording.

'Danielle, it's nice to see you again. May I wash my hands—don't worry, I'll find the bathroom. Call me when you're ready.'

'Yes, ma'm, pleasured,' Danielle smiled.

The house was L-shaped, cool and rambling. Sam passed the bedroom where she had lain on the occasion of her fall. The bathroom was spotlessly clean. She rinsed her face and sneaked the use of a comb that lay on the edge of the bath to tidy her hair. Passing back along the passage, she was tempted, and peeped through the open door of a bedroom. This could only be Mark's room; she knew with simple instinct that it did not suit Stephen. A divan bed covered with blue linen spread, wardrobe and a tallboy of drawers, a bedside table piled high with books and a well-worn black leather armchair.

Samantha stepped in to study the books. Mark was certainly versatile in choice. They ranged from light fantasy to volumes of classics and a plentiful supply of pastoral magazines. One book showed a marker and she picked it up to read the title ... *Mila 18* by Leon Uris ... She too had read this saga of those terrible, tragic days.

Samantha laid down the book and went out, down the passage to 'her' room and sat down on the bed. The room looked unoccupied. Memories flooded back ... A lifetime ago, it seemed, he had stood against that window and taunted her with some embarrassing facts and had made that first gesture of putting his hand against her cheek, flicking her hair across her face. Sam felt a sudden sense of suffocation and walked quickly out to the patio.

Danielle placed a bowl of green salad on the wrought iron table. 'I'se ready, mam.' She stood by, full of chatter and queries as to the health of her lubra relations and picannins at the other homestead. Samantha assured her they were all in good health. Mark's house was big and Stephen and he were the sole occupants. Did he consider having a big family, one day? Danielle said he often had business visitors and entertained with no mean hand, and was also precise, fastidious in the running of his establishment.

'But the boss am a good, kind gennulman, mam, if'n you follow longa orders'—the buxom woman grinned—'and I'se sure do!'

Even so, he was still a—a martinet! Samantha found the word and scowled into the distant reaches.

She heard high giggles and the clatter of dishes from the back regions. The men had evidently had their midday meal and the lubras were cleaning up. She sat idly for nearly an hour and strolled back to the bench under the tree, perceiving that the tally would probably end that day, at the pace Mark was setting. Golly, he owned considerable stock! Sam wondered what price wool was fetching. There must be quite a fortune in and out of his paddocks at present. Another tea break was called in the late afternoon and the men joined Samantha, to drink thirstily from the great mugs.

Mark smoked with them. He seemed withdrawn, yet his magnetic personality kept intruding on the girl's consciousness and she was vexed at this intrusion. Why couldn't she treat his presence with the same aplomb and easiness that she showed to others? He and she had started on the wrong footing right from the start, and he had not helped any with his arbitrary conduct. Samantha puzzled over the strange lack of rapprochement between Mark and herself.

This lack was brought home very soon. Allan appeared from the direction of an outbuilding, a large book on his arm. He strode towards Mark and a discussion ensued with the book opened between them. They both looked up to where Sam was seated. Mark made a decisive gesture and Allan shrugged his shoulders and lifted a hand in greeting when he saw that she was watching them. He walked to the utility, slung the book on to the seat, slid behind the wheel and drove off in a cloud of dust!

Samantha jumped up in alarm, for he was travelling in the direction they had come and soon only the dust in the distance marked his progress. Evidently he had not forgotten her, for he had waved to her; surely he was going back for some reason or other and could have taken her home? Nothing could be so urgent that the time taken to call her would have caused too much delay.

Remembering Mark's gesture, Samantha sank limply back on the bench. Drat him—he could have consulted her wishes, autocratic monster! She was not going to sit here any longer watching those dusty, silly creatures ... She jumped up and started to walk in the direction of the house, her body gracefully erect in the moleskin jeans and yellow shirt.

Mark, attracted by her quick, decisive movements, was momentarily distracted and watched her till she disappeared from view.

'Distracts even the invincible Mark Lane, eh?' Stephen spoke out of the side of his mouth.

Mark turned angry blue eyes. 'Tend to your work, cobber,' he said shortly.

Stephen stared in surprise. Mr. Mark Lane was getting raking touchy these days, so help him! 'Chew me no grief, Boss!' His retort was sarcastic.

Mark ignored the sarcasm and watched him unsmilingly. Stephen wanted to ask the reason for Allan's hasty departure, but refrained at the sight of a ramrod back as Mark turned away.

Samantha went to the bathroom and rinsed her face and hands again, with angry movements. She wished she were dirty enough to mess up the bathroom good and well! Danielle would probably get it in the neck, and she more embarrassment by some subtle, caustic remark. 'Stop being silly and childish, you dolt!' she spoke severely to her mirrored face, then caught sight of an enlarged snapshot that had been pushed between the mirror and wall. Sam pulled it out and a glamorous face stared back at her. The inscription across the corner read 'Mark, with love, Carol'.

Samantha put it back with fingers that seemed all thumbs suddenly. This girl must be very special to be taken to the bathroom so that he could study and admire her beauty while he shaved. Well, he was a good-looking man, so, she supposed, there were lots of girls who would fall down at his feet. He must be fairly well off financially ... that face on the snap looked like one who would go after what she wanted! Sam turned quickly and walked to the patio, settled into a deckchair and closed her eyes. Presently she stopped feeling so aggressive and inertia pervaded.

Sudden awareness of being under surveillance opened her eyes to find Mark, his one foot resting on a chair, studying her with eyes that were a striking blue in contrast against the dusty darkness of his tanned face.

Samantha started up. She definitely had not been asleep—how did the man manage to creep up so silently, so snakishly?

'It's the Indian in me, I guess,' he mocked her silent thoughts, and Sam despaired of ever cultivating a poker face against such strong odds.

'Have you—you finished so soon—is Allan back?' She must have slept, for the sun was a red rim behind the mountains.

Mark turned the chair with an easy movement and straddled it. 'Allan? Allan's not coming back, he has urgent notes to look up. I'll deliver the check tally to him, later.'

'But—but what about me?' she exclaimed.

'What about you ... hmmm?' He deliberately looked mystified and Samantha jumped up in frustration. She forced herself to walk to the end of the patio and back, controlling herself with difficulty, then measured out her words one by one.

'How—do—I—get—home?'

'How do you get home?' Mark repeated obtrusively, and then as if a great light had suddenly dawned, 'Oh, that! I shall have the honour of escorting you home, goddess. You do look very pagan—yes, very pagan——' and watched with interest as a furious girl tried her utmost to stand tall and imperious! He moved slightly and a dark smoulder started in the eyes that were watching her.

Simultaneously Danielle came out with a tray of glasses and Stephen strode up the steps. He smiled at Samantha. 'Hi, honey, I won't be here for dinner, Mark. Fiona commands and I obey ... after a much-needed drink.'

'You'll take the jeep, cobber, your car being bashed as usual, and I'm taking Miss Mac home in my car.'

'My word, what a comedown for me—Fiona will jilt me on the spot! Well, so be it.' Stephen was suitably shaken, but did not dispute the interdict. He mixed the drinks and offered one to Sam, who was still fuming at Mark's high-handed presumption that she be taken home by him. Allan would hear about this, deserting her ... She accepted the drink, fury making her eyes a luminous green.

'Could you give me a lift, Stephen? I'd hate to put Mark to all this trouble on my account, but Allan left so hurriedly, without even consulting me,' she asked with transparent sweetness.

Stephen glanced from her to Mark, whose hands had whitened in their grip on the back of the chair, and he looked somewhat taken aback at her sweet entreaty. 'Well, sprite, I wasn't going thataway, but can do so.'

'I'm taking Samantha back.' Mark spoke softly but distinctly.

There was a vibrant silence and Stephen swallowed his drink hurriedly. 'Okay then, I'll be off ... so long, everyone.' In the silence that ensued they heard the jeep start up and roar down the drive.

Samantha still stood with an untouched drink in her unconscious hands. Mark watched her with inscrutable, half-closed eyes. His hands slackened their grip on the chair and with a fluid step he passed her and lifted his drink off the table.

'Relax and drink, girl ... and stop hating me so actively. The gold spots in your eyes are positively bursting into flame,' he remarked laconically.

'How dare you!' Sam hissed through her teeth.

Mark moved closer, and laughed. 'How Victorian that sounds! My dear Samantha, I dare when and where I want to, even at peril of being attacked by a little outraged savage. I don't want to eat you, pretty one, and have no ulterior motive other than a desire for company.'

Samantha moved back. He was too close for comfort. 'An unnecessary drive——'

'On the contrary, I do have to go. I have urgent papers for Allan.' Mark took her arm and offered a chair.

His touch burned and she yielded to the safety of the chair. His attraction was potent and she shivered in revulsion at herself for allowing it to affect her to such an extent. Sam lifted her glass and drained the contents and her eyes watered as the fiery liquid burned her throat ... Stephen mixed with a heavy hand!

Amusement crinkled the corners of the man's eyes. 'Take it easy, Mac, that drink was meant to be sipped and savoured, not gulped as if your life depended on it.'

Samantha stared over his head in mutinous defiance. She would have to depend on him to drive her home, so she might as well accept the inevitable and compose herself with as much dignity as she could muster. Her obvious animosity only incited him to further salient, satirical remarks.

'Danielle will serve dinner early and then I'll deliver you, safely and undamaged, to the cloisters of home. I'll have a quick shower. Be a good girl and have another drink, drink it slowly—don't worry, I shan't be long . . .'

She sat limply, and felt as if her mind and body had been strenuously overworked, quite exhausted. Twenty minutes later Mark rejoined her and quirked an eyebrow at the empty glass. He mixed two drinks and passed one to her. Samantha accepted it without comment and he sat down opposite her.

'Accepted the circumstances of having to dine with me?'

'Have I an alternative?' Samantha asked in return.

'None whatsoever. I am therefore honoured at your grateful acceptance.' Mark lowered his head courteously.

She was genuinely astonished at his versatile nature. Mark Lane could be grim, sardonic, smouldering and then again courteous, tender and casual in a most bewildering manner. She tried her utmost to fathom him, to absorb his many facets and meet them with equanimity.

Danielle announced dinner and Mark was the perfect host as he seated his guest. The main course was as usual, mutton, served in a deliciously different way, and Samantha had a fleeting desire to ask for the recipe but, perceiving a raised eyebrow delving her mind again, hastily curbed her impulse.

Mark conversed easily, covering a wide variety of subjects, and she found herself responding, delighted that she could meet him with equal versatility. (Fantasy cloaked Samantha MacDonald with an exquisite creation with pearly floating panels, a glittering diamond tiara nestled on her proud head. Her host looking very distinguished in dinner dress, all his attention concentrated on his lovely guest in a soft glow of candlelight. He really was quite distractingly good-looking.)

Samantha looked down at her dusty jeans and shirt and hastily came out of this flight of fantasy, to concentrate again on her host's animated criticism of Australia's cricket tour to the Republic of South Africa, where they had lost the test match series. She had avidly followed the games via her radio and confidently interposed her own opinions, and watched Mark digest this amazing fact with a satisfied feeling of inner amusement.

When he finally guided her to the lounge she found that fully an hour had passed and not once had she felt discomfited by her companion. That said a lot for his perfect hosting. Could this be the easing of the relationship between them, the *rapprochement* she had given thought ... well, even if it was only temporary, it was nice, soothing.

'A liqueur, before we leave—brandy, hm?' Mark asked, and handed it to her as she nodded her confirmation. He lowered into an easy-chair and stretched long legs. The backrest cushioned his dark head and the tiny glass was almost hidden in the grasp of a sunburned hand. Over the rim of her glass Sam watched him close his eyes and a smile feathered her lips as he emitted a small grunt of contentment. She lowered her own lashes and contemplated the glowing glints of her drink and a curious hush, a stillness settled like an aura in the room.

Dark-fringed blue eyes opened a fraction to observe the girl, dreamily twisting the tiny glass in her slim hand; sheen of dark hair under the lamplight, soft firmness against the silk shirt, quite distracting ... Mark rose abruptly and walked to the window.

'Shall we go?'

Samantha came out of her reverie at his abrupt movement and her eyes widened at the curt query. Considerably shaken at the change, she mentally shrugged her shoulders. Back on the old footing, the calm interlude was over! She struggled to readjust herself and quickly got to her feet.

'I'm ready, Mark.'

The face he turned to her held a curious, enigmatic blankness and his arms lifted sideways in a puppet-like motion of accepted hopelessness. Sam was utterly bewildered by the change in him and her spine felt stiff as she walked ahead to the patio.

'Wait here, please—I'll bring the car.' His voice was grimly staccato as he took long strides into the darkness.

They rode in absolute silence and after a while Samantha opened her window to allow the cool air to flow in. Her happy sense of companionship had dissolved, disintegrated at the flick of a tongue, an implied manner of a few words.

A faint tang of shaving soap and tobacco emanated from the man next to her. Samantha moved restlessly and realised that he had a magnetic way of arousing strange impulses within her, some power that stimulated, infiltrated and crumbled the dormant structure of her senses. She had never before felt this physical and mental weakness—her forehead was damp and she moved closer to the open window. She would fight this wayward attraction, certainly it was not love, and her love was for John, so it could be just a potent attraction and the sooner she subdued it the better for all concerned, especially herself! The affinity she had felt at dinner was merely a civilised response to his polite hosting. Could it be that he sensed her troubled feelings and resented them? Samantha thought in sudden panic, did Mark think she was—what was the word—promiscuous—because she had cuddled in his arms at the foot of the mountain and that was why his treatment of her was contemptuous and mocking? But he must have realised that, at that time, any protective arms would have been just as welcome.

A sudden slackening of speed jerked her eyes to the man at the wheel and her thoughts to a stop. Mark pointed with a brief, 'Father, mother and little 'roos, over there.' And Samantha forgot all her problems in the fascination of watching two kangaroo families herding their little ones to safety with hops, skips and jumps. 'They're blinded by the lights and can be rather dangerous, often jumping straight at a speeding motor, so one has to watch out carefully.'

'Can they really jump far and kill a man with their tails? Just look at the tail of that one! It must be a male.'

Mark took his foot from the brake and the car started forward. 'A large 'roo can jump up to fifteen feet and more. They use their hind feet and tail and land in the same way, on their back legs and tail. They belong to the marsupial group, which means they live on grass and herbs, suckle their young and carry them in pouches. There are approximately one hundred and ten species ranging from the giant kangaroo down to the tiny fruit-eating jumping mouse.'

'And they're utterly unknown elsewhere?' Samantha enjoyed the change in him and wondered how long this would last.

'Mmm, but utterly.' Mark fell silent and soon the lights of the homestead shone out in the dusk.

They drew to a stop in the drive and Samantha put her hand on the handle of the door. Mark moved from behind the wheel, nearer to her, and put his arm across her slim body to hold the handle and her hand in a firm grasp.

He asked, softly, 'Can and will you tell me just one thing, Samantha? Are you happy, as things are, with John? It may be a long time before—before the marriage. Doesn't the future worry you?'

His sudden, intimate query caught her unawares, startled her so that she could scarcely answer.

'Certainly not! It doesn't worry me,' she managed at last.

'Why "certainly not"? You're a normal, healthy girl, with normal instincts.' His voice was gentle and so close that his breath mingled with hers.

Samantha felt a sudden breathlessness as questioning eyes searched hers.

'I'm ... I'm content as I am.' She pressed back against the seat.

'Are you, mate? My thanks for dining with me. 'Mark's eyes dropped to her lips. 'A kiss for that—and for your courage in your long, long wait?'

Sheer rage at his last words engulfed her, the faintness passed and the tiger spots in Samantha's eyes glowed like a cat's eyes in the dark.

'Mark Lane,' she grated, 'are you insinuating that I—I'm starved of—of—are you? Well, let me tell you that John is far from paralysed where kissing is concerned, so why should your kisses help—yours?'

'Oh no, Samantha, not that, ever.' Mark's eyes crinkled at the fury in her voice. He withdrew his hand and smiling suddenly, kissed her forehead. 'Now I've really upset you—sorry, Mac, I'm a raking brute. It's a fair cosh you're boiling mad, but your lips pouted so invitingly that I hardly realised what I was saying.'

He opened his door and before Samantha had regained her equilibrium, was out and opening the door on her side.

She sat for a moment, fists clenched, unable to move, and then slowly got out. Her legs felt weak, but she made a supreme effort to walk steadily to the front door.

John had a reference book on his lap and Sheila leaned over the back of his chair. Mame was also reading in her high-backed chair. They looked up as Mark and Samantha entered, and greeted them with varying expressions. John came slowly out of his depth of concentration, Sheila lifted her hand in an Indian salute and Mame's bright bird eyes went from one to the other in quick succession.

Samantha went straight to John. 'Hullo, John dear, it's nice to find you here instead of in your study. Makes a change from being cooped up in there all day.' She bent over and kissed him and he took her hands in his.

'Did Mark take good care of you, love?'

Sheila saved Sam from answering that problematic question. She stood to one side, her head cocked, regarding their display of affection with pensive reflection. 'Give me leave to show you, some time, how to greet your man with appropriate intensity when you've been away from him so long, lass,' she drawled with a smothered woman-of-the-world air.

'Why, Sheila! Have you really had lots and lots of experience in that line? Do tell!' Sam pretended breathless excitement, although her heart was still thudding and the lack of breath was not all pretence.

'In a pig's eye!' The dark girl bared her teeth in a leer. 'What do you think John and I do behind closed doors all day?'

'Write books?' Samantha showed ingenuous uncertainty.

'How right can you be?' Sheila slumped dejectedly. 'One simply can't make love to a slave-driver, one simply feels that hara-kiri is the only heavenly way out.'

Samantha tossed her head airily. 'Well, I don't see my loved one during the long days, and today's sojourn in another man's bower has appeased my lonely heart somewhat, so dear Johnny gets a leftover.' She turned to Mark in mocking supplication. 'Lover, chew me no grief, take me away from this house of would-be-suicides, practising sorcerers and'—with a fearful glance at the black-covered book on Mame's lap—'witches delving in the black arts!'

Mark stared at her in fascinated amazement, and read the devilish mockery of himself, in her eyes. With an oath he strode forward ... he could play too! He lifted Samantha high in his arms and glared ferociously over her body.

'Unhand the damsel, evil blackguards! Away with me, my beautiful one, to my vast, fast castle in the impregnable mountains!'

'Fast being the keyword,' snickered Sheila.

A thoroughly startled girl began to struggle in the hard arms. Mark held her firmly, spoke soothingly. 'Have no fear, little one, sweet princess.'

John supplicated, 'Oh, sire, give back my little one. I shall treat her gently, for she is my sole source of sustenance. I promise to eat only half a finger every second day.'

Sheila snarled at him, 'Scorpion! That limpid hand was promised to me ...' She sank down in front of him in despair. John gathered a knot of hair in his fist and tugged. 'Quiet, sataness, you shall have a succulent digit,' he soothed, and she breathed ecstasy. 'Oh, my lord!'

Mame watched their high-spirited antics with a smile. She was used to it and most often the pivot of their raillery. But now she caught Samantha's desperate appeal and spoke to Mark accusingly. 'Put her down, cobber, you're breaking every rib in the damsel's basket.'

Mark lowered his burden and as her feet touched ground Sam staggered slightly and he gripped her arms to steady her. Sheila drew in a small breath at the sheer anger that shone in Samantha's eyes, green and translucent. Mark dropped his hands, a muscle moved in his cheek, but his face remained inscrutable. Sheila's thoughts were suddenly speculative; what was between these two? That look in the girl's eyes was not simply caused by the horseplay, that was for sure, so why the glow of anger? She turned to John, her body having effectively screened his view of Samantha's face, and feeling a sudden tug at her heart drew a chair next to him and sat down.

John said ruefully, 'I'll try hard not to be such a slave-driver, my pet.'

'You could drive me up the wall and I wouldn't bat an eyelash,' her tone dropped earnestly. 'I love helping you, truly. It—it gives me an object to my silly frivolous existence.'

'Not silly at all, Sheila. Just being you is enough and justifies your existence. Besides, I need you to help me.'

'Ah, spoil it all now, you mercenary!' Sheila jumped up and looked at Mark, who had found a comfortable chair, at Samantha sitting rather stiffly next to Mame. 'The way of all males. I go now to see if coffee is being brewed in the witch's kitchen.' She disappeared with a flounce of her skirt.

'Did you enjoy your day, Sam?' John asked.

'Oh, immensely, thanks.' She managed superb sangfroid, not daring to look at Mark.

'I'm glad. Allan came back alone, with a message from Mark——'

'Oh yes, where is Allan?' Sam asked darkly. 'Sneaked off to bed, I'll bet.'

Mark shot up hastily. 'My word, I have some papers for him,' and he took rapid strides to the door. John called after him, 'He's still in the office, Mark. Mandy has gone to bed.'

'The coward!' Samantha muttered, and John looked at her in surprise.

'Mandy a coward?'

'No, not her—Mark. I mean Allan—oh, never mind.' She lapsed into silence

Mame filled the breach. 'We've decided on a barbecue for Saturday.'

'Barbecue ... Saturday?'

'Yes, Saturday.' Mame leaned over and passed her hand across Samantha's eyes. 'Come back, girl, it's your party.'

'Oh yes, a barbecue.' Sam became suddenly animated. 'It's what one does with raw, dripping meat. Cook it in a smoke screen so that others can't watch your savage, bloody instincts?'

John laughed and his grandmother embroidered the girl's gruesome description. 'One then eats the what-she-called-it mess with charcoal and sand, with watering eyes, washing the whole caboodle down with warm beer and singing songs in key flat. One then cheerfully howls "Wasn't that just fab and way out!" while inwardly cursing and wondering what to do about the scorch and grease marks on your nice skirts or smashing jeans!'

In the glee that followed this misconception Samantha decided she would like to meet other people, mix with them in the hope that she could, with other interests, get rid of the—exaggerated—feeling towards Mark and avoid him as much as possible.

Sheila, bringing the coffee, enquired about the laughter and Mame repeated her remark, to the great edification of that young woman. Mark and Allan came in and she handed the cups of coffee while the discussion proceeded on the subject of parties.

'Fiona's cousin is with them again, from Adelaide. The city lights don't seem so bright since she met you, Mark ... she's taken a sudden fancy to her country cousins lately,' Sheila whispered rather loudly to Sam. 'Carol Dutton. 'Pon my soul, Mark was dazzled the last time she orbited!'

'Aha, more glamour in the outback.' John whistled.

Slitted blue eyes pierced Sheila, but she returned the look naughtily. 'Is it a secret, Mark? Oh, my popping mouth!' she ejaculated flippantly.

Samantha had fixed a steely eye on Allan, promising dire things to come. She now switched her attention to Mark, at Sheila's illuminating remark, and watched him with derisive intensity. Carol, of the bathroom snapshot?

'No secret, even if it were possible to keep secrets with you around, nutbag, so pop away,' Mark drawled lazily, and studied the fingernails of a brown hand.

There must be some truth in the story, for he did not deny it. He was undeniably attractive and compelling, so there must be girls in his life ... or one special girl, the one of the 'To Mark with love, Carol'? Mark met her gaze and there were blue devils in his eyes as he got up and stretched luxuriously.

At the door he turned. 'I'll leave you now so that you can gossip about my many *amours*—delicious thought—while I go home and dream about 'em.' A roguish chortle sounded down the passage.

CHAPTER 8

THE sane light of day restored Samantha's discomposed emotions back to normal rationality. In the days that followed she drew a blanket of protective self-withdrawal around her whenever Mark appeared, which was not often, as he seemed to be avoiding her as well. The times when he did come over the door of the office would close behind Allan and himself, and often enough John would be with them as well. If he was still there at lunchtime then Mora would wheel the lunch-wagon to the office. Very seldom did Mark stay for dinner.

Samantha lived at Amanda's heels, begging to be shown

and taught how to run a home as large as the Lane homestead. Mandy willingly complied, for there were many chores and an extra pair of hands were always welcome, but she admonished Sam severely when she found her in the hot sun, industriously weeding the garden. 'All very commendable, but that chore should only be tackled in the early morning or after sundown. You're liable to sunstroke, hat or no hat ... don't argue, come in at once ... sneaking out like this when I fondly believed you were resting. Really, you need babysitting!'

To crown her embarrassment, Mark was just coming down the office steps and Sam knew he had heard every word because he stopped to look at them and his eyes raked over her in a cynical sort of 'when-will-you-ever-learn' way. He did not speak but merely tipped his hat further on to his forehead and walked in the direction of the pens. Sam felt there was a jinx on her; she only did things wrong when that man was around!

On the morning of the party she wrapped a large apron of Mame's round her middle and started work in the kitchen, helping Mina and Mandy with the preparations. Mandy watched her as she speared portions of meat, prunes and onions on skewers. The kebabs had marinated in a delicious brew of vinegar, curry, onions and spices, and the aroma pervaded the kitchen together with spicy smells from the oven, into which Mandy had popped dozens of meaty pasties.

A voice in her ear startled Samantha and she very nearly impaled her thumb when Mark spoke softly right behind her.

'That bit is upside down, chump.' He moved closer and put long arms around her, enclosing both her hands in his, skewer and all. Removing the cube of meat, he meticulously turned it, measured it, and stuck it back on the skewer.

'It must be centripetal too, otherwise nuclear fission will occur on contact with air and carburetted hydrogen, detonating in the hands of an unsuspecting grip. Could you stand that, knowing you were to blame, through sad lack of scientific knowledge?'

A thrill of sheer indescribable joy flooded her being and his soft voice sent a tingling echo right down to her toes. Samantha stood quite still, savouring this moment of bliss, sweetly unexpected.

Mark reached for another cube. 'Now watch carefully. I have a very good eye for the spearing of meat ... and other things!'

Scarlet flags raised their banners in her cheeks, but she too answered softly, in a stammering whisper, 'My sad lack of knowledge of science would then make me a murderer? What a dreadful prospect! Mandy should have warned me in my ignorance. Show me again how you spear things, scientifically, Mark?'

'Pleasure, lass. Thus ... and thus,' Mark skewered two more and suddenly nipped a rosy ear so temptingly close to his mouth, '—and thus!'

About to open the oven door, Mandy, cloth in hand, stood as if transfixed at the jumble of words and actions. She suddenly came to life. 'Hey, cobber, unhand at once or you'll find your raking coiffure in that bowl of slush and that should marinate you to a fine degree! What's with this scientific jazz, the poor girl looks real dazed?'

Samantha thought dreamily, yes, poor girl, really and truly dazed. And came out of her entrancement as Mark dropped his arms and her uncontrolled hands landed in the basin with a splash!

Mark stepped to the other side of the table, out of reach of his threatening relative. 'Simmer down, kookaburra. Imparting knowledge to dense females is very trying and I'm badly in need of sustenance ... this one looks good.' He perched on the corner of the table and bit into a large cornish pasty, his eyes on Sam's trembling hands as she continued skewering.

'See now, there went the tip of your pinkie. Keep that one for my declaration tonight ... sort of love potion, you know?'

'A slice of my finger doesn't come in that category, it only works with glamour girls, like your Carol, is that her name, and—others.' Satirical sweetness was in her tone and Samantha immediately regretted it, for there was no venom in her at this moment. She felt, instead, unexpected exhilaration, and the satire had come involuntarily.

'Well, well, is the lady jealous?' Mark studied her sardonically while he wiped his hands on a cloth.

Amanda took up defending cudgels. 'Who could be jealous of a chump like you, Mark Lane? I have a hunch you're riding the girl, so kindly belt up!'

'I assure you there's only kindness in my heart. Any items needed from the store? I'm going to the village.'

'No, thanks. What are you going for, or shouldn't I ask? Can't wait to see your Carol, is my guess. Are you bringing her back with you?'

'Fiona and Carol are coming back with me, so business mixed with pleasure commands me to the village. Stephen wanted to relieve me of the pleasure part, but a bit of man talk soon convinced him that he was regrettably indisposed. Watch it, Mac, those wires can be dangerous. We can't have our guest of honour becoming an accident case on this great day!'

Samantha's eyes were the colour of smoky gum-leaves as she watched him walk out. She puzzled over her own behaviour as she worked. She was spoken for, and she did not care overmuch for the tall, arrogant man, yet she did not want anyone else in the picture... Dog-in-the-manger, she scolded herself, and reached firmly for another clutch of 'dangerous weapons'.

Samantha leaned forward to apply a film of pearly lipstick and then stepped back to view the whole effect—her short, flounced candystripe skirt, topped by a soft white peasant blouse, her only ornament a cairngorm brooch which was an heirloom from Mary-Gran. Slender gold sandals and high piling of her hair made her look taller, and regal, she hoped. Her hair really needed cutting, she had experienced great difficulty in arranging it to her satisfaction (quite a few unladylike curses had drifted out of the open window!) A touch of eye-shadow emphasised the gold flecks in her eyes.

She came out of the room and walked briskly to John's study.

Those two miscreants were still batting away on the wretched book. Sam surveyed them and remarked sweetly, 'I've forgotten... did I invite you to a party or didn't I?'

John looked startled. 'My word, is it so late already? Sam, you look good enough to eat—Sheila, why didn't you remind me of the time?'

'Time... what's that?' Smudged carbon on her chin and nose and fly-away dark hair made Sheila resemble a scruffy urchin. She looked hard at Samantha. 'Yeah-bo! if I have to compete with this gorjus gipsy, I'll skedaddle longa right now.' She banged the cover over the typewriter and whisked out of the room.

John said sheepishly, 'Sorry, love, Mora has been hovering around and grunting about "bigfella boss changing plurry quick." Send him in and I'll join you in the swing of a shrike's tail.'

'You needn't rush, John, only Mame says some of the visitors usually come early, so she and I have dolled up in order to be ready for the first arrivals. Can I help you?'

'No, thanks, Mora is quite capable, and I can still arrange my own cravat.'

'Well then, I'll send him to you.' She walked out slowly.

John was kind and jovial, but somehow he had become sort of remote, far from her since he had become so immersed in his work. Sheila and Mora, in their particular spheres, were all the help he needed and apart from her therapy ministrations in the mornings she hardly had any close contact with him. Come to think of it, John hadn't had a fit of depression or moodiness for a long time. Sam sighed, yet she must be glad, because that was what she wanted, his interests to keep him busy and happy. Luke would be there tonight, he was coming with Tommy Crawford ... would he bring news of Getsenberg?

Mame joined her on the veranda.

'Mmm, you look and smell nice.' Samantha sniffed at the old lady's neck.

'So do you, MacDonald, stop sniffing like a puppy. Ready for the ordeal?'

'Don't worry, Mrs. Mame. You see before you a typical example of a sophisticated highly-born lady awaiting her guests.' Samantha watched the first car draw to a standstill. 'The gentry, I presume?'

'Indeed not, 'tis but humble peasants, except that old one in front, who clacks and harumphs and tries to run South Australia singlehanded.'

Donna Bennet, Fiona's grandmother and Luke's 'old bag' of the sessions. Her family bringing up the rear, she stood and surveyed the foreigner from Scotland. In just such a way on a former occasion had Mame Lane studied her, and Sam caught a vagrant twinkle in the blue eyes of her companion.

Miss MacDonald became very demure and withstood the

scrutiny with bland sagacity.

'Harumph!' was Donna's verdict.

Sam fought a mighty instinct to giggle and Mame hurriedly introduced everyone, her own mouth curled suspiciously at the corners.

In rapid succession other cars and utilities pulled up and she was drawn into a whirl of introductions. John wheeled into the mêlée and was greeted with genuine pleasure. They were all aware of his disability caused by the accident, yet innate courtesy made them tease and laugh with and at him, without causing any embarrassment. Sam's estimation of Australians reached its peak as she watched and experienced their frank, generous friendship and caustic wit. She happily absorbed these qualities, loving it.

The veranda had been chosen for the scene of combat. It was cool and spacious and chairs were arranged in clusters. A large table at one end served as the bar and willing hands were distributing glasses of sparkling thirst quenchers to the chattering families. Danielle was squatting happily among the children who were playing on the lawns and Samantha sent her a smile of greeting. The buxom lubra pantomimed with expressive hands, 'Not for this lubra black woman to longa miss a dinkum party!' Stephen must have brought her in the utility ... Sam's imagination baulked at the idea of Danielle on a horse!

The drone of the mail plane was heard and very soon after, Luke Mannering and Tommy Crawford came striding up the steps. The pilot's greeting to Sam, 'Ha, by jove! 'Struth, she's a beaut ... bonzer, I'll say?' made his moustache wiggle alarmingly and caused quite a few smothered chuckles. She met his admiration with quiet ease and then he made off, with suspicious haste, in the direction of a rosy-cheeked girl who had kept her eyes glued to his face from the moment he had walked up the steps.

Dr. Luke took Samantha's hand. 'Our lass is even more beautiful than I remembered.' His eyes paid tribute, but he seemed strangely withdrawn, there was a remoteness in him that puzzled her. Sam's heart skipped a beat, her fey senses warned her to be prepared.

A loud 'harumph!' sounded in their ears.

'Howdy, doctor, how's them babies of your'n?'

Luke's shoulders settled resignedly. 'Fine, Donna mia,

proper corkers. Two more expected next week, on the same day. I do get around, don't I?' He scowled wickedly at the old lady's shocked face and gave her a naughty tap on her posterior as he moved along to greet John.

Samantha mingled with different groups, people who drew her readily in their midst, friendly and ready to accept her with the casual way of a close community.

Outside, lighted fires had settled into glowing charcoal, ready for the trays of succulent meats. Mora was supervising the braising of a whole sheep that was slowly revolving on a spit over hot coals. It was almost done to a turn, crisp on the outside and quite mouth-watering. Other abos were tending the braziers with elaborate care, strutting with importance as lubras and picannins watched from the shadows and chattered shrilly and incessantly.

Stephen wondered aloud, 'Where the devil can Mark be with the girls?'

General laughter ensued when one wit remarked, 'Having a wayside flirtation with both of 'em, before you get the chance to dig your salacious claws in, that's a raking bet!'

Samantha caught Luke's eyes across the veranda and a cold, frightening feeling enveloped her. He had such a strange air of preoccupation ... had something happened to Mark? She stilled the thought almost immediately. If that were so then Luke would not hesitate to inform the family at once. He was probably mulling over some difficult medical problem, but it was so unlike him.

A murmured request from Mame sent her down the steps to the fires. She was still passing on the message that Mora could now start on the skewered meats when she heard Mark's car pull up. Samantha stood quite still and watched as he walked up the steps, a girl on either side of him.

They were greeted hilariously and Mark smiled as taunts were tossed at him, for their late arrival. His hand rested easily on the shoulder of the blonde girl beside him, the other one—who must be Fiona—was whisked away by Stephen. From the flickering shadows Samantha studied the girl at Mark's side. Tall, blonde, and her sophistication simply oozed in waves of glamour while a silvery material sheathed her body quite seductively. A sarcastic thought, with more envy than malice, crossed the watching girl's mind; didn't that beaut know that such a rigout was not for a barbecue?

Surely Fiona, who wore a full-skirted, sleeveless dress, could have wised her cousin on suitable apparel? But then Miss Dutton looked the type who would sneer at a country cousin's advice!

Supreme disregard for the obvious discrepancy in her attire showed in Carol's manner. She smoked incessantly, a long holder between crimson-tipped fingers. Most of her attention was concentrated on the man at her side, who seemed to be lapping it up in his own superior way, and from where Sam was standing, Miss Dutton looked exactly like the feline that stole the cream. She turned her back determinedly and gave herself a mental shake; since when and why had she herself become so priggish, cattish and critical?

Samantha leaned back against the trunk of the blue gum, the glow of the fires flickering across her face. Rubbing the silver bole with the palms of her hands and hooking one heel back into a notch of the tree, she continued to watch Mora lay the meat on the grating.

Mark steered Carol over to where Mame was sitting and there was a slightly wicked slant to his smile. 'Sweetheart, Carol has been dying to meet you. I told her you were the love of my life and she's simply curling with jealousy. Carol, meet the adored Mame.'

Carol Dutton looked surprised. 'Oh, I thought Mame was a ... how do you do, Mrs.—er——?'

'Mame Lane. Does she not justify my description?'

'Why no, you said ... I mean, of course ...' Carol covered her faux pas with a nervous flick of the holder in her hand. Mark had deliberately misled her about the girl he had described so vividly, she had felt quite jealous, and that fiend of a cousin, Fiona, had listened to his teasing and never once let on!

'How do you do, Miss Dutton.' Mame's cool blue gaze was shrewd and the blonde girl felt for all the world like a gawkish, awkward schoolgirl. She turned with relief when someone else spoke to her and very soon regained her sangfroid.

Mark bent over Mame. 'Where is our star guest?'

His grandmother gestured and he straightened up to look through the screening. Moving with indolent sureness, he walked down the steps. Samantha was still leaning against the tree, she had the look of a gypsy, with the firelight burnishing her hair to molten copper. She lifted her eyes and saw him, a few yards away, and the firelight reflected or matched, she was never quite sure, the dark smoulder in his blue regard.

Samantha brought her foot down abruptly from its resting place and took a step towards him. 'Hello, Mark.' Her voice betrayed a sudden huskiness, as if she had inhaled wood smoke.

Mark Lane made a queer gesture, like one trying to shake off a threatening web. 'What do you see in the flames, witch? Forget the fortunes of others.' A hard hand clasped hers, he made a sweeping gesture with his other hand. 'Soon all this hard work will be demolished by the hungry horde. Come along, I can mix a juicy drink and hasten to assure you that my hand is not so heavy as Stephen's.'

Samantha's exhilaration of the morning suddenly returned, his hand felt cool and firm, he had thought of her, and come to look for her and was still being nice. She smiled her assent.

Carol Dutton scrutinised Samantha languidly as Mark came up the steps, still holding her by her hand. She edged her way towards them as Stephen, Fiona in tow, touched Sam's shoulder.

'Hi there, sprite, where have you been hiding? Meet our voice, Fiona.' Stephen stepped back a pace and collided with Carol. He steadied her with an apology. 'And this is cousin Carol,' he added rather offhandedly.

The blonde girl glared at him icily for a long moment and then returned her attention to Samantha.

'Can you bear it——' she began, and was sharply nudged by her cousin as Fiona interrupted what was sure to be a hurting remark about John's condition, relative to Sam's feelings. She knew her cousin only too well.

'I'm glad to meet you at last, Miss MacDonald—Samantha—I've heard reams about you from Stephen.'

'Hello, Fiona, Stephen does ramble so. I just knew our nice session voice would fit you, someone like you.' Mark handed Sam a glass and her smile touched him in brief thanks. 'How do you do, Miss Dutton, are you enjoying your vacation here?'

'Oh, so-so, could improve later.' Carol looked invitingly over her shoulder at Mark.

Sam stiffened slightly and felt Mark's leanly hard body at her back. 'I love it here, it's a wonderful life, so much to do and see,' she spoke with deliberation.

Carol looked meaningly at Stephen and Mark, 'I guess there shore is'—she drawled—'rather handicapped, though, for you, with a fiancé——'

'Carol! You're so fond of the city, you would never appreciate the joys of pastoral life.' Fiona interposed, with a searing stare at her cousin.

'With the right—er—background, dear cousin, I too would settle for country living.'

Mark threw back his head and laughed. 'Well, come with me, I'll start teaching you right now ... with a large chunk of dripping, juicy steak!' A brief touch on Sam's shoulder as he moved past her and took Carol's arm, propelling her forward.

His was the cue for a general exodus to where the inviting, spicy aroma of barbecued meats wafted in the night air and tickled questing noses. For the next hour old and young alike enjoyed themselves savouring the various meats, salads, pies and fruit salads. Samantha sat with Mame and John and thoroughly enjoyed her first taste of charcoaled chops and kebabs. She became a firm believer in the cult and sampled until she felt bloated!

The men circulated among the guests, seeing to their needs, although it was really a free, easy, help-yourself affair. Tad and Mike and a couple of their jackaroo cronies disappeared into the night with loaded plates and drinks balanced precariously. Carol forgot to be supercilious, got her lovely dress full of grease spots and plenty of attention from the boys. Boys who still wore outback garb, almost a uniform, of elastic-sided boots, check shirts and tight jeans, the only difference being that they were now spotlessly clean and their hair was slicked down in various current fashions.

Luke seemed to avoid Samantha, or so she came to believe, because whenever she wanted to talk to him or drew too near the group in which he happened to be, he would withdraw, find some place elsewhere to occupy his time. She did not think she had offended him; the doctor definitely had a problem and it had to do with his avoidance of her, of that Sam was sure. She determined to corner him, very soon.

Mark attracted her attention, for he was looking directly

across at her. Mandy was with him and Sam saw her hand Mark a kebab dripping with tomato sauce. He held it up, indicated his little finger and pressed it on the tip of the skewer. He closed his eyes and started to eat the meat while Mandy put her hands across her eyes in mock horror. Samantha caught on and dropped her eyes while putting a hand on her heart. The bleeding 'love potion' ritual was on!

Carol looked at Mark and wondered aloud, 'Is the man that fond of tomato?' and the leering grimace he directed at her puzzled the girl for a long time Sam was thankful to see that Mark did not divulge the secret.

Soon the radiogram came into its own and couples started dancing on the polished cement of the side veranda. The older generation sat back to watch in contented repletion, it was not often that they had the opportunity to be together and there was much chatter and gossip. John sat in the latter group, happy with his friends, and urged Sam to join in the dancing. She demurred, feeling she could not lift a foot and her waistband was too tight ... oh, that lovely food!

It was not to be. 'Oh no, you don't—gird your loins, pull in your tummy—away we go!' Stephen pulled her up and to the gay sounds of Trini Lopez enthused and infused her with his expert footwork. And Sam, no mean dancer herself, swayed with him, did the shake with him and gyrated till she felt heady and dizzy. The record ended and she tried to slip away, but shouts of 'No go!' and she was effectively stopped by the lads. They had discovered the newcomer could 'trip the course ... she could dance a proper piece, she could.'

Carol was also very much in demand; she was 'hep' with the latest and everybody was eager to learn. Mark and Luke sauntered over to watch and Sheila enticed the doctor, they whirled away. Next, a freckle-faced youngster was persuaded to try his hand on his piano-accordion and started off with a nostalgic tango. Tommy Crawford cleared his throat and politely invited Samantha; this was his coup, one dance he could do well. Mark checked a movement to Sam and took Mandy instead. They glided away. Soon they were the only two couples on the floor, the others stopping to watch the gliding fluidity of grace in the hands of learned experts. Halfway through the dance Tommy sloped Samantha expertly, sensuously, and when she came up he passed her without a break into the waiting arms of Mark. Mandy was simultaneously whirled into Tommy's firm grip.

Samantha gasped and almost missed her footing, but her new partner's steady hand guided her and he was smiling into her startled eyes.

'Smashing, aren't we, Tom and I?'

'Smashing's what will happen to Mandy and me!' gasped the breathless girl inelegantly.

They danced in perfect accord and Mark's lithe guidance thrilled her and put wings on her feet. The music ended and, skirts billowing, Samantha was lifted high in climax by two hands at her waist. Held high as if featherweight, clear blue eyes very close to her own. Mark lowered her slowly to spontaneous shouts and clapping. Under cover he sang softly, 'Why don't we do this more often, just what we're doing tonight——' His masculine fragrance was potent and her wide eyes begged for mercy, not only for release from his grip but to still a turbulence that was quite incomprehensible. Mark loosened his hold on her waist.

Tommy slapped him on his shoulder. 'Team work, what say, feller?'

'Jolly bango, what say, cobber?' Mark turned from Samantha.

'Mark Lane, don't you dare do that to me ever again! I almost had a heart attack—an old lady like me!' Mandy stormed at him.

'My bower bird, you're still good for many years.'

'Tell that to Allan, I'm just his baggage. We sure did show 'em, though,' Mandy said, and smiled complacently.

Mark seemed to avoid Sam thereafter and paid marked attention to Carol. Samantha did not mind in the least, she was not left alone as the evening sped on, and she had discovered that the cool, competent, most often infuriating man could be lots of fun when he let his hair down—and his ego.

Luke claimed her for the next dance and Samantha brought her wayward thoughts into line, remembering his behaviour earlier on.

'Sam, after this dance, would you sort of amble away ... to your room? It's private there and I want to speak to you,' Luke forestalled her questioning.

'All right, Luke,' she answered instantly.

Mark Lane noted but could not hear the whispered injunction. He watched the girl's face as Luke left the room and wondered what had been said to bring on that pensive, troubled expression. Carol claimed his attention and when he looked back Samantha was nowhere to be seen.

Sam entered her room in some trepidation, to find Luke sitting on her bed. He gestured and she sat down, her legs suddenly very shaky.

The tall doctor studied her silently, intently. He sighed involuntarily.

'Hans Getsenberg will be in Adelaide on Wednesday.'

'Luke!' Sam paled, her fists clenching spasmodically.

'He'll be ready for John on Friday.'

'Luke ...?'

Doctor Mannering moved quickly. 'Here, put your head down on your knees ... so. Keep it there ... come up slowly now.' He held her, a long arm around her shoulders. 'I'm sorry I shocked you so, Sam. I'll never learn the soft approach. I've had this on my mind all evening.'

'Why ... why didn't you tell me sooner?'

'I thought it might upset you ... all these people milling around.'

Minutes passed as Samantha regained her composure.

'Just the place for a quiet tête-à-tête?' Mark drawled from the open doorway.

Samantha looked at him mutely. Luke glanced up briefly and then spoke to the girl. 'Feel better now, Sam?' and kept his arm around her shoulders.

With deceptive calm, Mark advanced into the room. 'Is Samantha ill?'

Luke did not reply and Sam was biting hard on her lower lip.

'Well, Luke?'

'Well what, Mark?' Doctor Luke was about to continue, but stopped when he looked at the man confronting him. Mark Lane was in a cold, deadly rage and his narrowed eyes were slitted icebergs. Samantha did not see this, for she was meticulously folding the hem of her skirt in tiny pleats and her eyes were lowered. She finally looked up in the heavy silence and voiced the words that were on Luke's lips.

'Mark ... Mark, Luke says Mr. Getsenberg will be in Adelaide next week. *Next week*, Mark!'

'Does John know?' Mark had turned abruptly, with his

back to them and his thumbs hooked into the pockets of his trousers. He expelled a long breath and faced them again, repeating his question. 'Does John know?'

Luke said, 'I gave Sam rather a shock, she nearly passed out. No, I wanted Sam to know first, it might have excited John too much. Should I have told him?'

'No, Luke, you've done the right thing. The news may well have preyed on his mind all evening, exciting him too much. Possibly despairing him—his hopes that all will be well—oh, I know him so well——' Sam leaned forward pleadingly. 'Don't be angry with Luke for telling me first, I know you were the first one he should have come to. And please, Mark, don't tell John just yet, wait until the family are alone.'

She was very pale and her eyes, looking up at him, were large and luminous in their appeal. Mark took a long stride and sat beside her, to take two trembling hands in his warm, strong clasp, willing them to be still.

'It can keep a while longer, Samantha. When did you hear from Hans, Luke?'

'I received a cablegram from him this morning. John must be in the nursing home by Tuesday, for preliminary preparations. The big job, if all goes well, will take place on Friday.'

The two men were talking across Sam's small figure. Mark raised a questing eyebrow, asked tersely, 'Plane or car?'

'Plane. Far quicker and better for Tom to bring him. A long car trip at this stage may be detrimental.'

'You're the doctor. I'll take Samantha by car, not enough room in the plane for all of us and we'll need the car anyway.' Mark took the fact for granted that he and Sam would be with John.

'That's fine, Mark, you need only come through on Thursday,' Luke said.

'Does that mean we shan't see John ... visit him before the ... before Friday?' Samantha's voice trembled with stifled anxiety.

'It would be advisable not to, he'll be under tranquillisation most of the time and we don't want anything to upset him, my dear. Perhaps on Thursday you and Mark can pop in for a few minutes.'

Allan stood in the doorway. 'What's the big confab about?'

Mark briefed him on coming events and the big sturdy

100

man listened in silence. At the end his only comment 'My word!' conveyed a surprising range of emotions.

On Sunday morning after breakfast, the family sat on the veranda, each one immersed in their personal mail. Samantha read the news sheets to John in a subdued voice while he lay back with his eyes closed. Her mind was not on what she was doing and she wondered if he was listening and what he was thinking.

John had taken the momentous news with wonderful fortitude and calm. His later comment, after the family had been called and told, had brought the tears very close to Sam's eyes and a large lump to her throat.

'Well, I guess it's about time. I hope they'll let me do some book work while I'm incarcerated. It will be a bore if I can't continue this exciting thing I'm on now,' John remarked, and kept any doubts of ultimate recovery well hidden, showing only tender concern for his grandmother when she nearly broke down at Luke's news. 'Keep the good little pecker up, kooks, not to worry, everything's going to be hunky-dory.'

Samantha faltered in her reading as she thought about it.

'I'm listening, chick.' John did not open his eyes and she resumed with a slight tremor in her soft voice.

Mark looked up from the letter in his hand, her voice invading his consciousness, and heard the tremor in the soft tones. He studied the girl with half-closed eyes. Her lashes fanned down on youthful, high cheekbones as she looked down at the print. What were her thoughts on the coming ordeal; did Samantha MacDonald realise what was in store for her, either way? She had great faith in the eventual restoration of vitality to John's limbs and most probably hoped for the day when they could live a normal happily married life.

With the ease of active muscles Mark moved from the low-slung chair and walked down the steps into the sunlight.

Samantha's eyes followed him and she faltered once more in her reading. John opened his eyes at the cessation of her voice.

'Tired, girl? Leave off for a while, nothing of interest to relate anyway. A sad lack of juicy scandals these days! Stretch your legs a bit and go and see what the lazy lubra is

101

doing, it's long past tea-time. Better still, follow up that swagman out there and cheer him up. Mark's hardly opened his mouth today ... burdened with a smashing hangover, I'll bet!'

Sam stood up and stretched her cramped limbs. Mina appeared with a loaded tea tray and John sighed in satisfaction. 'Fetch the guy, Sam, tea and aspirins will help at this stage.'

Samantha reluctantly walked in the direction Mark had taken. She really did not feel like talking to him; he definitely looked grim and she feared more sardonic or curt remarks if she intruded her presence and that was something she simply could not face today. John was uppermost in her thoughts, and Sam suspected that the same thoughts occupied Mark and the rest of the family. They all, including herself, showed composed exteriors but speaking for her own insides, well, it was positively tied up in knots ... Samantha prayed humbly, asking God to be with her, to give a helping hand when the time came.

She found Mark hunkered down on his haunches under a tree, idly making patterns in the dust with a gum twig.

He shot a narrow-eyed look up at her when he heard her coming and then concentrated again on his drawing. Samantha leaned against the tree and watched the movements of his tanned hand. She shifted her eyes to the top of his bent head ... dappled sunlight played on the dark hair and a stray, pirate lock escaped down his forehead, dark brows frowned in concentration and ... Samantha experienced an uncontrollable urge to run her fingers through the thick springy hair, to smooth back that vagrant lock.

'Tea's ready, Mark, and you shouldn't go out without a hat in the sun.' She was surprised at the gentle tone of her own words.

'Thanks, Mac.' A slight deepening of the indentation on a brown cheek was almost a smile. Mark continued his intricate pattern and Sam watched him for silent minutes, then some inner courage asserted her to speak again.

'Mark, you're worried about John—I guess we all are. I know he's going to be fine when he comes back, so please, Mark, don't worry too much——' she pleaded to the top of the dark head.

He straightened up slowly, still not looking at her. 'You

102

really believe that, with your whole heart?'

'Yes, I do.'

'How come?' The cleancut lips were taut.

'Well, I just feel that way——' Sam hesitated.

'And are your feelings always foolproof?' Mark twisted the stick in his hand with curious intensity.

'No, Mark, not always. This is a certain ... call it an almost spiritual feeling that I have, or rather feel——' Sam laughed shakily. 'I have no other word for it.'

Deep blue eyes regarded the intense young face, eyes that were direct and level. "Keep a green bough in your heart and God will send you a singing bird", Mark quoted softly.

Samantha's eyes widened and became luminous with surprised delight. She repeated his words slowly. 'That's beautiful, Mark. May I ask the origin?'

'A Spanish proverb, a quotation that I overheard some time ago. Your words and your remarkable faith surfaced it from my subconscious, I guess.'

'Thank you, Mark.' She was deeply touched.

'Thanks to you, little one, for jolting me back to sane, hard realities. We all learn to accept them, in time.'

A strange overtone of bitterness in him puzzled Samantha. Just what was he thanking her for? There was no sarcasm now, of that she was quite sure, and yet humility or bitterness did not agree with her conception of him as autocratic and therefore imperturbable. She had a secret feeling that Mark was beginning to relent towards her, accepting the fact that she was here to stay. There was still the enigmatic blue in his eyes whenever they strayed her way, but a definite softening approach which, paradoxically, sent a queer tug hurtingly through her breast. Sam remembered the flood of joy that swamped her only the morning before, in the kitchen. This man had an uncanny knack of playing her emotions like strings of a harp.

For the first time there was a kind of peace between Samantha and the big Australian as they walked back to the house.

John sorted the books that he wanted to take with him and passed them on to Sam. It was the following day and she and Sheila were helping John, packing what he would need, plus the books he insisted on taking. He became quite fretful if either of them were out of his sight for too long, so they pampered him in turn, Sam in her quiet way and Sheila diverting with gay chatter.

Watching the lissom dark girl with the wind-blown curls, Sam became aware that beneath her merry gossip ran a strain of anxiety which John apparently did not notice. He teased her often and there was a close bond of affection and a sort of restrained vitality on the girl's side in their passage of words. Was she, Sam, unwittingly causing deep hurt and heartbreak for this girl, and what must it cost her to hide her love with everlasting gaiety?

Samantha felt an inexplicable guilt in her own heart and could not shake it off; after all, John had chosen her and, having known Sheila long enough, should be sure of his choice. If Sam had known Sheila before John's proposal, as she knew her now, would she have accepted him, causing hurt and trampling on another girl's feelings without a qualm? Well, it was done now, when John had asked her to come with him he had mentioned the girl back home in a light, unconcerned way, to him Sheila was just the girl that Mark and the family expected him to pair off with, to marry eventually. What price her guilt then?

With a murmured excuse Samantha left them and walked outside. Instinctively her feet carried her to the summer-house. Somehow it had become a refuge, a quiet place for contemplation and musing when she wanted solitude.

Mame watched as the girl walked unseeingly past her window and noticed the bent head and troubled look. With quick decision she put down her crochet work, picked up her cane and left the house in the wake of the slender figure. Sam was standing, hands deep in her skirt pockets, staring through the screen of creepers. She turned with a forced smile as Mame entered.

'Come here, child, sit next to me.' When Samantha was seated, Mame went on without preamble, 'I might be intruding, but you'll always find me ready and willing to listen to your troubles or any confidences you may wish to disclose. Out with it now, make-believe I'm your Mary-Gran if you like.'

The sweetness in her smile made tears spring to Sam's eyes and she bit hard on her lower lip.

The old lady took her hand in a firm clasp. 'You do miss

her badly, girl. Tell me your troubles and I'll do my best to be as wise as she would have been.'

Samantha looked at her through a mist of tears. 'You're so much like her, dearest Mame, it comforts me to know I have someone to confide in—only I don't quite know what I want to confide.'

'Can it be John? Are you worried about him?'

'Well, in a way it is, not about the operation ... not that...' Sam hesitated.

Mame felt cold fingers curl around her heart. Samantha MacDonald wanted to leave, she was not in love with John any more; would she wait until everything was over? So ran the thoughts, like creepy earwigs in the grey head.

'Tell me, child.'

Sam lifted a determined chin. 'Mame, did Sheila expect to marry John, was it all cut and dried? Tell me really and truly?'

An audible sigh of relief escaped in a soft gust. 'Is that what's worrying you, my dear?'

'It is. I know it's rather late in the day, but I have an awful guilty feeling that Sheila cares more than she lets on.'

'You shouldn't feel guilty. After all, John made his own choice.'

'But what about Sheila? You haven't answered that question ... I can't bear to think I've barged in and spoilt everything for her. John must have cared enough to let the plans for marriage go undisputed. He told me she was the one everybody expected him to marry!'

Samantha's statement was considered gravely. 'We did have expectations in that direction, she always favoured John and he treated her in a lordly, possessive manner. But remember this, he went away and met you, and the final choice was his, not ours. So there's nothing we can do about Sheila's feelings, is there?'

'That sounds so hard and callous, Mame. She's still the same person and one can't just cast out love—when your man turns to someone else.'

'Are you trying to convey, or making yourself believe that John may be merely infatuated with you ... to find later that Sheila was and is his true love? Oh no, that I can't believe. John's attitude towards you is very evident!'

Sam was shaken at this new aspect that Mame had dug

up, for she had never doubted John's love for her. Mame's words left her floundering in sudden uncertainty. 'I'm afraid I wasn't thinking of John's side of it, only Sheila's.'

'No, Samantha dear, I'm not being hard and unfeeling. The fact remains, you are John's girl, and Sheila must accept that fact, however hard it comes. You must forget that there's any guilt on your part and concentrate only on John. He needs you now and especially within the next few weeks.' Mame's bright eyes were earnest and pleading.

'Yes, I guess he will need me . . .' Sam's voice trailed off in a whisper.

They sat in silence for a while, then the old lady asked with sudden husky intensity, 'Sam, just how much do you care for John?'

The gold-tipped lashes flew up. 'Mame, what a question!'

'I mean, really and truly—the way I loved my Jonathan? Is there glory in your heart at the mere thought of him?'

Samantha allowed her lashes to drop, to fan from sight the cloudiness of green eyes. 'John is a wonderful man, I care for him more than anyone else in the world. I guess glory only comes to a chosen few, like you, Mame. I care enough to think only of his happiness, even at the cost of mine or any one else's.'

'That's rather contradictory, my dear. There should be no cost to yours if it's wrapped up with John. Your happiness is naturally assumed if you love him and he is contented.' Mame was shrewd.

'Yes, you're right, I'm all mixed up . . .' Sam stammered, and shifted the subject. 'Mark is taking us to Adelaide on Thursday. Mame, come with us. I'm sure John would want you just as much as we would want you to be there too. Could you—would you?'

Her soft pleading shook Mame. 'My dear, how I've hoped to hear those very words,' she blinked hard and controlled her mouth before continuing. 'I've wanted to go with you, but Mark didn't say anything. I was hoping, actually willing you to invite me along——'

'Oh, Mame, how silly of you, of course you're coming. Fancy waiting to be asked! He's your grandson and I'm sure we'll all need you. Mark simply hasn't asked you in the mistaken belief that the journey will be too much, which is just so much ballyhoo . . . the road's not bad, the car is comfortable and you're a tough, healthy feller. You can even sit on my lap, but I do think the seat will be softer than my bony legs and I promise to clobber Mark if he drives too fast. Darling Mame, I love you!' Sam put her arms around her companion and nuzzled her face in the startled old lady's neck.

'Humph! Clobber him? Then we'll never get there!' Mame studiously ignored the moisture on her neck when Sam drew back. Tears?

'We'll soon surmount that difficulty! While the smashed male lies supine on the rear seat, supplant him will I, to drive with skill and daring, och aye,' Sam's eyes were sparkling suspiciously as she stood up with a valiant flourish. 'Scots awa' to the rescue!'

'Rescue? When it be the same Scots lass that does the clobbering? Hmm ... surmount, supine, supplant and smashed ... must I supervene with supplicating sighs for you to surcease your sadistic surges?'

'While your love lies bleeding on the back seat. Cor, he bleeded a proper piece, he did!' Sam gazed in horror at the couch and Mame rose hastily.

'Let's celebrate your coup de grace with a cuppa. I feel quite bilious, you bloodthirsty swagger!'

A slender hand joined the blue-veined one on the walking stick as they strolled back. Mame glanced sideways at the girl. 'Don't get soft in the head now, stop worrying about Sheila. She'll get by, she has the Lane streak in her. John is the one to think about, to concentrate on, and he's probably wondering right now at your desertion.'

Samantha nodded quiet agreement. Sheila met them at the door.

'Where have you been, Sam? His nibs has been shouting the house down. I'm going out for a breather ... anybody mind if I stay for the night so that I can also see the old slave-driver off in the morning?' She smiled disarmingly and walked into the garden without waiting for a reply.

They watched her until she was out of sight and Sam gave an involuntary sigh. A stern blue glance made her turn swiftly and walk to John's room.

CHAPTER 9

'Look after the girls, Mark.' John's affectionate glance enveloped Mame, Samantha and Sheila and roved on to Mandy and Allan.

Mark stood with long arms around Mame and Sheila's waists. He moved them forward to where Samantha was standing slightly apart and the hand on Sheila's waist was extended to grasp hers in a firm clasp. 'It will be a job, old chap. I need to be an octopus!'

'Thank goodness you aren't, there's no answering for the consequences. See you soon, travel carefully.' John looked down calmly as Tom Crawford took his place in the cockpit.

'*Pax vobiscum*, cousin,' Mark said.

John smiled. 'Thank you, peace be with you too.'

The plane revved to a high whine and moved down the runway. Soon it was a tiny speck in a cushion of blue brilliance. Mandy, Allan and Mame climbed into the utility and Mark restrained the two girls from following suit. He spoke to Allan.

'Samantha and Sheila are coming for a long gallop. Several sheep have strayed across the north boundary, and I want to check the lines.' A look of understanding passed between the two men, a 'right, chum' from Allan as he took off with a flourish.

Samantha watched the receding vehicle in amazement, then turned to the tall man, who stood in unconcerned ease with his thumbs hooked in trouser pockets.

'I'd rather not, if you——' she began, to be cut off peremptorily.

'Oh yes, you are. I need your and Sheila's help. Afraid of a little hard work? Easier to crawl into your hidey-hole and mope?' That confounded sardonic smile was back on well-defined lips.

Instant resentment kindled in Sam's breast, but Sheila intervened before she could reply. 'Mark's unfailing recipe, or technique for restless souls. Bow down, Sam, there's no out.'

'Is that so? Well, I know of plenty!' Samantha started to walk.

A lithe, lazy stride and her way was blocked. Sam stared

at a shirt button that was near enough to tickle her nose while casual words sounded above her head. 'I could be most obliging and carry you to the horse if my lady has no wish to walk. Quite easily, having done so before ... if you'll recollect?'

'Thank you, I have every wish to walk—home.' Samantha spoke to the uncompromising button.

'Oh? When woollies are obstinate we sling 'em over a strong, manly shoulder. You're not a silly sheep, therefore one must carry you in the approved manner, Miss Mac.' With sudden dexterity Mark bent down and Sam felt her knees give way. The next moment he was striding along with a thoroughly startled girl in his arms. Sheila was hard put to keep pace and, for once, she too was bereft of speech.

'Put—put me down at once!' Samantha gasped.

'Only if you'll come with us,' Mark retorted, unabashed.

'You're—you're much too fond of p-picking me up—at the slightest provocation!'

'My word, you're right ... third time now. Are you provoking me, lass?'

'Put me down, Mark!' Sam reiterated with passionate insistence, for that insidious, magnetic aura was affecting her again, and anger was mixed with a pounding tide of feeling.

'Do you agree to ride with us, to be a good girl?' He stopped walking, blue eyes deceptively disengaged.

'Yes ... yes! Put me down!' the angry girl agreed, and Mark deposited her with a thump on to her feet.

Samantha stepped back violently. 'You—arrogant—backwoods—savage!' Green eyes sparked with furious animosity.

A jaw muscle tightened and Mark's features paled to a lesser degree of tan. Sheila felt a constriction in her throat as she watched him take a step nearer to Sam. Once before, she had seen white anger on Mark Lane's face ... anger at the aborigine who had mistreated one of his horses. That frightened darkie had never again dared to put his foot on Lane property.

Samantha stood, with feet apart, and waited for the onslaught. Tumultous fury swamped any fear she may have had.

'Backwoods ... savage, MacDonald?' With alarming calm he stepped still closer, towering over the slight figure.

Dauntless, unanswering, Samantha faced him—and felt a

rising exhilaration as her heart started to thud with a mysterious, flawless passion. Almost as if she waited with bated breath, with a sort of ecstasy, for an expected blow.

'Savage, Samantha?' Mark raised his hands upwards, to the dark hair. A gleam of white teeth showed between tautened lips on the sun-browned face.

As if in pain ... Pain? Not anger? Dimly, through her flooded emotion, Sam recognised the face of pain, and made an instinctive gesture towards his upraised hands.

'Hold it, Mark! That's John's girl. You're supposed to look after her.' Wide-eyed, Sheila made a desperate, valiant, laughing effort.

And succeeded.

For long moments Mark looked down at the defiant wisp of a girl, so close to his broad chest.

'John's girl? You don't say?' His hands dropped and Samantha would never know if his intentions were to pull her hair out at the roots ... or stroke it.

She took a pace back and tucked her loosened shirt back into her jeans with shaking hands. 'I'm ready, what are we waiting for?' she asked of the graven image before her.

Normally her sense of humour would have come to her rescue. If anybody else, Stephen for instance, had picked her up bodily, she would have seen humour in the situation and treated it as such. When this man, imperious and commanding, did so, she was immediately galvanised into fury and frustration. His temerity aroused her and some instinct compelled her to fight back or—submit to the potent attraction he had for her.

Mark's intention had clearly been a kindly desire to take her and Sheila with him in order to stop them from dwelling too much on John's coming ordeal, to occupy their minds elsewhere. Most noteworthy of him ... and most reprehensible of her to call him the names she had practically spat at him! She was the savage, for allowing Mark's dominant ways to bring uninhibited rage to the surface so easily. Never before had this facet of her character revealed itself and Sam was appalled at the hidden capability of her nature. Mark was the only one who could, somehow, incite her to such an extent.

Mark had full control of himself and the familiar enigmatic look was back in the blue depths.

'For happier days, I hope!' It was Sheila who answered Sam's last query. Her words carried more relieved fervour than she realised and Mark's eyes rested her way in a slitted summing-up.

'Yeah, I guess so,' he drawled. 'What a slender hope, with backwooders littering the Australian horizon.' He turned away. 'Coming?'

They walked in silence to the paddocks. Samantha knew she had hurt him with that derogatory word. An apology quivered on her lips, but she was unable to utter it. She helped in mute silence to the saddling and then mounted in quick agility before anyone could give her a hand. Mark surveyed her and the horse, thumbs in their usual resting place, then moved with a lazy stride to shorten and tighten the stirrups. She lifted her foot quickly and a derisive smile played briefly as he patted her horse and then mounted Frost with lithe ease.

He set the pace with an easy gallop and Samantha pulled her linen hat forward, more firmly on her head. She would keep pace with these two experienced riders if it killed her. They rode mostly in hot, wind-blown silence. Sheila's occasional shouted comments were whipped away in the wind and Sam could not catch them, but Mark's ears were more attuned and he answered with gestures and deep voice which carried well.

This was his life, and every resilient muscle in him revelled and responded to the indolent grace of his horse. As he forged ahead of the girls a picture of natural power and beauty was formed. The tall figure suddenly reined in and his hat was waved aloft in an outstretched arm. Frost reared up on his hind legs and Sam caught her breath in involuntary delight at the magnificent artistry of man and beast.

The girls joined him and looked down the valley. Another rider was just visible, herding a small flock through the lower reaches that edged a coppice of gums and slow-trickling billabong.

'Tad has evidently found them. I have the repair kit in my saddlebags. We'll join him for a spot of rest under the gums.' Mark studied his timepiece. 'It's noon, we've certainly made good time. Nice going, girls, we'll make an Aussie of you yet, Mac.'

Sam felt a glow under her ribs. By rights, Mark shouldn't

111

even want to talk to her, much less throw a word of praise, after her scathing lash at the airstrip. Somehow, before the sun set, she would muster up the courage to apologise for her lapse of manners.

They cantered down to the stockman who had dismounted and was leisurely rolling a smoke in the shade of the silver gums. Sam dismounted with the others but remained close to her horse, playing with his ears, while she regained her land legs. They felt wobbly and her back ached, but she was not going to complain or allow the others to discover her weakness, especially after Mark's remark.

Sheila was not so discreet, flinging herself down on a mat of dried leaves with a loud groan. 'Oh, my aching back ... honestly, Mark, was it such a matter of life and death after all? My legs just don't belong to me!'

Samantha felt soothed by the thought that she was not the only one with aching limbs. She joined Sheila with a sigh of relief and sat down very gingerly.

Mark accepted a home-rolled from Tad and lowered his length on to an exposed root. He studied the girls through the curling smoke. 'Softies, Tad? Where are the days when a riproaring lass would ride backwards on a wild 'roo and not bat an eyelid?'

'Sneers won't break my bones, Mark Lane, they slither off my already broken back. My dearest wish, to wake up and find myself back home, filled with tucker and long cups of delicious tea ... oohh, I'm thirsty, Tad, pass the waterbag. How long would it take to slit a woolly's throat, make a fire and roast said woolly? On second thoughts I'd even devour it raw and drink the blood—I'm hungry!' Sheila wailed piteously.

Mark motioned to Tad. The stockman walked to Frost and started to unbuckle the saddlebags.

'We get the message, loud and clear, so rest your wagging tongue. Samantha can't even speak, so great is her need ... eaten your tongue, softie?' Mark's question came in an insinuating whisper and Sam sat up indignantly. A groan escaped her as her back protested at this sudden torture.

'Ah, it speaks with foreign tongue.' Mark took the parcel from Tad and, with great care, began opening it. Two pairs of astonished eyes watched as he revealed cucumber and tomato sandwiches, rolled smoked beef and ham and rosy apples. Tad plonked the inevitable tea flask next to the heavenly spread.

'Why, you planned this outing before you left home! Mark Lane, you deliberately let me rave on, you ... sadist ... you ornery platycephalic ... platypod ...' Sheila wavered.

'—duckbill!' Sam finished knowledgeably, and then gasped as she realised that the very first word she had uttered was another insult.

Mark gave Tad a meaning look and slowly started wrapping up the spread again while a grave faced Tad picked up the tea flask.

'What—what are you doing?' Samantha stuttered, and Sheila squealed in despair.

Mark speared both of them with a steely eye. 'I may be a flatheaded, broadfooted platypus, but at least I'll not share my tucker with softheaded insulting females!'

'Oh, Mark, I'm truly sorry. I was just—exclaiming. Forgive, please, and forget.' Sheila came to her knees and watched with ravenous, mesmerised eyes as he went on wrapping with slow deliberation.

'Forgiven, dear girl.' Silence as he continued his task. Samantha closed her eyes and swallowed.

'I'm waiting for the party of the second part,' Mark remarked casually.

Still with closed eyes, she moved forward from her sitting position and crawled on hands and knees till she sensed she was near enough. Not daring to open her eyes, she spoke. 'Your pardon Mr. Lane,' she lowered her voice, '—and for this morning too, please?'

A warm, feathery kiss touched her eyelids. Startled green eyes flew open to stare straight into twinkling blue pools. 'Granted, bonnie MacDonald. A most gratifying apology.'

Sam moved back hastily; one could easily drown in those dark-fringed blue pools, they had a hypnotic effect on one. No man had any business to possess such beautiful eyes, a girl would give her eye-teeth to be able to flutter those sooty lashes. She forced her own eyes down to the spread which was now open to the public and anticipation rumbled deliciously under her ribs. Sheila was already demolishing a second morsel and Samantha wasted no more time.

Over his second cup of tea, Tad studied Mark curiously.

'What's biting you, cobber?' the lean, sun-browned Australian eyed him.

'How do you do it, boss? Two of the slinkiest sheilas this side of Murray river have just been on hands and knees to you, and you take the scene casually!'

'Commonplace, mate, commonplace ... rather trying after a time. Through the stomach, you know, the greedy tum-turn. Keep them starved and they come a'crawlin'.' Mark's expression was beautifully superior.

Contrary to her abject apology minutes before, Samantha exploded swiftly, 'Probably the only way you can get them!'

'Oh no, miss, I have other alluring charms, covered and otherwise, you might say undiscernible to the naked eye. I'll be happy to enlighten you.' Mark grinned maliciously and put a hand to the top button of his shirt.

Sam choked on a mouthful of tea and Sheila pounded her back solicitously. 'No, thanks, Romeo, we'll take your word for the hidden charms.' She bent over Sam and hissed, 'Why can't you keep your big mouth shut, you want to land in a dire situation?'

'Well, you started it,' Sam retorted.

'Oh no, Scottie, you did ... very early!'

Mark eased to his feet and jammed his hat above his eyes. 'I grieve that said charms must remain unseen, but this is where I depart before accusations start flying my way. Tad, lead to those fences while these cool cats fight it out.' He lifted expertly into the saddle and 'Won't be long ...' was borne back in the dust of his hasty departure, Tad hard on his heels.

Sheila lay flat on her back and idly chewed a twig. 'Big deal! Thought we were supposed to help.'

Sam stretched and rolled on to her stomach. She dug her fingers into the soil and breathed deeply of the fragrant, aromatic smell of eucalyptus that warmed the earth. Time sped on wings of dappled sunshine and rustling leaves.

Faintly but pure came the trill of a singing bird ... 'God will send you a singing bird ...'

Samantha got up quietly, the other girl seemed to be sleeping, and walked through the canopy of tall trees to the edge of the billabong. Gnarled roots dipped into the shallow water. The girl climbed down the bank and sat on a root. The banks were fairly high and made a sweeping turn at this point; she guessed it would be quite a banker during the

'Wet' as the natives termed the rainy season. She debated for seconds, then leaned down and slipped off her small, laced boots, hitched her jeans up and slid down the root until her feet touched water. It was cool to her skin and Sam leaned back and closed her eyes.

'Sam?' The whisper penetrated, she opened her eyes to find Sheila regarding her from the top of the bank. 'Mmmm?' Sam smiled sleepily up at her.

The girl slithered down and settled beside her. They both watched stray leaves and twigs twirling and floating somnolently on the surface of the water. Sheila at last voiced what was uppermost in her mind; she spoke without turning her head. 'Sam? Can we talk about John?' She felt rather than saw her companion's nod, hesitated, then asked, 'Sam, aren't you just a wee bit worried? You seem to be so sure of—of everything.'

Samantha sat forward and took the hairpins out of her hair. She ran her fingers through the long tresses and removed bits of grass and twigs, then began to plait methodically before she replied, choosing her words carefully.

'I'm not infallible, mate, but I am clinging firmly to the conviction that all will be well. John has simply got to walk again. I'm not allowing myself to think further than that point, it's as simple as that.'

'Maybe your conviction is just wishful thinking.'

'If it is, then my heart overflows with wishes.'

'What if expert handling fails, or can't cope with—this particular case?'

Sam considered this as she started on the other plait. 'If, by some mischance, that should happen, and I'm not going to believe it for one moment—well, John is big and will learn to accept, and so shall I.'

'If he should—die——' Sheila brought her dread out with difficulty.

'He ... will ... not ... die!' Samantha measured her words slowly and firmly.

A sigh of relief escaped the other girl and she shrugged off her haunting fear with a shaky laugh. 'I wish I could clamp my mind as firmly as you do, Sam. Anyway, I don't think I really meant all those silly things I said about marriage, about not wanting to tie myself to a man unable to provide the physical side—you remember how I ranted that

115

day in your room?' Sheila did not look up, intent on the peeling of the stick in her hands.

Samantha watched the slender brown hands. Was Sheila only saying what came to her mind or was the meaning of her words deeper? Sam became convinced that the other girl was inadvertently revealing her love for her childhood mate, and if her words were not an outright hint, their meaning was clear; she would be willing to love and cherish John if the operation was not successful and he remained as he was now, a cripple for life.

She said, delicately, 'Sheila dear, I know you didn't mean them, we all have our moments of bravado, when we say things we don't mean. If my coming has caused heartache, please believe me, I'm deeply sorry, but'—Sam spread her hands hopelessly—'what must I do?'

Sheila broke the stick into tiny bits, stood up and flung them into the water. 'Do? I say, chum, did my slip sag badly? It was only a hypothetical case anyway. But if ever it could happen and you wanted out, remember little me in the background. I like you, Samantha MacDonald, but I feel there's something missing somewhere... I can hear the horses coming back.' She scrambled up the bank and, after a slight hesitation, Sam followed her.

Mark's eyes rested on the dark plaits, on a troubled droop to the softly curved mouth and circled to Sheila's slightly defiant chin. A touch of strain was in evidence. He refrained from comment and merely passed the flask and they finished the last of the tea.

'We found the break in the line, kept us longer than we expected. I suggest we start back now so that we catch the evening session. Luke may have some word for us...' He tightened his saddlebags, ignoring the quick look that passed between the girls while rightly assuming that some dicussion on John had caused apparent strain.

They started back at a more leisurely pace and rode four abreast for a couple of miles. A sudden spurt from Sheila put her to the fore and Tad flicked his horse to join her. He started whistling a catchy tune, slightly off tune, the wind carried back to Mark and Sam in the rear and she raised an enquiring eyebrow. Mark started to hum in deep baritone and after listening intently Sam joined in softly. Her companion stopped humming and filled in the score, singing louder for her benefit.

'Tie me kangaroo down, sport ... Tie me kangaroo down...'

Humming the verses, Samantha sang the chorus with him, her normal soft husky undertones accented in her singing voice. 'Tan me hide when I'm dead, Fred ... tan me hide when I'm dead...'

'A genuine Aussie song in a Scots accent ... not a bad combination,' Mark stopped long enough to remark. Over and over they sang as nimble hooves ate up the miles. Sam stopped eventually when her throat began to feel dry, and Mark carried on whistling through his teeth. After a while she became aware of lack of sound and lifted her eyes from the scrub ahead to look at him. His dark head was turned and he was looking at the plaits that swung from under her hat. Either the sun or some hidden thoughts caused a smoulder of unseen fires to cloud the heart-stopping blue eyes that were now on her face. Samantha's heart lurched alarmingly at that level gaze; if she did not hang on to her animosity, nurture it, she felt she could quite easily fall under the spell of cobalt pools caught in sunbrowned strong features ... Sam abruptly hammered down on chaotic thoughts, dug her heels hard and shot away from the disturbing influence. Her heart kept time with the drumming of Champagne's hooves, as she streaked past Sheila and Tad.

Mark started in pursuit, catching up with her as they neared the homestead. He shouted angrily at her as they raced at breakneck speed, but the girl wilfully ignored him. Her hat blew off, the two plaits came undone and, in the afterglow of sunset, her hair streamed as the wind whistled past.

At the rear of the stables Samantha stopped with an excited flourish. Mark was off and at her side before she could dismount. He lifted her down roughly, held her in tight, shaking arms.

'You damned little fool!' he stormed angrily, and stopped abruptly at the sight of dishevelled, dark coppery hair that fell in all directions and two lambent green eyes that managed to shine through the cascade with unfathomable depths of emotion.

'Mac, Samantha, haven't you ever heard of potholes—wombats? What came over you, are you trying to kill yourself?' Mark loosened his hold, only to grip her upper arms. Again Samantha waited for a blow that did not materialise.

A gentle hand brushed the hair off her face, cupping it for a moment before pressing it against his broad chest, while the other hand encircled her waist. Rebellious spirit suddenly quelled and acquiescent, Sam stood quite still. Her face pressed firmly against his shirt, she breathed the masculine aura of the man. His heart throbbed in her ear and his iron-hard body tensed against hers.

A leaping, pounding tide of feeling responded with shocking suddenness through her limbs. Samantha lifted her face from the protecting hand in blind, mute appeal ... and stars exploded while the world stopped to watch for breathless moments, as Mark inexorably brought his lips down to meet hers ...

A sublime litany of song was in her heart when he finally released her.

Mark stepped back and rested his arms on the rump of his horse, so did not see Sam stumble slightly after being released from his embrace. She had regained her balance when he turned to face her again.

His voice came deep and gruff. 'Forgive me, Samantha, for trespassing—that was unforgivable of me, but absolutely irresistible. Accept my apologies for allowing my—savage instincts—to overcome me.' The blue fire had quenched in his eyes ... and the wings of melody in her heart died down as well, to a heart-rending dirge of broken feathers.

The slow trot of horses pierced her tumbled emotions. A rough rod of invisibility straightened her back while Samantha faced an irrefutable fact. For her, Mark Lane had explosive physical attraction which could open flood-gates of passion and hidden depths of which she had been unaware ... till now.

As casually as possible she lifted gold-tipped lashes and forced herself to speak rationally. 'Not to worry, Mark, it happens to the best of us—sometimes. Your trespass is forgiven,' Sam added softly, impulsively 'and it was not ... savage.'

'Mac! I——' Mobile lips clamped and eyes were hooded as Mark turned to watch the approach of Sheila and Tad.

Sam closed her eyes in quick disbelief; for a fleeting moment she thought she had glimpsed the embodiment of truth, the heart of a man in his eyes. Self-hallucination could play the devil with one.

Sheila handed Sam her hat and watched the departing man and horse in surprise. 'Where's he off to in such a hurry? I thought he was staying for dinner and session—what's Mark done his block over now?'

Catching sight of Samantha's face, a shock of near enlightenment passed through her and she caught her breath.

'Gees! Take care, honey, your slip's showing now.'

A warm, understanding hand took Sam's cold one and Sheila led the unprotesting girl up the path to the house.

Luke's voice came over the transceiver, 'John is quite calm and well and sends his love to all. Hans is here and preparations are in hand, all is well. See you, Mark and Sam, on Thursday, over.'

Allan spoke. 'Thanks, Luke. Mame will be coming as well. Love and regards to Johnny.'

Listening in with the family, Samantha took comforting pride that, after Sheila's soft warning, she showed composure and calm in their sharp-eyed midst. The voice that came now almost broke that hard-earned composure.

'Mark here, Luke. Received your message, see you Thursday. Mame, please note, I'll be there before picanniny dawn, so be ready. 'Bye.'

Regaining her calm Sam thought, not a word of apology for his brusque departure earlier on; he was his own master so did as he wished. She resented his high-handed manner for the family's sake. (They obviously took it for granted, so who was she, after all, to resent anything concerning Mark Lane?) He was not coming over tomorrow, so at least she would have a full day's respite from ... unsettling presences. Time to build up a determined blockade against her stupid weakness. Her beloved John would need all she could give of her spirit, and it must be undivided, not torn apart by other problems.

Sheila already suspected the turmoil caused by Mark's kiss; fortunately she had not witnessed the cause, only the effect, hence the urgent warning. Samantha inwardly cursed the transparency of her own nature. Once John was fit and she could live a normal life with him this mad, primitive infatuation for his cousin would surely die. This ... sweet torment!

As from this moment onwards she was not going to let Mark touch her or allow his insidious attraction to affect her so deeply.

All very noble, Sam's thoughts ran wryly, he had his own dynamic way of cornering her into explosive situations! Could she possibly have a (quiet?) chat with him, explaining that she did not want to be cornered, or would that only show up her feelings too blatantly? Mark was wickedly shrewd and would read between the lines and she would only reap further contempt. Sam shrank from the thought.

What could he be thinking, right now, of her ardent response to his kiss? Samantha's cheeks burned as she recalled the episode. Mark had only recently taunted her with the fact that he could easily kiss her, and he had proved his point. He must be gloating right now, or had already forgotten what was just another incident in his day. A car whirling into the driveway brought Sam back to her surroundings with electric awareness. 'No, not so soon!' she wailed inwardly, and knew exactly how a wounded fawn would feel, seeking escape and being utterly paralysed.

Stephen walked in and Sam remembered, with a relieved sigh, that Mark had spoken on the transceiver so it could not possibly be he. She was endowing him with uncanny powers!

'Hallo there.' He ponked down next to Sheila. 'I've been commandeered by your pater to escort you back to the home fires. They've died down ... the home fires, not the parents, and need the skilled hands of their truant daughter to lighten up their lives again ... the parents and home fires.'

Sheila studied him critically. 'You speak perfect English, Stephen. Why not consider it as a profession? You'd wow the college types.'

'I have my lifetime profession mapped out; to discover sheilas and devour them, swiftly and surely. Of course'— Stephen indicated Samantha—'if they were all like that sprite, the job would lengthen to a slow, beautiful torture! I hate cruelty,' he sighed piously.

'No wonder Fiona looks so ragged and tortured.' Mandy became thoughtful.

'She does not, she's gorgeous——' Stephen started indignantly, and subsided red-faced at the jeering laughter. He focused Samantha. 'Mark sends salaams and regrets he was unable to attend dinner. Something came up, but what it was is a mystery to me, evidently very grim, judging by Mr. Mark's phiz. Okay, Sam sprite, chew me no grief, I'll try to respect my elders. Mark ordered me, with cold politeness, to convey his respects and message, and he would contact his waiting clan on the dingbat. Did he make contact?'

'Yes, thank you.' Again Samantha was proud of the cool impassiveness in her voice. She stood up. 'I think I'll be off to bed, the ride today has bushed me good and proper.' Her eyes turned to Sheila and the appeal in their depths touched that young woman's heart with a queer twist. 'Do you mind if I don't wait to see you off, Sheila? Are you coming over tomorrow? Will I see you before we leave?'

'No, I'll not come tomorrow, so will say goodbye now. Keep us posted on—events, there's a dear.' Sheila hugged Sam impulsively and her eyes gave assurance that any suppositions would remain just that.

Samantha murmured a goodnight and walked out of the room. For no known reason Mame Lane sighed deeply.

The long, powerful car ate up the miles smoothly, with comfortable ease. By late afternoon they were barely fifty miles from their destination. Mame had chosen to sit in front for the first half of the journey and now, after stopping at noon to stretch their legs and enjoy a hamper lunch, she was drowsing on the back seat.

Samantha sat in front, head nestled against the back-rest. Mark had been as impassive as ever when he called for them in a grey dawn and she was grateful for that, it helped strengthen her own composure in the face of past happenings. From under her dark, gold-tipped lashes she watched his hands on the wheel, radiating confidence in their firm touch. Gentle hands, steel hands ...

'Covering roughly forty acres.'

'I beg your pardon, Mark?' Sam swivelled her thoughts back. His hands had drawn her and her conscious mind had momentarily lost the gist of his commentaries.

Mark glanced at her, a quick touch of amusement in his eyes. 'Bored?'

'Oh no, not a bit, do go on, please.'

'I was mentioning the Botanical Gardens which cover

forty acres and contain the world's finest collection of water-lilies. You must find time to visit them, also the National Gallery. They possess the finest range of coins I've ever seen. The Sound Shell concerts at Torrens Lake are quite fabulous. I'll take you to see the black swans on the lake.'

'When are we going to deliver the ton of tucker that Mandy packed for the scamps?' Mame asked.

'It will be rather late when we arrive ... I'll deliver in the morning, after we know how—know the outcome—tomorrow some time.' The man behind the wheel cleared his throat. 'That's the Murray river and bridge in the foreground. We can stop for a breather, see if we can spot a paddle-wheeler, the *Coonerwarra*, perhaps.' He pulled up on the verge of the road and Sam walked with him on to the bridge. Mame declined; she was too comfortable to move her bones, thank you.

Samantha accepted a cigarette from Mark and they smoked in silence. He pointed to a flat-bottomed boat leisurely paddling down the calm waterway. 'Can't recognise her, probably a hired houseboat from Renmark, that's where the citrus orchards are.'

'It looks lovely, the boat, so peaceful and restful ... where are the fabulous vineyards, what direction?'

'Barossa Valley? About forty miles north of Adelaide. The valley has a very continental flavour, or character. Germans settled there originally. The grapes are harvested from March to April and they have a spanking Vintage Festival, most colourful.'

'You know your country, Mark. Have you travelled extensively, I mean here, not overseas?'

'I've been around somewhat ... the Northern Territory, to Brisbane, Queensland. The Gold Coast (that brings back memories!), Sydney, New South Wales to Melbourne, through Victoria back to S.A. I can't honestly say I know Western Australia very well, only flew to Perth once and it wasn't a sightseeing trip.'

Samantha suddenly wondered what his age could be; no one had ever mentioned it. With unconscious intensity she studied his face while she calculated; John was thirty, Mandy slightly older, Mark and John were childhood confederates, so that would make him ...

'Did I forget to powder my nose or are you merely overawed by an aristocratic countenance?' Mark returned her intent gaze with a quizzically raised eyebrow.

Sam flushed. 'I was trying to work out your age,' she answered honestly.

'Now what brought that on? I guess my extensive travels have aged me somewhat, but don't let that fool you, kid. I'm as old as Lofty Mountain and as young as—I would cite you, but, having just called you kid, I must admit to a superior age.'

'How involved can you get! You're worse than a woman at disclosing the age secret!' Sam exclaimed. 'Anyway, you needn't tell me. Mame will enlighten me ... if I'm interested enough to ask,' she managed a disinterested drawl.

'You're a canny lass, to be sure. Dare to ask her, then see how I can retaliate!' A remembering look started in his eyes.

Samantha hastily trod on the stub of her cigarette. 'It's getting late, we have at least fifty miles still to go.' She whirled on a dainty, buckled shoe and walked quickly to the car.

Mark drew on his cigarette, then flicked it into the water. As he settled behind the wheel a whimsical smile hovered on his lips.

Samantha watched the passing scenery with studious intentness. A hand on her knee startled her and Mark remarked casually, his eyes on the road, 'Relax, Mac, we're nearly there. That is Mount Lofty you're trying so earnestly to annihilate ... plenty of time to freshen up before visiting John. Relax, nothing to worry about.' He lowered his voice and, gangster style, continued out of the corner of his mouth, 'That, of course, depends on keeping your mouth shut.' He removed his hand.

The tips of her ears started to burn as she slipped him a defiant glare. She turned round to Mame and her own voice surprised her with its gushing falsetto. 'Are you all right, Mame? I bet you'll be glad to have a nice hot shower ... or do I mean a cold one?'

Mame was surprised as well. 'Why this sudden gush of concern, child? I'm not complaining, quite comfortable, thank you.' What had that godless relative of hers growled in undertones to make the girl suddenly turn with such gusto, pretty ears blooming? She simply could not follow these volatile young people, cool and wise one moment and

123

the next highly excited or embarrassed. Mrs. Jonathan closed her eyes in exasperation.

Mark joined the traffic into North Terrace and soon they were gliding up the driveway of the hotel, to be received and welcomed with typical Australian charm. The tall, sun-browned man was evidently well known and liked, judging by the attention he received—quite the pastoral magnate, in fact! In a smooth space of time Mame and Samantha were ensconced in the airy suite reserved for them. Mark's bags went into the adjacent single room.

'Such luxury!' Sam turned from the window, from which a breathtaking view extended over the city. Shimmering waters were discernible in the afterglow of sunset, through lace etchings of tree-tops. She peeped into a pink bathroom with spotless, shining fittings. 'I feel like visiting royalty, or a very V.I.P.!' She sank luxuriously into an easy chair and, unbecoming to a self-styled personage, kicked off her shoes. A pert young maid was expertly dealing with their baggage in the bedroom. The private sitting-room where Sam now sat was tastefully furnished with soft green hangings and a tan wall-to-wall carpet.

'You have first go in the bathroom, Mame. I'm glad Mark managed rooms for you and me to share. So much more cosy having you close.'

'So do I, quite likely to get lost on my own. Good thing I did come along anyway, you'd likely need a chaperone.'

'What ever for?' Samantha was aghast. Mark's room was right next door, did her companion think for a moment——!

'Well, I saw, with my own gimlet eyes, plenty of speculative looks cast in your direction when we entered this establishment.'

'Oh, did you? I wasn't aware of looks floating around.' Sam's giggle was slightly hysterical.

'Believe me, with Mark around it wouldn't go beyond speculating ... they wouldn't dare!'

'Yeah,' drawled Samantha, 'one cool, deadly look from his pretty eyes and all my chances disappear in a puff of blue smoke.' She added hopefully, 'Any girl-friends here, who could work on his iron heart, maybe break it so that I'm left in peace to speculate back?'

'His heart is breaking already.' Her unguarded tongue

voiced a subconscious thought and the old lady hurriedly pushed the self-amazing thought back to subterranean depths, for later inspection. She continued, 'Carol is here somewhere, Mark will know her whereabouts. There's also a married couple he visits when time permits, Jack and Angie Breem and their new baby. We may meet them, Mark is very attached to them. And probably other attractive females he's met here ... so, you see, you'll need me after all.'

'I get your point.' Samantha smiled wryly. Mark's heart breaking? For whom? 'Off to your bath, woman, pretty up for our John ... and leave some of those heavenly bath-salts for me!'

She changed into a housecoat and took a cigarette from the miniature treasure chest, placed for the convenience of guests, and her heart quickened at the thought of seeing John again. What did he feel, did he have confidence in the coming miracle? Closing her eyes, a silent prayer came from the depths of Samantha's heart and winged upwards, to the One who watches and waits with eternal, everlasting Love.

They were both ready when the knock came and Mark and Luke walked in. The doctor took his old friend's face in his two hands and kissed her lips. Sam stood up as Luke approached her and for some reason her eyes misted. He put a long arm about her waist and tilted her chin with his other hand.

'Hello, beautiful.' Brown eyes smiled into hers and saw the green mist. 'You'll meet Hans tonight and, by jove, he'll make your John so right ... just for the honour and satisfaction of having you thank him!'

'Luke! I thought the French had the monopoly of flattery, but you Aussies have them stone cold. Now, lead me to the great man, let me play him on my hook.' Samantha dropped her light banter. 'He is ... is he confident of the outcome, Luke?'

Luke dropped his arms. 'Hans Getsenberg doesn't talk much, Sam, but knowing him as I do, the less he says the more confident I get. He's the greatest in this particular field ... trust him.'

'I will,' Sam promised huskily.

Doctor Mannering courteously took Mame's arm and escorted her to the door. Mark advanced and casually held out his snowy handkerchief. Samantha accepted it, dabbed her eyes and handed it back (this all-seeing man) while he waited impassively. Cobalt eyes had narrowed fractionally at Luke's affectionate embrace, but were blandly serene as he and Samantha followed Mame and the doctor to the elevator.

CHAPTER 10

'AND he handled me like a rag doll, the old reprobate. When I get out of this situation, just watch how I'll retaliate. Just you wait, Mister Hans Higgins, just——' John's flow of words stopped in mid-air as the old reprobate spoke from the doorway.

'And the good luck to you, Meester Lisa John.' Hans Getsenberg scowled from under bushy brows. 'The best theeng in my life will be to the back see of thees—cobber, you say?—walking out on his flat foot from the suffering long nursing home!'

'My word!' Every inch of visible skin on John Lane was flaming red.

Samantha's heart leapt at the brusque certainty of this man who held John's happiness in his long, slender, incredibly sensitive hands, one of which now held hers while piercing black eyes scrutinised her face with a curious intensity.

'This is the sweetheart, no? Humph.' The man looked down at the hand resting in his, turned it palm upwards and studied it with eyes that were almost hidden under bushy eyebrows. He dropped it suddenly, turned to Mark and Mame and ignored Luke, who edged up to Sam and murmured, 'That means he approves. The brusquer he gets the higher the approval rates.'

Samantha had not had a chance to speak. She seemed to be continually struck dumb since her arrival on this continent.

Hans heard Luke's aside and said disdainfully, 'Young pipper-snatter, too big for the bloomers.'

'Whipper-snapper—breeches,' Luke corrected him absently.

'That is what I say.' Hans turned back to Mark. 'And you, my friend, so long I have not seen you—ah, these were the

126

good days when I teach you the ski in my snow countree, eh? and the pretty fräuleins try to take from me the job!' A deep guffaw followed.

Sam sat down quickly and again dark eyes focused her. 'You have the tongue, no? Ah, it is mute from the contact with thees manswag,' indicating his frustrated patient.

'Swagman,' Luke explained.

Mark said, in unexpected defence of Samantha, 'John's dear lady is dumb-struck with awed admiration of your beautiful brow thatch, Hans. It seems to draw the ladies like a hairy magnet. Even those fräuleins were after only one thing—your eyebrows. Tell me, what do you use, or is it a secret not for divulging?'

Sam was amazed at the teasing familiarity of Mark and Luke towards the great man, and waited for an explosion. It came. Another great guffaw filled the room as Hans Getsenberg stroked his brows with fond fingers. 'So jealous, thees man, not having the beauty I possess.' His fingers cupped Mame's elbow. 'Mrs. Jonathan, I will dine with only you, for you alone will consider the handsome—to attract, not so—of my brows.'

'Charms?'

Luke drew favourable attention. 'That is it, put well, Doctor—my charms of the brow to appreciate. Now, Johnee, you feel better for seeing your so beautiful girl, the mute one?'

Samantha simply had to say something, four pairs of eyes were turned her way. Her mind was a complete blank, she batted long lashes at the man from Switzerland and strange words left her tongue. 'Dear Doctor, Australians are so ignorant, I find ... can you tell me if it's possible to ride a wild kangaroo backwards?'

'Ah now, that is a very good question, shows you have the seeking to find intelligence.' The bushy-browed surgeon hesitated and desperately searched his meagre knowledge of kangaroos ... out of the corner of an eye he caught Luke's amused expression, and his suspicions were aroused. This pretty fräulein was spotting the ribs off him! 'So, I cannot answer a question of such importance under ignorant eyes. Mrs. Jonathan will forgive while I take instead to dinner this lovely seeker of knowledge after riding the marsupial!'

And Luke had said he was a man of few words!

A spark had leapt in Mark's eyes as Samantha put her innocent-seeming question. Unobtrusively he moved nearer to her as the two doctors turned to study John's chart and Mame bent over John to answer a query. He leaned over casually. 'And to think it was I who leaped to your defence just now! You baby doll ... how would you like to be skinned?'

'Mark, please,' Sam whispered back. 'I simply had to say something and I don't know where that came from—forget it, please,' she smiled blandly as Luke glanced at them. 'Mark is annoyed because I called the Aussies ignorant, and I've just apologised very nicely.' Sam's smile flashed back to her tormentor. 'Oh, thank you, I knew you would forgive me, so perfectly sweet of you.'

Mark returned the smile. 'Not at all, Samantha love, think nothing of it. We Aussies are big-minded ... as you will find out.' Only Sam could see the syrupy malice in his eyes!

Getsenberg flapped his hand at John. 'We go now and leave your fräulein the privacy of a word with you.' A world of kind wisdom and affection illumined his face and Sam knew her faith was not displaced.

Mame kissed John with a bright smile. 'Sleep well, my boy, God be with you.' She looked lovingly at him, patted his head and turned away.

Mark saluted. '*Amigo*. Till tomorrow, and we'll put the champagne on ice for the celebration.' Samantha gave a start at the mention of iced champagne and slipped her hand into the outstretched palm that John offered her. Mark noted the questioning and answering smile that was exchanged, knew that, inadvertently, his words had brought back a memory known only to them.

'How is my girl?'

'Your girl is fine, John. And you, my dear?'

'Rarin' to go, for sure. My word, I did get a shock when the old man walked in. Wouldn't have been a bit surprised if he turned me down in a huff.'

'He's a good man, John, and will justify our faith in him.'

'I do believe you really mean that.' John looked at Sam, his eyes shining.

The door opened and the night sister stepped in. 'Your injection, Mr. Lane. Won't take a sec.' Warm eyes smiled at Samantha.

'That's how mean they are, Sam, the moment a pretty lass steps in they stick pins into me—to put me to sleep, I'm willing to bet!'

'So many lasses, he looks like a tea-strainer, the poor wee man.' Sister did her job efficiently, swiftly. At the door she whirled. 'Sleep well ... in just two minutes.'

'There you are, you see what I mean!' John was indignant. 'You better kiss me now, before I fall unconscious.' Sam kissed him lingeringly. 'Mmm, that was nice.' John's arm tightened around her shoulders. 'Do it again. Mmm, very nice!'

'You're a fraud, John Lane. Nice, is that all you can say?'

'Nice ... lovely word.' John smacked his lips and opened his eyes wider, to ward off a heaviness of the creeping variety. 'Damn that woman ... Sam?'

'Yes, John?' she ventured as he lay silent, his eyes trying to focus on the wall behind her.

'How—how is Sheila, is she well? Did she send any messages ... message...' John closed his eyes.

'Yes, darling, she sent her love,' Samantha assured the sleeping man.

For the umpteenth time Samantha peered at her watch by the ray of pale moonlight that floated through the window. After that long journey and sitting up so late, she should be tired ... she was, deadly tired, but simply could not fall asleep. What was the matter with her? Hans and Luke had dined with them and they had sat for a long time in the private sitting-room, Mark and Hans talking of old times, drawing the others into their conversation. It was near to midnight before she and Mame had at last climbed into their respective beds. She was surely not, at this late date, worrying about John? Overtired, that was it. Mame was in a deep sleep across the room. In the faint light Sam's watch pointed to four-thirty a.m.

Cursing inwardly, she climbed out of bed and went to the bathroom, washed her face and brushed her teeth. Quietly she gathered her clothes and walked to the sitting-room, closing the interleading door. She switched on the soft table lamp and dressed, deciding to sit there until the light became stronger and then go for a walk. Distant sounds of traffic reached into the room, a car in a near courtyard was started up with a terrific revving. Sam frowned; somebody was being very inconsiderate.

The door of their suite opened and a tall figure in a dark blue dressing-gown materialised. Samantha stared up at the frowning face of Mark. He lowered on the couch beside her.

Startled, she whispered, 'Mark, did I waken you, or couldn't you sleep either?'

He regarded her, his brows creased. 'That confounded fiend outside woke me and I saw your light from the balcony. Did he ... no, you've been up longer, you're fully dressed. What's up, Samantha, don't you feel well?'

'I simply couldn't sleep. I'm quite well, it's just ... I don't really know,' she answered forlornly.

Mark took her hands in a warm clasp. 'Your subconscious worry about John is the most probable cause of sleeplessness.' He rubbed her hands, deep in thought. 'I've got it! A brisk walk to really tire you out thoroughly and then back to bed for a couple of hours.'

'But I can't sleep while John——'

'I'll see you're there in plenty of time.' Mark consulted his wristwatch. 'Five a.m. That gives us a good four hours. Stay put while I get decent. Put on a coat,' he patted her hand and strode out.

The minutes ticked by and he was beckoning from the doorway. Sam switched off the light and joined him. Mark had taken time to shave and she sniffed the fresh, masculine fragrance. They used the smoothly silent lift to ground level and a smiling night porter let them out. The morning air was very fresh and Sam was thankful for Mark's suggestion that she wear a coat.

He tucked her hand with his into a jacket pocket and led off with long strides, shortening them again immediately when he felt the drag of her arm. Early toilers passed them. Already the traffic was speeding up. Mark pointed out various buildings on North Terrace ... Parliament House, the National Gallery and Museum.

The sky was a golden pink when their circuit walk brought them back to the hotel. Sam's cheeks matched the glow and long afterwards she would recall the briskest walk of her young life!

Mame was still sleeping and Samantha refused to open the intervening door, fearing it would awaken her.

'You must sleep, Samantha,' Mark insisted, but she remained adamant about disturbing the old lady. 'My bed ... you can pop in there,' he suggested.

Samantha was horrified. What would the staff think!

'Little prig! Don't forget I, for one, have seen you in far more intimate circumstances,' Mark whispered. 'Do you recall a certain woolly dressing-gown?'

Here he was, cornering her again! Sam stalked to the couch and sat down, not daring to answer, for it would surely start something again. The man watched her, amusement and a certain tenderness in the gleam of a smile. She was such a proud little atom, it was wicked to goad her. He sat down beside her.

'Dare I smoke, or do you think it will drift through the door to dear Mame's tender nostrils?'

'Smoke by all means—not for me, thanks.' Samantha leaned back. There were other chairs—why must he sit next to her? Should she move away from him? Oh, bother it, she was too tired. Under lowered lashes she studied the dark hair, crisply damp, the high, tanned cheekbones. His jacket had been flung aside and a steady pulse showed a rhythmic beat at the base of a strong throat. Blue suited him ... her eyelids drooped.

Mark stubbed his cigarette and leaned over the girl. 'Take off your coat.' He assisted her, turned her so that her shoulders and breast cradled against his chest while one long arm lifted her legs on to the couch. He settled back. Sam sleepily started a protest, but Mark said firmly, 'Hush your pretty mouth, sleep little one. Papa will watch over you.'

What price resolutions now, why fight against anything? This was so cosy and the Aussie could be so gentle and thoughtful. No wild feelings showed signs of churning ... Samantha snuggled closer into the hollow of shoulder and neck while wings of memory fluttered—'dear one, you are safe', gentle hands, soft, whispering voice. Elusive sleep came at last ...

Much later, quite unabashed, Mark Lane grinned at the astonished maid when she entered with morning tea and the grin extended to his elderly relative, who had discovered the empty bed and now faced him with anxiously enquiring eyes on the sleeping girl. One dark eyebrow shot up, but the composure on his face reassured her and with a disapproving sniff Mame busied herself with the teacups.

'They've been in there an awful long time,' Mame addressed her nephew's back as he stood at the window of the waiting-room. Her nerves were tautly on edge and she marvelled at the outward calm of Mark and Samantha. It was impossible to read the girl's feelings, for Sam was sitting in the deep armchair, calm and serenely immobile with closed eyes and soft lips firmly relaxed. There was a sort of dedicated look about her.

Mark's only indication of stress was his incessant chain-smoking. He kept his back turned, obviously interested in the passing traffic, or so it seemed. At her nervous statement he turned at last and came to her side.

'To those who wait, time drags painfully, my dear. It seems like hours, but in fact, it's quite some time——'

The door opened and Sam was on her feet; three pairs of eyes were riveted on the white-coated man who entered. He look at each of them in turn as he slowly flexed his tired wrists.

A deep, outward breath of accomplishment left Hans Getsenberg's lips and the assurance in the smile that followed was surely the most wonderful, the sweetest expression that three waiting people had ever beheld!

Mark moved to quick encircling support of a pale, unsteady Mame, while Samantha stood stiffly, her eyes glowing with unshed tears. Tears that a smile from a man who had not yet uttered one word could only bring. She lifted a tentative hand in unconscious, grateful simplicity, and the man in white strode over and enfolded the slim, shaking figure in his arms.

'My dear, all is well. God in His goodness is with us and in the short time John Lane will be as before. He will walk.' His statement came simple and steadfast.

'We thank you, Hans ... God bless you,' Mark answered. He gently forced Mame back into her chair. 'Can you prescribe something for our two girls? The waiting and reaction is upsetting—a tranquilliser, perhaps?'

'But of course, it is a painful and exacting time—to wait.' Hans released Sam and put his thumb on a wall press-button. To the staff nurse he muttered a prescription and she hurried away to carry out his order.

'Now, the days coming are veree important. The strict therapy for Johnee will be of the baby to take his first steps. I presume you, Miss Samantha, are staying here?'

'Mrs. Jonathan and I are staying.' Sam looked at Mark. 'I think you mentioned going back?'

'Yes, I'm staying for a couple of days, but must return for the shearing operations. I'll be back when John is ready to come home. Luke will keep us posted on his progress, etc.'

'Good. John is in post-operative, you cannot see him just yet, but he is in good shape, so do not worry. Come this evening. I shall be in attendance all day, so you may contact me any time.'

Sister came in with two small glasses of milky fluid and Sam swallowed hers gladly, for she felt a shaky reaction setting in. Almost immediately she felt calmer and noted a similar effect on Mame.

Hans departed and Mark shepherded Mama and Samantha out of the hospital to his car and they returned to the hotel. He ordered drinks and lunch to be served in their rooms when Mame remarked her disinclination to appear in the dining-room. After lunch Mark left them to attend a business conference, promising to join them again at tea-time.

Samantha moved around restlessly and Mame, busy with her crochet work, admonished the girl to sit down and relax. Sam complied and became immersed in a visitor's guide to Adelaide, to drop it from nervous fingers as the room phone shrilled.

'Samantha? I'm phoning from Jack Breem's place. I contacted the hospital. John is well but still groggy, may be out of it by evening some time. I've also spoken to Stephen at Fiona's post office, and he'll notify the rest of the family. The children's hampers were also delivered, I promised them we would see them tomorrow. Anything I can do for you or Mame?'

'No. Thanks for phoning, Mark. I'm glad the family will know soon, they're so far away and will be grateful for your prompt easing of their minds.' He certainly held all the reins in a firm hand. 'Mame told me about your friends. How is the baby?'

'Angie's baby? She's gorgeous, I've booked her exclusively

133

for the next forty years! I told Jack I would bring you and Mame to see and approve of my choice. I also saw Luke. He's beside himself with pride for having assisted Hans. Relax, honey, you can let your hair down now.' A curious, almost caressing note entered those last words and he rang off abruptly.

Sam stood looking at the telephone in her hand and thought of the simple beauty that could be infused in the word 'honey'. She met Mame's glance and replaced the receiver carefully.

'John is doing fine so far. Stephen has been contacted and the children's hampers have been delivered. We're to see them tomorrow.'

'Oh good.' Mame returned to her crochet work.

'Mark is with the Breems, their baby girl is gorgeous.' An unexpected lump obstructed further talk.

'Well now, Mark is probably drooling over her. He adores girl babies and did say at some time or other that he would like at least half a dozen of his own crawling all over him and dribbling down his neck.'

'All at once? And what about sons?'

'He evidently expected them all at one shot! Sons? I guess each man has a wish for sons, deep in his heart.'

Samantha thought of Mark with his own children, and there was a sudden void under her heart as she tried to visualise the wife who would share life with him. Sam was suddenly very sure that the chosen one would be adored and cherished, in spite of his arrogance; vital capacity for love vibrated under the outward surface of composed inscrutability, the hard exterior that Mark Lane wore like a glove. Sam had sensed this phenomenon quite a few times when he had suddenly changed from a hard-bitten Outback man to a gentle, thoughtful one, especially when it concerned his family or the animals under his care. He was a hard man, but his wife, if she was the right sort of girl who knew how to handle her man, would reap deep, subjected love and tenderness. How she knew this, Samantha could not puzzle out herself, except for the time he had handled her when she had fallen off her horse and this very morning, when his muscles must have become agonisingly cramped, holding her while she slept for two solid hours! So he had done all this for someone he did not even love. What would he be like towards the woman he chose for his wife, to bear his children?

Sam gave a deep breath and turned her thoughts resolutely to John's and her own future. A future that would now become established with John's recovery, when she could be thinking of her own babies and a loving husband in the background. Did John want children? Surprisingly, they had never discussed it, and since the accident that delicate question had never been raised or thought of by herself and John had been equally mute on the subject. Well, soon she would know. The thought was accepted with a queer reluctance by Samantha MacDonald.

She picked up the guide book and studied it with a fierce concentration. After a few minutes she flung it aside and reached for the phone. She gave her name and Sheila's and requested the receptionist to send two bouquets of flowers, with love, to John. Sheila had asked this favour of her before they left home.

Mark returned and, in the early evening, they visited the hospital. John was sleeping soundly and restfully. Hans Getsenberg assured them he would not awake before morning. If he did come round and wanted any of his family, he, Hans, would let them know immediately.

Luke Mannering joined them for dinner and mentioned that the opera company at Sound Shell did a fabulous production of *Carmen*. Mark instantly decided that the girls should be taken, and when Sam raised a protest, that quizzical eyebrow shot up. 'It will be good for you, Samantha.'

'Good for what—surely not my morale?' Her question was sarcastic.

'Rather say, good for me—you'll sleep better and I won't have to play nursemaid again. Or do you fancy another early walk and a comfy sleep in Papa's arms? I really think I'm spoiling you, rather.' Mark's eyes gleamed.

Samantha turned to Luke. 'On second thoughts, I would love to see *Carmen* after all.' She managed a disdainful side glance at Mark and, to her surprise, he dropped his eyes and studied the empty coffee cup as though it contained hidden treasure!

Luke was momentarily puzzled at Mark's words, but did not ask for an explanation. As a matter of fact his friend puzzled him quite some these last few weeks; he had known Mark for many years and sensed the change in him. He had become withdrawn, with an irritating veneer that covered his true qualities. A glimmering of truth beckoned, but the doctor snuffed it out as mere conjecture on his part.

Mame insisted that she was no 'girl' and would much rather snuggle into her bed. Mark did not press her, ordered Sam to take a wrap and they set off to enjoy their fill of the opera.

Seated in the open air with her two handsomely tall escorts, Samantha lived and yearned with Don José in the haunting Flower Song and was transported with the fiery rhythm of the Toreador Song, which conveyed so dramatically the violence and passion of long-ago Spain. The sleeve of one man sitting next to her brushed her arm and caused an unspeakable, unattainable yearning of her own to merge with the music, touching her, making her feel with a deeper intensity.

She had never before heard such a fantastically beautiful performance of Georges Bizet's masterpiece, had listened often but had never been so deeply moved, and came away in an absolute daze. Her escorts were also strangely silent.

Back in her sitting-room Mark rang for drinks and they sat in comparative silence, each unconsciously reliving their reception to the sound of music.

Luke rose reluctantly, stretched his arms. 'I guess it's bed for this man. I have had a great day, the most gratifying day ever. To work with that great chap—oh, man, that makes me feel good. I'm calling in to see my friend John.' He patted the top of Sam's head. ''Night, love, sleep peacefully and no fancy nursemaids, mind. Watch out for that sort!' he snorted in mock concern as he took his leave.

Samantha's eyes were drawn to Mark as he stretched long legs and leaned back in his chair. Smoke filtered past his eyes as he stared reflectively at the ceiling. Deep blue depths, with those extraordinary long lashes and contrasting tan. His lithe, lean body looked relaxed, and yet there was an unfamiliar, almost sad droop to his mouth, as if his thoughts were deep and burdensome. The welfare of John must be an ordeal for him as much as it was to the others, if not more? Mark cared for him, almost as a brother; the effort to hide his feelings, to keep a calm exterior must be very great.

A sudden sympathetic impulse drove Sam out of her chair towards him. His eyes moved to her face and the introspective look faded to be replaced by an alert brightness. She sat on the arm of his chair and put her hand on the back of his head in a compassionate gesture, the first voluntary move of affection Samantha had made towards this man since their meeting.

Mark stiffened slightly at her touch, but without a word Sam started stroking from the top of his dark head down into his neck, over and over. She had studied this relaxing manipulation at the hospital back home, had often used it on Mary-Gran.

Every nerve in the man's body came alive at her touch. Mark opened his mouth, but Sam formed a silent 'hush' with her lips and pushed his head back into position. Gradually he relaxed completely, sighing only once when her dress brushed his shoulder. 'Your nursemaid method is far better than mine. I did walk you off your feet, poor child. This would have been far better, if I'd only known . . .'

'Shush up, Mark, you're not supposed to talk, it puts me off my delicate stroke. Anyway, your method was effective if somewhat drastic.' Samantha faltered in her smooth timing as she recalled the aftermath of that walk . . . sleeping in his arms like a baby!

Silence as she continued. Presently he asked drowsily, 'What makes you think I need nursing?'

Sam tweaked his ear gently. 'Call it that mysterious, over-rated woman's intuition if you like. You've been so wonderfully good to all of us—especially to me—apart from a few flare-ups——' She faltered again.

'My word, is that what you call——'

'—And I do appreciate everything.' Her voice was firm again. 'Now, I think you're ready for bed—before you start coiling up again. Off with you!' A last pat and Samantha got up and walked quickly to the door of the bedroom, turning with her hand on the knob. Before the man could rise to his feet she put a finger to her lips and blew a kiss. 'I shan't need you tonight. Put out the light when you leave, sleep well.' Hastily she slipped through and closed the door as he started towards her. She leaned against the door, aghast at her audacious gesture, and heard the outer door close as Mark left.

John's eyes managed a pale sparkle as they entered the

next morning. He looked fresh and clean-shaven, a bit on the pale side. A valiant effort was being made to down the tasty breakfast set on the wheeled invalid trolley across his chest. He gripped Mame and Sam's hands as they stood on either side of the bed. Mark watched from the foot-end and waited through the kissing process.

He flicked his finger against the cradle. 'What have you here, more tucker or a neat blonde?' A queer constriction made the question more gruff than he expected.

'Both, for all you know.' John's intake of breath was deep and shuddering. 'What I can and will tell, impress on you is—th-there are two big toes under there that can wriggle most satisfactorily!'

Mame sat down and brought forth a large handkerchief. 'I'll howl as much as I want to and nobody is going to stop me, but nobody!' She buried her face.

'Can I join the gang?' Samantha gulped, and John drew her head down and made a great fuss of wiping her eyes with his own cambric.

'There, there. To think that two big toes can cause such fluster in the female breast! They're quite ugly, the toes, I mean, but if they can cause such upheaval, just imagine what the rest of me is going to do!'

'Poor unsuspecting popsies,' Mark retorted, and turned to Mame. 'Would you like to come with me? I'm going to sign the kids out for the day and I'm sure Samantha would like to stay with John. We'll be back before lunch.'

Mame assented with a last vigorous sniff.

Mark continued, 'We'll see Tom Crawford first, to confirm my flight back tomorrow. I'm leaving the car for your convenience, Samantha.'

'That's very thoughtful of you, Mark,' John thanked him. 'When you've finished your business bring the scamps in for a quick hello.'

John looked at Sam when they were alone. 'Thanks for the flowers, dear, they're lovely ... Sheila's too. Now pull up a chair. I have a proposition to put before you.'

She sat down and waited while John stared at her assessingly.

'Sam, how would you feel about living here, in Adelaide?'

'Live here? Whatever for?' Samantha blurted in astonishment.

138

'Hold your horses, let me finish. The position is this; it would be most convenient as far as my work, my writing is concerned. As you know, I have to keep in constant touch with the universities and my publishers and it really is a bind having to correspond every time certain questions or points are raised——'

'But, John, how could you bear to leave the homestead? Why, I——' The shock of his proposal overwhelmed Samantha.

John smiled wryly. 'I could bear it quite easily, but it seems you're shocked to the core. I do think you love Blue Hills more than I. Anyway, it was only a scheme I had in mind, and not for the world would I drag you away if it causes distress ... selfish of me, but I never realised you loved the place so much.'

The very thought of leaving the Outback, the home she had come to regard with love, the family who had taken her in their midst so wholeheartedly, to leave all that for a flat or house here in the suburbs made Sam feel quite ill. She stifled a sense of nausea and spoke as serenely as possible.

'Not selfish at all, John. After all, it would be convenient as far as your work is concerned. Your suggestion came as a shock. Give me time to digest it,' she pleaded.

'Right, girl,' he studied her obliquely, 'now that I've spoken about it, I seem to realise that it may not be such a good idea after all. You belong there and I can't envisage you in suburbia. Leave it be, we'll have another chat when I'm up and about.' He patted her hand comfortingly.

Thereafter they talked in a lighter vein, for they were constantly interrupted as nurses bustled in and out on various duties. Hans and Luke appeared with two well-known doctors who were interested in John's case. Samantha took a walk in the hospital gardens when the physiotherapist arrived who would be in charge and responsible for exercising and strengthening the legs of their patient. An hour later she shared his tea and soon afterwards a very solemn Ham and Twinkles appeared, followed by Mame and Mark.

Twinkles kissed John with decorous awe and immediately moved into the circle of Samantha's welcoming arms. Ham's eyes were bright as he shook his uncle's hand. 'Uncle John, I'm so glad ... by gad, that Doc is sure with it!' He kissed Sam and stood at the back of her chair with both hands resting on her shoulders. Her heart was touched with tenderness. How could she ever leave the homestead and her very own, well almost, loving family? She stifled a rising emotion as she caught Mark watching her, an unreadable expression in his cobalt eyes.

They left John with the understanding that they would visit again in the evening. A delightful afternoon was spent at the Botanical Gardens and all too soon the time came to return the children to their respective hostels. Mame chose to stay at the hotel while Samantha and Mark set off for the evening visit. Mark greeted John and left again. He would call back later for Sam.

An hour later he returned and they took leave of John. Mark remarked casually as they walked to the car park, 'Carol is waiting in the car. I met her in town this morning and invited her to dine with us tonight.'

'Carol—Carol Dutton? Oh, why didn't she come in to see John?' Illogically, for no reason at all, Samantha was annoyed at the intrusion of an outsider into her family. But the Dutton was not a stranger.

'Too soon for strangers, or should I say friends, to visit. The family is enough at present, and you, of course.'

So he was beginning to accept her; Samantha felt a warm glow at his statement. She said, unthinkably, 'Carol is also an old friend of yours, I believe. You even have a picture of her in your bathroom, of all places——' She could have bitten her silly tongue.

'Any objections?'

The derisive, quizzical tone stung her to a sharp comeback. 'Why should I object? You have a perfect right to date whom you choose and stick them wherever you want to—th-their pictures, I mean!'

They were at the car and Sam smiled extra sweetly at the blonde girl in the front seat. 'Hello, Carol, so nice to see you again.'

Mark had his hand on the door, fully expected her to share the front seat, but Sam opened the back door and slid in before he could object. 'I'm quite comfortable here, thanks. I do hate being squashed, don't you, Carol, and your dress is so elegant ... a pity to crush it.' Her smile ignored the dark slant of narrowed eyes.

'Hi there! I'm glad to hear the good news about John, you

must be thrilled to bits. Like my dress? Cost the earth.' Carol smoothed her thighs complacently as Mark settled behind the wheel and dexterously handled the car through the heavy traffic. 'Yeah, a fab sum, like there's so little of it,' she added.

'I'll say!' was Samantha's inward comment. From her back-seat view of the girl's bare shoulders she very much doubted if she had seen a dress at all!

'You kept me waiting nearly an hour, Mark Lane. If it were anyone else ... Have you decided where to take me dancing after dinner?' Carol pouted and touched his arm with a caressing finger.

Mark slanted a surprised glance at her. 'Who mentioned dancing? We'll have a drink before dinner then, to give Samantha time to dress up, or'—his eyes blinked at her scanty attire—'or down as it would seem.'

Carol looked startled and opened her mouth.

Samantha forestalled her. 'That is sweet of you, Mark, but thanks, I'd rather have an early night. This afternoon at the Gardens was quite delightful, but walks always make me frightfully sleepy.' Her drawl was a masterpiece of disinterest. Just let him order her to go with them, just let him try!

'Humph!' Mark's sole comment sounded so like a certain relative that Sam had to clamp down hard on a rising bubble of laughter. Her silent dare was not accepted and she felt most reasonably let down. Well, it had only been a polite gesture on his part, and what loving twosome would want to be saddled with a tiresome third? No wonder the blonde had looked startled, had opened her pretty mouth like a—a fish out of water.

At dinner, Carol sparkled and her quick, glib repartee amused Mark and seemed to draw out a sophistication that equalled hers. He was extraordinarily handsome in his dinner suit and Samantha saw a new side to this hard brown Australian. Mame too had become every inch the autocratic dowager, presiding with distinguished aplomb, now that her fears and worries for her nephew were allayed. Samantha's lips curved and a hidden dimple appeared as she thought of the day of her arrival at the homestead, her audacity in requesting this very grande dame to count her teeth!

'Joke?' Mark noticed the dimple.

'No. Mame,' Sam said.

'Mame?'

'Yes ... and horses.' Green eyes were alight with amusement as they met the bright look the grande dame shot across the table.

'Mame and horses?' Mark intercepted the sly wink that was passed between them and sighed in exasperation as Sam nodded dreamily, making no effort to clarify her statement. He turned to Carol in sorrowful conclusion. 'The poor girl's around the bend and Mame is heading that way fast. I foresee a raking crash when they meet on that blind corner!'

He politely escorted them to their suite before leaving with Carol. Long after the old lady had fallen asleep Samantha lay watching the fancy shapes that a filtered moonbeam etched on the wall. After much turning she thumped her pillows once more and resolutely pushed persistent thoughts of couples dancing in close proximity back into the deep stream of unconscious thinking, from whence it came, and shut her eyes with angry determination.

CHAPTER 11

THE mid-morning sun sparkled and drew tawny flames from the depths of Samantha's hair as it hung on her shoulders. A patterned green and white dress accentuated the green of her eyes, the gold flecks in them like captured sunshine. She and Mark were at the airport, waiting for the plane that would take him home. The man leaned against the car, watching in a bemused way as a light breeze played truant in the silky hair of his companion. He took a step closer, lifted a brown finger and flipped long strands on to her cheek.

'Stop it, Mark! I should have tied it up this morning.' Sam felt suddenly irritated at the flash of feeling his casual gesture caused.

'Don't ever cut it, Mac. If I had the authority of a fiancé or husband, I would forbid that sacrilege, and insist on this style at all times, even at night. Can one just imagine all this draped across my manly chest, slightly ticklish, perchance?' Blue eyes flamed wickedly at her startled gaze.

'It's absolutely silly to wear it like this—like a teenager, so untidy.' Casual words to cover confusion at his remark and the strange flame that danced in his eyes. Sam had seen it before, that devil flame, when Mark Lane was being derisive or saying outrageous things to her. It was possibly a sign of enjoyment. He was plain wicked, and the sooner she became used to his ways, the better for her peace of mind.

Tommy Crawford appeared and Mark bent down and kissed Sam's nose. 'Take care with the car, mate. No dents in it as yet, so mind your reckless ways. Look after yourself as well, I can't always be with you.' He deliberately flicked her hair. 'I still like it this way.'

Before Sam could think up a suitable reply, he and Tom were sauntering across the tarmac. She watched the sun winking on the wings of the moving plane, and the serenity of the morning gave Samantha MacDonald no warning that, before the day had waned, her world would be shattered by the words of a complete stranger.

She started the car and drove rather slowly until she found the measure of its powerful motor and then relaxed with confidence and pleasure to wend her way to the hospital. John was in fine spirits; Sam stayed with him until noon, then left with her promise to see him again in the evening.

After a tasty lunch in the dining-room, she and Mame lazed in their room, chatting desultorily and listening to the radio. When tea had been served, Samantha stretched and walked to the window.

'All that super food and sitting around has made me feel very sluggish. I'm going to walk to the river and back, to circulate my lazy insides. Coming?'

A somnolent Mame declined lazily. Sam blew her a kiss and walked downstairs. In the foyer she stopped to study a rack of new magazines, unaware of appreciative glances cast her way by two men. The one stopped talking for a moment as they approached her and then continued as they came behind her, on their way to the entrance.

'—Mailplane, crash landing. Passenger chap owns sheep-station—north-east somewhere—Fatal injuries—Lane, I heard, well-known——'

His words penetrated Samantha's preoccupation with sudden, blinding explosiveness. She turned swiftly, but they had already disappeared through the swinging doors. Her paralysed legs were rooted to the floor and a roaring sounded in her ears. With great difficulty she unglued her feet and stumbled towards the lifts. Dimly she tried to remember what the man had said ... 'Crash landing—fatal injuries—Lane.' No ... No!

The pounding in her head was almost unbearable and Sam did not know how she found the door to their suite, to stare blindly as Mame started up.

'Samantha! What's the matter, child?'

Teeth chattering, she tried to drink the water that Mame held to her lips after she had led the white-faced girl to a chair, her own face paling in concern and apprehension.

Mame's frightened face came and went in a fog as the roaring rose to a crescendo and Sam fought for control. She must not frighten Mame, she must not ... The pounding in her ears died down to an insistent throb.

'The mailplane——' She choked on the words and brought a shaking hand to her lips. How, what must she say? Sam had no need to say anything, for her words were repeated by the masculine voice of the news announcer: '—The mailplane made a forced landing, pilot and passenger were brought back by flying service. The pilot was slightly injured, but his companion sustained multiple injuries, though not as serious as first feared. I repeat their names, pilot and passenger respectively: Benny Croft and Martin Lang. The undercarriage of the plane was badly——'

Samantha's body went limp. She could only gaze mutely at Mame's hands as the old lady tried to rub warmth back into her cold ones.

'My poor baby, tell me, I'm strong ... is it John? Or something to do with that report, someone you know?'

'Not John ... the news report. I—I heard a man downstairs, h-he said Lane. And then walked away.' Her voice was a sobbing whisper of relief as she gripped the comforting old hands tightly. 'Dear God, I thought it was Mark—what name did he say?'

'Lang, Martin Lang. Not fatal injuries, thank the dear Lord for that, whoever he is. You thought it was Lane? You poor child, it must have been a terrible shock.'

'Shock? I wanted to die, Mame. My dearest beloved hurt, maybe dying or—dead.' Samantha sat forward and buried her face in her hands, body shaking with reaction, quite unconscious of the revelation she had just made. 'Forgive me, darling Mame, for frightening you so.'

Mrs. Jonathan Lane's eyes dimmed and her heart was heavy as she watched the girl bracing herself for the inward battle against the sudden knowledge that had hit her like a blow in the solar plexus. The truth had at last been revealed to Samantha and no subterfuge could hide the fact that she loved Mark, loved him with all her being, far different from the affection, or the love she thought she had, for John ...

Samantha stood up suddenly and walked to the window. Strange, she had done this self same thing surely not twenty minutes ago. What had happened to the scenery? She gazed out unseeingly and then turned back with a travesty of a smile on pale lips.

'I think my walk is still indicated, and i-if I see that misinformed m-man again, I shall walk up to him, clobber him one and retire haughtily.' Her face softened as her eyes focused more clearly on her elderly companion. 'I'm sorry, Mame dear, would you rather I stayed with you?'

'Of course not. A walk right now will do you good and I'm perfectly all right. Go for that walk, dear.' Mame waved her away, knowing only too well that Sam wanted to face the shocking revelation alone, away from other eyes. She would come back with a new measure of control. Samantha would fight her battle and pride would be her greatest defence, Mame knew this with sure inward certainty. John would never know, not from either herself or the girl. Would Sam, with inborn integrity, be strong enough to stand a marriage with only affection for her future husband? There was no comparison between fondness and passionate love; the substitute was a mockery. Mame's thoughts, with this extra burden of knowledge, circled in hopeless desperation and compassion.

A deadening, traumatic fog enveloped Samantha, as she walked with inner blindness and turned automatically into King William Street. Only when she reached the river did she stop to look around, instinctively seeking privacy.

Children were playing some distance from her and took no notice of the solitary girl who sat down on a grassy slope. The cushioning fog dispersed, exploding into painful realisation, and Sam MacDonald rolled on to her stomach and dug her fingers deep into grassy soil.

All this had lain below the surface and she had scornfully

145

derided it as mere magnetic attraction. It had taken a stranger's passing remarks to shock and hammer home the truth. A final recognition of a deeply known fact; she loved Mark, body and soul. The litany of song when he kissed her, the joyous warmth she had felt in the kitchen, the comfort of his arms at their very first meeting. That was surely her soul calling, warning of love, and she had wilfully ignored it, unaware of its portent.

Relaxed at last, it flowed over her in waves of remembrance, painfully illuminating. Love for him rocked her body with tormenting sweetness. Tormenting, agonising because, instead of rushing to meet it with joyous outflung arms, she must stifle and quench this flame in her blood that burned her with longing.

'Dear One, help me, please help me,' Samantha whispered despairingly, and buried her face in her arms.

Very much later she became aware of another presence and lifted burning eyes to see Luke Mannering standing a few yards away, watching her.

Samantha sat up stiffly and he dropped down beside her. Without comment he wiped her wet forehead with his handkerchief and brushed tangled hair back with gentle fingers. Luke then drew the girl into the circle of his arm and gazed, reflectively, at the still waters, willing her to further composure. The sun had set and dusk was a soft mantle.

'Mame sent me. She seemed to know exactly where you would be. I called to take you to the hospital. Mame is there now, I'll fetch her later.' Luke held Sam firmly as she gasped in contrition, 'No, you're not visiting tonight. Mame will tell John you're slightly indisposed, that I've bundled you off to bed, which I shall do, presently. She told me of the—shock —you had today.'

'Luke, I'm such a fool!' Unshed tears burned.

'My dear Sam, doctors can only prescribe for the body, but are sadly limited when it comes to this sort of thing. I'd give my right arm to lighten your burden because I know what you must face. Does it hurt so very much?'

Samantha opened heavy lids to look at him in wonder, and saw only kindness—and knowledge of her love for Mark, in his dark eyes. Compassionate eyes that saw and understood, that encouraged the floodgates of relieving tears to burst at last.

146

'You're all so kind and good to me ... and I behave like a fool,' Samantha sobbed against his shirt. Luke sat quietly until she stopped, again offering his hanky.

'Blow hard,' he ordered in a noncommittal voice, which nearly brought on another flood.

Sam stood up, straightened her crumpled dress and walked with Luke to his car. Back in her hotel room he urged her to have a hot bath while he sat down and waited. When she had complied and came out in her belted dressing-gown and hair tied back in a high pony-tail, Luke handed her two pills and watched as she swallowed them, too exhausted to protest. The man's breath caught in his throat at the fragile beauty and tragic droop to her soft lips.

'Be a good girl and climb straight into your bed while I fetch Mame. I'm taking her to my place to talk to the folks at home over my transceiver. Any messages?'

'No!' Samantha steadied her voice. 'You won't mention the—misunderstood news—I heard today?'

'No, poppet. Neither Mame or I are that dumb. See you later, if you're still awake, which I doubt, knowing the potency of those little pills.'

Samantha stood looking out of the window as she slowly removed her gown. Somebody passed below, whistling a familiar ditty: 'Let me abos go loose, Lou——' She gave a gasp of pain and whispered into the night, 'Yes, Luke, give him my love.' She climbed into bed and before her weary thoughts had collected, the pills started their soothing anodyne.

The day came when Samantha walked into the hospital room and John stepped forward to meet his fiancée, a cane in each hand and a smiling nurse in attendance.

True, only five steps, but on his own two feet!

Sam watched him wordlessly, her heart so filled with gladness, affection and thankfulness that she was utterly unable to speak. She came to him in a deep silence, her eyes luminous with the message she could not articulate.

Sister Adam broke the silence with a discreet cough. She moved a chair behind the proud man and tapped him on his shoulder. 'Sit down, young man. Enough for the time being, or you'll find yourself flat on your pretty face ... quite the come-down that will be! Watch him, Miss MacDonald, you know the saying "Pride comes before a fall".' Pride of achievement shone on her own face as she waited for John to sit before leaving them.

Utter silence followed her departure and finally John said, 'Quite the gushing sort, aren't you, baby? I've never been so overwhelmed by chatter as I am at this moment!'

'Darling John, I've never said so much in such a short time as I'm saying now.' Sam found her voice.

John squeezed her hand. 'Yes, I read it all in your eyes, we'll take it as said. Kiss me.'

Samantha complied, tenderness flowing through her.

Since that afternoon when she had been shocked into the awareness of her true feelings, she had acquired a new protective cloak of dignity, and only at unguarded moments did depths of agony glimmer deep in tawny green eyes. Her love for Mark held no peace and she was constantly on guard when in the presence of John and others. Luke and Mame were fully aware of her misery, but she had spun a tight cocoon of silence on the subject. They respected her withdrawal and were wary of intrusion.

Her ultimate decision to live in Adelaide with John had cost her dearly. After heartbreaking days and nights Samantha had reached this solution; it was the only way out of an agonising situation. At least there would be no chance encounters with Mark, which would surely happen if they stayed on at Blue Hills. She knew, only too well, the strength of her endurance and vulnerability. Mark was extremely perceptive and, with his ready aptitude, would soon discover her secret. It tore at her heart to leave the loved family and homestead but a coward's way was often the wisest course.

Sam now brought up the subject with an eagerness she did not really feel. 'John, remember your proposition about living here when we're m-married? I feel it's a marvellous idea. I-I like it here and there's so much to see and do. The important thing, after all, is your work. I've walked and explored Adelaide very completely since we've been here. It's a lovely town and there are nice, quiet suburbs where you could work in peace. We can see more of Ham and Twinkles, the family can visit and we c-can visit them——' She faltered on that thought.

John smiled wryly. 'Methinks the lady doth protest too much—are you trying to convince me or yourself? You're much too fond of our Outback.'

Sam tried again. 'No, truly, darling, I do love the homestead because—you handed me a family and you, of course, were there. Don't you see, if you're here and I'm with you, why then, this will be home to me. I can grow fond of any p-place.'

'Sure and what a fickle child you turn out to be.' John looked at her thoughtfully, only half convinced. Why this sudden change of heart, this eagerness? Maybe her stay in town had changed her affection for Blue Hills. It could be rather lonely for her when he was busy with his books, but then it would be just as lonely here, especially without the family. Sam had never shown signs of loneliness and John had a queer feeling that the idea of a family of her own had turned the scales in his favour when she had consented to marry him. He had a swift, inexplicable feeling that the girl facing him had somehow changed, become older, aloof and untouchable. 'Fiddlesticks, you demented joker,' he derided himself, but the thought persisted.

'I'm almost persuaded, my love. We'll ask Luke to keep an eye open for suitable premises, but in the meantime, we'll go back to the jolly old homestead for—shall I say, until the great day.' John studied her intently as she lost colour and his voice shook slightly as he asked, 'You should be blushing. Am I scaring you, or would you rather opt out?'

Could this be an opportunity to ask for release, to tell him she wanted to go back to Scotland? Back there no one would ever know she had lost her heart to someone who didn't need it. How would John take it if she told him, not about Mark, just a declaration that what she felt for him was not love but great affection, and she was not prepared to marry on those terms? While he was crippled or if he had remained crippled she would never have opted out, as he called it, even though she loved another. Even as these thoughts ran wildly through her head her lips were answering.

'I haven't forgotten. You're not scaring me and I'm not opting out, as you put it.'

'Right, my innocent, I——'

'Don't call me that!' she came back hotly.

John looked at her in surprise. 'Sorry, darling, I didn't know you were touchy about it. We'll fix matters as soon as possible—don't be shy.' He reached out and turned her averted face, a hand cupping her chin, and saw unconcealed misery in her eyes. 'You really are scared! Please don't be—I'll not rush your fences. Having waited this long, I've learned extreme patience. Anyway, Dr. Hans and I had a long confab on this delicate subject, and a reprieve is indicated for a while longer. Want to be reprieved?'

'I'll be ready ... when you are, John,' Sam offered gravely, then forced a note of lightness. 'By the way, you needn't be so delicate, I've heard about the birds and the bees. Now, be a brave boy and tell me about Hans' talk and his diagnosis of your—er—love-life.'

She listened with clinical interest as John told her, stumbling embarrassment clouding his voice, making his case rather muddled and incoherent. When he finally stopped talking Samantha studied him with amusement.

'Is that a true diagnosis? If so, it's probably in code and a mere layman like me would have a job sorting out the jumble, or should I say mumble. Your case sounds like some obscure, incurable malady!' she laughed at him.

John lifted and dropped his hands in a hopeless gesture. 'Like when your girl gives with that cold, calculating, clinical stare, when she should have a warm glow of compassion —it kind of puts a feller off, like.'

'Well, this feller girl is making with the push-off. If I don't go now, Mame will have the whole force beating the bush for the body. Like I kiss you goodbye now?' Sam kissed him with sudden fierceness. 'Mame will be sorry she wasn't here today to see her baby walk. Oh, John, I feel I want to go into the nearest chapel, to offer my thanks.'

'No need to, Samantha MacDonald. God received your thanks long ago when you showed unfaltering faith in Him and my recovery.' John's voice sank to a confidential whisper. 'He won't mind at all if you make a second offering, He likes bonuses.'

Three more days and then they would be going home.

Home ... Samantha's head ached as she brushed her hair and static caused shining strands to whip across her face. She sighed at memories that refused to stay dormant. Impulsively, she walked to the phone and made an appointment.

Two hours later she left the salon, hair cut just above shoulder-length, a smooth, swinging cap with the ends flipped out and up. Her head felt very light and was tilted rather defiantly. Defiance in anticipation of future acid comments on her impulsive action.

An involuntary gasp of reproach escaped Mame as Sam walked in at the door. After inspecting the girl's head from every angle, she declared it looked quite nice but made Sam look awfully young!

'Of course I was doddering on the brink of senility, so now I'll have a few more years of grace before toppling over,' that young lady retorted sarcastically. She moved her head from side to side, liking the free swing of her hair. 'Just think, no more old-fashioned pins, no more plaits. Hooray for the suffragettes!'

'Down with them when the family catches sight of you. The boys——'

'To hell with the boys. Squares, chew me no grief!'

'Samantha! What language, you sound like a—a hippy! Speaking of the boys, Mark sent you a message the other night when I was with Luke——' Mame stopped as Sam, on her way to the bedroom, halted in her tracks.

'Well, what was it?' Sam kept her back turned. 'Go on, what was the message?'

'He said to tell you he still liked it that way, teen-style, whatever that may mean.'

'Now you tell me!' Samantha studied the point of her shoe critically for a few seconds. 'Doesn't mean a thing really, one of his jokes.' She disappeared into the bedroom.

Samantha stood with her back to the window, and her heart contracted as Mark leaned down to kiss Mame. She wanted to rush over to him, to touch and feel the reality of him. He turned to her and she gripped the window ledge firmly, quite sure that the beat of her heart was visible.

Mark stopped abruptly and dropped the box he had brought with him on to a chair while cobalt eyes studied her.

'Hello, Samantha.'

Her lips formed a casual 'Hello, Mark' while her heart whispered 'Hello, stealer of hearts!'

Mark sighed and leaned forward to kiss Sam full on her lips. 'So wilful a witch! One word from me and she jumps in defiance to oppose that word. In future I'll not dare to

ever mention that you have a pretty neck, you're quite likely
to cut it off. Did you condone this sacrilege, Mame?'

'Sam can do as she wishes.' Mame's retort was sharp. 'It
was heavy, and causing her headaches.'

Mark sat down without further comment, opened his
cigarette case and leaned back with ease. His contradictory
nature always surprised Samantha. She had been fully prepared for a blast of disapproval, even anger, and all he did
was kiss her with a sigh of regret. A kiss that still tingled on
her lips. (Mame had said, long long ago, 'Never kiss unless
you really mean it.')

'Tom and I called on John. He looks bang-o and strutted
around chockful of pride, his sticks whirling dangerously. So
we go home tomorrow. The shearing is done, everybody is
looking forward to your return.' Mark indicated the box.
'Mandy sent this, on instructions from John, which I duly
passed on to her . . . a dress, I believe.'

Taking the covering off, Sam exclaimed, 'It's my dress, my
Paris dress! I don't need it. Why should John want it?
Whatever——'

'John seems to think you need a night out before you go
back. I have instructions to escort you and help paint the
town a pale pink,' Mark enlightened her dryly.

'But I don't want to!' Sam's cry was genuine, for how
could John know of the fiery coals he was heaping on her
head!

Up came a sardonic eyebrow. 'With your fiancé's full
permission, who evidently thinks you're entitled to a fling
before being stuck in the wilds again. Unfortunately he chose
my company to supervise the scene.'

'Unfortunate for you. What a terrible chore it must be—
how can you bear it?' Sam wilfully chose to misunderstand.
'John is a clot, I don't need entertaining.'

'Well, you don't have to go——' Mame sought an excuse
for the girl.

'Not a chore at all, beautiful, a pleasure. I've booked a
table in the Colonel Light, dancing to follow, so we can
practise our tango. Accept with grace as it will be some time,
perhaps the last time, that I'll be your escort. I'm leaving for
the Gold Coast. The travelling bug is biting.'

Samantha's heart turned in her breast . . . he was going
away. Well, would that not be better; to be free of his con-

tinual magnetic presence while she was still at the homestead? If and when he returned, she and John would be safely settled in Adelaide. If? Of course he would return, it was his home. Another staggering thought surfaced and brought more turmoil to an already crowded heart; as head of the clan Mark would make it his business to be present at their wedding—he might even be the one to give her away, as stand-in for the father Sam did not have! 'Please, Lord, keep him away, let not this happen,' she pleaded silently, desperately.

Mark waited her reply with polite interest.

An insistent, reckless inner voice urged Sam to go with him tonight. There would be no danger among a crowd and it would be another precious memory to store. The sweet tormenting thought of his arms around her brought sudden weakness to her limbs.

'Very well, Mark, I accept with pleasure.' The understatement of the year! Imagine his surprise and mockery if she should truthfully reply, 'Thank you, darling, I accept with delight your invitation to heaven, be it only for this one night.'

'We'll drink to that.' Mark reached out and phoned for room service. He removed his jacket and settled back, stretching his long legs indolently.

'Mandy sends thanks for taking the scamps out so often. You two have evidently visited all places of interest. I'll take a bet that Ham and young Twinkles have learnt more about this town than ever before.'

'How do you know all this?' Samantha was curious.

'I have a special line in spies, Luke for one. I know of every move you made, all your dark secrets.' He looked mysterious and knowing.

'Oh no! Luke wouldn't——' She was alarmed, but a warning cough from Mame checked her outburst and her heart returned to its normal place, leaving a huskiness in her throat. 'Luke is a nasty doublecrosser. Hovering around like a hen with chicks, and now I find he was only spying, not admiring!'

'You sound as if you really have something to hide, little chick. Has Luke been too enthusiastic? Tell Papa?' Mark's eyes darkened.

Tell Papa indeed! Papa would be galvanised out of that

comfortable position in seconds if she disclosed one dark secret and South Australia would see him no more. A hysterical urge to blurt it out and watch his reaction almost overwhelmed Samantha. She walked hurriedly to the radio and fiddled with the knobs.

'Doctor Mannering has been most circumspect. He really is a darling, and so attractive. As an escort he's tops and I adore him. The girls are sure slow in allowing such a guy to roam free. Why someone hasn't snapped him up long ago I just can't——' Samantha could not stop chattering senselessly.

Mark stopped her. 'Cut the jazz——' he began sharply, and stopped as the waiter entered with a loaded tray.

Sam was relieved at this timely intrusion. He sounded quite angry and she realised, belatedly, that she was getting into hot water again. Flippancy on her part all too often aroused his mockery, and she was certainly leading with her chin right now. Surprisingly, Mark did not follow up his sharp exclamation. Either his sharp humour had left him or he was disinterested enough not to bother with silly flippancy. She wondered if he had planned to take Carol out and now, at John's request, he was stuck with her.

The waiter poured the drinks and left. Over the rim of his glass Mark studied the girl unsmilingly. Sam felt prickles rise in the nape of her neck and walked, glass in hand, to the window and back again in restless movement while Mame studied both of them unobtrusively.

'Shake out your glad rags, Samantha, they'll need pressing,' Mark suddenly commanded her.

Sam stopped pacing and regarded him in awe for a few seconds.

'Yes, my lord, immediately, sir!' Mocking intimidation, she put her glass on the table and lifted the dress. 'Of course you know all about fabrics,' she said loftily as she held it up and gave it a shake. 'Not much pressing needed with these crease-resisting materials.'

Mark was staring at the dress in wonder. 'My word! Did Mandy pack the screws?'

'Screws? Oh, that stays up on its own.' Bubbling laughter exploded at his unbelieving expression.

'I can't believe it ... you have to breathe, just one deep breath ... and your top will surely be topless?' The

154

astounded man looked from her dress to her bosom. 'Yes indeed, just one slight emotional upheaval and I'll be dancing with a topless girl—I mean with a topless—how could I possibly go on dancing? Wear it at your own risk!' he grinned audaciously.

Sam flushed and clutched the dress against her as if she was already exposed. 'Did Carol's dress come unstuck?' she asked, flags of colour starting in her cheeks.

'Carol's dress? Mmmm——' The wicked grin was more pronounced. 'You can't expect me to give away trade-fashion secrets, kitten. Although you've made a point there. I guess there wasn't enough emotional, or shall I say not enough frontage to upheave——'

'Well, I'm not going to be disturbed by heavy breathing.' Sam looked at him suspiciously, and the flags flamed higher. 'Or are you suggesting that my-my f-frontage is bigger than——'

'Hold it, Mac!' Mark was alarmed at her fire. 'Don't let's get worked up. Your—er—front is very nice, but it's already working overtime!'

It certainly was, for Sam was recalling a talk Sheila and she had had about this selfsame dress. 'Wear it only when you're with your beloved and alone together, then you can breathe as deeply as you like,' Sheila had teased her. Sam drew a deep breath as imagination ran riot and her confusion greater.

Mark got up slowly, amazed at the effect of his light words. He took the dress and laid it carefully across the back of the couch. While his back was turned Samantha forced order to her thoughts and the heat faded from her cheeks. Mark kept his back to her when he spoke again.

'A lovely frock, Mac, and will be still lovelier when you're in it. Mame, another drink?'

Mame's accusing eyes watched him almost in anger. He smiled back, inscrutably, a tiny muscle tightening in a brown cheek.

'Yes, and stop ribbing Sam. You're absolutely incorrigible.' Mame handed over her glass, her eyes glimmered a warning. He did not know what she, Mame, knew and his teasing was tearing the heart from the girl.

'Don't worry, Mame, I can take it.' Samantha had recovered and spoke coolly. 'Fill mine too, Mark. I promise I 'shan't shock or disgrace you, even if I turn blue in the face.'

'That's my girl! I must warn you, though, nothing can shock me. I like being shocked, depending——' Blue eyes were naughty, but he was still puzzled at the confusion he had caused. 'John would like to see you and I promised him we would call before going on our painting spree.'

'In that case I'll get ready earlier.' Sam accepted her glass. 'Mame, I'm not happy about leaving you alone on our last night here. Why wouldn't Hans let John come out today? He's strong enough to go home, so he could quite easily have joined us.'

'I did look into that, Samantha. Hans thinks too many moves would be unwise, tire him unnecessarily. John will be taken direct from the hospital to the homestead. John declined to join us tonight anyway, he wanted you to enjoy the evening without worrying about him.'

'John is a darling, so thoughtful and I—I care very much for him.' Sam dropped her eyes to study the glass in her hands. She had meant to say 'love', but the word simply refused to be uttered. She missed the narrow-eyed slant of Mark's eyes on her as she walked to the bedroom.

He was waiting when Samantha finally emerged from her room and his dark lashes lifted a fraction as he beheld the slender figure in the much-maligned dress. Her hair hung in a shining helmet above gleaming, bare shoulders, her make-up was light. In fact Samantha resembled a cool, frosty— snow maiden. Only her sun-flecked sparkling green eyes gave promise of hidden fires that lay dormant in their depths.

She stood still as their eyes met, waiting for just a small word of approval. It came. An impudent eyebrow lifted, a very blue eye scanned the vision.

Mark Lane said 'Great snakes!' and held out a well tailored arm.

Mame saw them to the door and at the last minute grabbed Sam's beaded little bag, dropped two safety-pins into it. 'Just in case,' she winked.

The man on the hospital veranda watched admiringly as the couple walked towards him. This cousin of his was a beaut, so tall and distinguished, and the girl beside him, his girl, looked quite ethereal, a special heavenly quality tonight. That dress certainly did things for Samantha MacDonald! Quite unaccountably John's thoughts vied away from the oncoming couple and hovered for seconds on a dark-haired pixie with a carbon smut on her nose. Mark and Sam did not stay long, for John was preparing for an early night in order to face the trip home on the morrow. He jokingly forbade any hangover from either of them and pride and affection glimmered in his eyes as he watched them walk away.

Samantha looked around with interest when they were seated in the glass-walled room. It had been named after Colonel William Light, South Australia's first Surveyor-General, who had planned the city in 1836. Dancing and floor shows were held nightly.

A courteous waiter popped the champagne cork, Mark tasted, nodded his satisfaction and their glasses were filled. He raised his glass in a toast.

'*A vostra salute, cara mia.*'

'*A votre santé,*' Samantha wished him in soft accent, colour mounting at his use of Italian endearment.

Dinner was served with skilled, unhurried excellence. Mark was the perfect, attentive escort, seeming proudly aware of the many admiring glances that settled on his partner. His command of wines showed the superb knowledge of a connoisseur. And Sam had called him a backwoodsman!

Meanwhile, her flight of fantasy was becoming a reality. Except that she did not wear a tiara—and her escort did not love her . . .

Samantha, unused to all these wines, was beginning to feel light-headed when Mark finally asked, 'Care to dance, Miss MacDonald?'

Sam held her breath as his arm encircled her and a hard brown hand clasped hers. Fortunately the band had chosen *Cochita* and she had to concentrate on the intricate steps as the drums throbbed exotically. Even then she was intensely aware of his firm embrace and restrained vitality and felt more light-headed than ever.

After the first dance Sam's thudding heart slowed down and she yielded her senses to enjoyment of music and delight at Mark's lithe guidance when they danced. Warm joyousness made her eyes sparkle and her gay mood infected Mark and they became just another twosome, bent on passing the hours happily and carefree.

The lights dimmed. Mark held her close and his muted voice vibrated against her hair as he put words to the music.

'She ... was like the snow-bird ... Mmm, a whole lot like the night ... She ... was like the willow, and calls no man her master, but the day she ... went away ...'

A sudden void where her heart should have been made Sam falter. He felt her stumble and loosened his hold to look into her face. She kept her eyes lowered, but the man felt the stiffening of her body. The music ended, he released her and they walked back to their table in silence.

'I feel in need of fresh air, Mark. I'm feeling slightly stuffy.' Sam managed a casual air.

'More likely just a wee bit tipsy, my snow-bird?' Mark smiled and held out his arm. They walked out into the starlit freshness of the night. Sam breathed deeply and Mark watched her with some concern.

'This is the wrong thing to do, Mac. Fresh air coupled with drinks are not conducive to sobriety, if you're not used to the combination——'

'So who cares?' Samantha's head did not belong to her, she felt as if she was floating, a coloured bubble floating ... floating. She whirled gracefully and held out her arms to Mark. He stepped forward and they danced, waltzed dreamily across the lawns in the dusky, velvety silence ...

'Mark?' Her whisper trembled in the darkness.

He stopped and she moved closer, lifting her face.

'Kiss me,' Samantha demanded softly.

'Samantha ...' Mark held her arms with quiet force.

'I said kiss me!' she repeated fiercely, and closed her eyes.

The grip on her arms lightened, long moments passed. Sam opened her eyes and found him watching her in grim silence.

'What the devil are you up to? Are you trying to prove something?' Mark broke the silence harshly.

'I want you to kiss me,' Sam repeated stubbornly.

'Could be you're testing the stability of your dress?' He ran a light finger across the soft skin above the dress.

'No.' She shivered, and waited.

'What, then? To confirm your belief that I'm—fascinated —with you?'

Samantha looked at him mutely.

'If I do, it may prove that fascination can be mutual—and dangerous.'

'One little kiss can't be dangerous?' The lilting invitation

158

unnerved him.

'Can't it? You unbelieving, tipsy two-timer!' Mark shook her suddenly, his hands hard on her arms. 'It can be dangerous as hell! Thank your lucky stars that I'm at the receiving end, not some other gummy. Don't try me too far, though ... you may get what you're asking for, sweet MacDonald!' He let her go abruptly and walked away, stopped to light a cigarette, drawing deeply.

Sam thought wildly, he was the only one who would ever be at the receiving end of any request of hers. What was she trying to prove anyway?

She said, almost choking on her words, 'I guess that's what I am. A-a two-timing double-crosser and—and high, just for luck. Now that we've officially listed my sins, may I have a cigarette as well? It's rather unnerving and ... tempting, to find an attractive man whispering love songs in one's ear.' She sat down on a convenient bench.

Mark turned back, lighted a cigarette and handed it to her. The flame of his lighter left an echo in smouldering blue eyes.

'In other words I tempted you? Forgive me if I caused that inviting plea. That makes me a co-driver.' He sat down and touched her gently on her bare shoulder. 'Samantha, can we deny that there is a certain volatile—attraction—between us? Let's face it.'

Sam lifted her eyes to meet the warmth in his.

'I know quite well that you love John. Forgive me for calling you names. The fact is, you're very desirable and—if I hadn't brought John to the fore, made myself angry, I might have lost my head, and the devil knows what would have happened then.'

Still she did not move or speak. Mark sighed and rose to his feet, held out his hand. Samantha forced herself to take it and he drew her to her feet.

'May I put it on record that I'm honoured by your request? In other circumstances I would have reciprocated with great pleasure ... Shall we go in?' Mark put a light finger under her chin. 'I promise not to provoke further indiscretions. We're enjoying the evening, I would be devastated to have it end so abruptly.' He lifted an arm around her shoulders and they walked back.

In the foyer they came face to face with Carol Dutton!

The man accompanying her almost collided with her as she stopped with a cry of surprise. 'Well, fancy meeting you here! Hello, darling. Hi, Samantha. Hitting the high life as well?' A quick, critical glance passed over Sam's dress and hair and a pencilled eyebrow rose at sight of the protective arm resting on bare shoulders.

'Succeeding beyond our wildest expectations. Hello, Carol, evenin', Lance.' Mark greeted them and prepared to pass, while Sam smiled at Carol.

The blonde's escort blocked their way, eyes fixed on Samantha. 'I say, old chap, make with the introduction?'

Mark dropped his arm, said briefly, 'Samantha, meet Lance Bannister—Miss MacDonald.'

Lance's eyes widened as he took Sam's hand and saw the ring on her finger. 'Well, tie me down, sport, you haven't gone and done it——!'

Carol interrupted with quick exasperation, 'Of course not, stupid. Samantha is John Lane's girl. Mark is nursemaiding, I guess, in a big way, by the look of things.'

'My great pleasure, ma'am, to be doing just that.' It was said with supercilious politeness and an unwilling dimple peeped out as Sam watched the other girl's mouth open and close—it really did resemble a fish out of water.

Bannister's eyes were still on Sam. 'How about joining forces, Carol? We can—er—relieve Mark of his heavy—duties. That is, if you don't mind, Miss MacDonald?'

'If Mark wishes.' Samantha sensed disapproval.

'Come on, Mark honey. This clot is boring me, let's have some diversion,' Carol invited suggestively. 'I'm sure Sam won't mind. It must be fatiguing trailing a cousin-to-be.'

'Don't be so bitchy, Carol,' Lance grinned, unabashed at the icy stare directed at him.

'Very well.' Mark's acquiescence was brusque. He took Sam's arm and walked on. At his request the floor waiter found them a table for four and they sat down to watch the ensuing cabaret.

In the dimmed light Sam glanced at Mark and found him watching her. He leaned closer and whispered, 'Say the word if you'd like to leave. This is commonly known as being bull-dozed.'

An impish impulse seized Sam. 'Fancy Mark Lane being bulldozed! No, we won't leave just yet. Carol's dying with curiosity to know where we've just come from and she's crazy over you. Don't sing in her ear unless you want to follow up the consequences,' she whispered back under cover of the music.

'I'll follow up our little whatsit right now, if you'll move closer.' His face came nearer with grim intent.

'Mark!' Samantha leaned forward and picked up her evening bag. She smiled sweetly at Carol and Lance. 'War-paint needs renewing,' and she walked away as the lights brightened and the cabaret ended.

Lance Bannister was alone at the table on her return. 'Sit this one with me. I'm rarin' to make closer acquaintance with you, doll. Where do you hail from?'

'Scotland. That's where I met John.' Most Australians were outspoken, but Sam did not care for this one's intimate manner.

'Mark's a lucky guy.' Lance folded his arms on the table, eyes raking.

'Mark?' Sam looked at him in astonishment.

'Yes, Mark, sweet baby. Nursemaiding must be a raking pleasure with babes like you. All good things must end, though. Carol tells me John is due for the take-over.'

Samantha studied him coolly. 'How deep are your sewer drains here, Mr. Bannister?'

It was his turn to look astonished for a full minute and then he banged his fist on the table and laughed delightedly. 'Sewer drains! Quite a girl you are, baby. Rats like me go for dolls with a bit of spirit!'

'Take care, your teeth are showing. I believe they have means of exterminating ... alien bodies.' Sam disliked him intensely; no wonder Mark had shown disapproval. She was sorry now for the impulse to tease Mark, to stay longer. Mark had been so very sweet about her other impetuous impulse, in the gardens, and now this man was making her feel degraded.

Lance had stopped laughing and venom was in his eyes as they travelled over her features, coming to rest pointedly on the soft flesh above the line of her dress. Venom disappeared, replaced by sensuous excitement in the light, hooded eyes.

'You and I could stop the world, sweetie. The first pleasure being to teach you how to put honey on your tongue.'

The music ended and Sam glimpsed Mark and Carol talking to a couple at a table across the room. Lance intercepted her glance.

'Carol's pinched the boy-friend, you'll have a job getting him back.' He stood up and took her hand. 'Dance with me.'

Sam remained seated and he bent over her. 'Or shall we make a little scene, mmm, baby?'

She moved into his arms reluctantly. He was an excellent dancer but inclined to show off at every opportunity. Sam wondered where Carol had met him. He gave her, Sam, an unclean feeling. She searched the room and caught sight of Mark's tall figure, and her telepathic plea must have reached him, for he started to steer his partner in their direction.

'When are you coming to town again? I'll be at your service and always available.' The sibilant whisper was full of assured self-love and Sam shivered in disgust.

Mark tapped him on his shoulder and, completely ignoring the dark protest, changed partners with a deftness that surprised Sam.

'Anything wrong, baby?'

The sound of that particular endearment on Mark's lips came like a breath of spring freshness, after hearing it only moments before rolling off the other man's muddy tongue. Samantha moved closer to Mark and smiled up at him so tenderly that his eyes darkened to midnight blue. 'Not now, Mark.'

'Are you starting to provoke now? I warn you ...'

'Oh no, I simply feel ... clean. I do *not* like Lance Bannister.'

'Has he been annoying you?'

Samantha shivered, but dared not tell this hard man of the other's suggestive insinuations for fear of arousing his wrath. Goodness knows what would happen then!

'I don't like him. He has ... sordid eyes. Do you mind if we leave now——'

Mark did not wait for her to finish, stopped and drew her to the table where she had seen him talking earlier on.

'Angie, Jack, meet Samantha. Keep her here, I'll be back.' He strode away.

'Sit down, Samantha,' Jack Breem beamed and his wife chuckled, 'Masterly ways for sure, has our Mark!'

They watched his progress, saw him gather Sam's wrap and bag with a word to Carol. He ignored Lance, whose eyes roved the room to come to rest on Sam. She turned away quickly. Mark was back, his hand on Sam's chair.

'Thanks, Jack. Ready, honey? Let's shake up a cup of coffee somewhere.'

'How do you do, Angie and Jack. Pardon this tornado. I hope to meet you properly some time. Have I time to ask after your baby?' Samantha stood up and Jack held up a restraining hand.

'Hey, bide a wee, we're also going. Come and see the bairn and Angie will supply the coffee.'

'Please do, it's high time we wandered home. My sister Mick is baby-sitting—our second anniversary, hence the night out,' Angie seconded her husband's invitation.

Samantha and Mark extended their congratulations, then he looked at her questioningly. 'Yes, please, Mark,' Sam said. 'I'd love that, and I simply must see the girl who can steal the stone heart out of a man.'

Later, she held little Angela while the baby's mother prepared a bottle. 'She's not supposed to have one, but now that Mark had to waken her she'll need consolation.'

'Is the coffee in the sugar canister, lass?' Jack called from the kitchen.

'It's in the tea caddy, dear.' Angie winked at Sam and thrust the bottle in her hands. 'I'm coming, Jack.'

Samantha looked at the bottle and then at the baby in her arms. This was one nursing experience of which she was ignorant. Mark watched her, shook his head and lowered his length to a kneeling position in front of her.

'Let her lie back on your arm, so ... yes, now up-end the bottle so that her intake will be milk and not air ... just so. I never tire of watching an infant or new-born animal suckling, enthralled at the strength nature gave those tiny mouths and jaws. You'll have to burp her now, hold her up against your shoulder and pat her back. She's been too greedy. Put this flannel over your shoulder so she won't mess your nice dress ... There, up it comes, a jolly burp that was! Now she can have the rest.'

They watched as Angela sucked in happy contentment. Mark put out his finger and she gripped with a tiny strong hand. Sam sighed in bliss at the dimpled bundle in her arms and said wonderingly, 'Thanks for the first lesson, Mark. Surely you didn't acquire your domestic knowledge just from watching nature, and sheep don't sling their young over their backs to de-wind them?' And looked up into blue eyes which were regarding her with magnetic intensity.

A fleeting moment passed between them which transcended differences and swayed dizzily on the edge of knowledge. Mark's eyes lowered to the baby, he said thickly, 'Didn't you know? I have dozens of these and it's becoming a bore having to run around burping everyone.'

'I'm so glad about John, Samantha, you must be thrilled now that he's well again. Here's the coffee, give Muffin to me. Mark, you'll turn my girl's head with all that adoration. She's promised to you anyway, in time.' Angie lifted her baby out of tense arms and carried her away.

'Oh, thou misguided prophetess!' The cryptic declaration fell softly and hovered into elusive silence. Jack bustled in, cheerfully unconscious of the fleeting shimmer of angel's wings. 'Yes, dear old John, now the boy can begin to live again,' he followed up his wife's remarks. 'Samantha MacDonald, let's get acquainted.'

Samantha tightened the belt of her dressing-gown and walked silently down the passage to the kitchen, closing the door behind her. She lit the kerosene lamp on the dresser and then lifted the cover of the Aga stove. The plates were still hot, and she placed the kettle of water on one. While waiting for it to boil she unbolted the back door and stood outside on the lower step, feeling the cold slate tingle through the soles of her bare feet. The stars were beginning to dim, but it was still very dark and a stillness that could almost be felt lay over sleeping nature. Very far in the distance came the sound of a motor. Someone other than herself was awake at this unearthly hour, or it could be a generator of some sort. Nobody started work quite this early.

Sam went in and sat at the table. Two days had passed since their return from Adelaide. The trip back had been untoward and John had stood it very well. Yesterday he had taken short walks in and out of the house, but for the most part of it had rested on the lounger that Allan moved to the cooler part of the veranda.

Mark had remained with them for only a short while after

their arrival and had not put in an appearance since. He would be busy straightening his affairs before leaving on his proposed trip.

Sheila had spent the day with them, almost beside herself with the wonder of seeing her girlhood champion on his feet again and Sam felt a constriction in her throat when she thought of the girl's dark eyes as they rested on John. Sheila had sat with him for hours, chatting about his writing and other past events that Sam knew nothing of, things that they had shared in the past before she, the sranger, had come. Sam left them to it eventually and joined Mandy, who could at least give her news of the homestead that she could appreciate and understand. Even Mandy would suddenly stop whatever she was doing or saying to take another look at her brother, to absorb the fact that he could walk again. All in all, yesterday had been a most trying time for Sam emotionally, and she had finally gone to bed to sleep in deep exhaustion. Now here she was wide awake, before dawn, and thirsting for a cup of tea.

She made and poured her tea, standing at the kitchen dresser while she sipped and tried to bring jumbled thoughts to order. An impossible task, for they seemed to whirl within reach and then away again; Sheila, John, Mandy and funny little Twinkles in a tutu chased bewilderingly across the perimeter of her mind. Mame and Luke, the keepers of her secret, were closer, and the centre of the vortex was a tall, sun-browned, blue-eyed, gentle, autocratic, inscrutable Australian. Who held her heart in the hard palm of his hand ... and would never know it.

Samantha had her back to the door and almost dropped her cup when that same Australian blocked the opening and whispered, 'Does fate always couple our sleepless nights, or would you call it coincidence, Samantha?'

Sam's cup clattered as it met the saucer, she whirled in fright, a bare foot hooked under the scatter rug and Mark said 'Whoops!' as she staggered into his arms.

'Now that's what a feller likes, a real warm welcome when he leaves his bed at three in the morning to——'

'Mark! You frightened the wits out of me!' Sam stuttered, swallowing hard on the heart-shaped object that was theatening to choke her.

Mark steadied her at arm's length. 'Something wrong

again, or is this merely becoming a habit?' He released her, walked to the dresser and selected the largest cup he could find, poured the tea with a good helping of sugar.

Samantha's ruffled feathers smoothed down and the thing in her throat moved back to it's rightful place. 'I—I was awake and felt thirsty. How did you get here? I never heard a horse. Why are you up so early anyway?' She remembered what she had thought to be a generator, but that sound had stopped some time ago . . .?

Mark put the cup down and pulled a pack of cigarettes from the breast-pocket of his green and blue checkered shirt. 'I'm on my way to North Bend billabong, to check the water level. This lamp can be seen for some distance. I was curious to see who was up at this hour; one does become disturbed at the unusual. I stopped the Land-Rover at the turn of the road and walked here, not wanting to disturb unnecessarily.'

'Oh.' Sam poured more tea for herself and sat down at the table opposite him. 'Where's North Bend? I've heard talk that you've started a small cattle herd there. Do cattle and sheep raising mix well?'

'North Bend is well beyond the range where I so heroically saved your sweet life. Normally sheep crop close and cattle are unable to graze on what is left. The range is a natural boundary and I have run a fence where necessary, beyond this is where I have started a small herd. Come with me, Mac, and if possible, I'll show you a thrilling phenomenon.'

'Phenomenon, what do you mean? I can't just disappear without a word. The family——' she objected, while sudden excitement at his invitation quickened her pulse.

'What's the family got to do with it? You're still your own boss and you'll be perfectly safe with me. Don't be chicken, Mac.' Mark slanted a derisive smile.

'I'm not chicken and——' Sam started in a rising tone. Mark stopped her with a finger on his lips.

'Hush, you'll arouse everyone. Stop arguing, slip into jeans and shirt and bring swimming gear. I know of a super hole in the billabong. Danielle packed tucker to feed an army. I'll pen a note and place it strategically, explaining your absence. Come on, Samantha, don't dither, I haven't got all day. Off with you!'

Within minutes she was back. Mark turned the lamp down and they sneaked down the road like a couple of swaggers.

166

He started the Land-Rover and they were well on their way when dawn opened sleepy eyes to greet the first flush of a rising sun.

They left the open road and turned into what could barely be called a track, started climbing towards the lowest neck of the range. Mark handled the bucking Rover with experienced ease. Sam spread her feet and legs firmly against the bouncing jolts and clung to the handgrip on her side. She was a lightweight and quite a few times had almost landed on the driver's lap. Said driver's mouth would then quirk in amusement at her discomfiture. Nevertheless, Sam was enjoying this truant ride and a mounting excitement sparkled in her wide-eyed survey of lush country as they descended beyond the first range and down the next one.

The track eventually meandered down into a valley bisected by a long green line of bush and tall trees. In the distance Sam noticed a shack of sorts with a thin plume of smoke rising in the still air.

'Who lives there, your mysterious phenomenon?'

Mark laughed deeply. 'You could call Rolf Mason that, although he's not the one I have in mind. Rolf is a loner and would fight every inch of the way if you could manage to shackle him and drag him to civilisation. He minds the cattle and in return I've given him the right to prospect. He doesn't find much, but it keeps him happy, digging away.'

The old prospector was indeed a sight to behold as he watched the Rover draw to a standstill. Sam could only bring to mind the old hillbillies of American cartoons to describe him, the wild grey hair that stuck out in all directions, the foul pipe clutched between toothless gums. Which same pipe now threatened to fall out as the leather face split in a grin of welcome for Mark.

The welcome was wiped off magically as Rolf Mason beheld the passenger.

Mark lifted a hand in salute and it was returned in thick silence. Not a word was passed between them and the old back was a ramrod as it disappeared into the shack, reappearing after a full minute had elapsed with two camp chairs which were plonked down under a wattle. Mark indicated and Samantha sat down while he produced the makings and started to roll a homey. He paused in his task to hand the squares of paper and tobacco to the old man.

Sam watched the ritual and waited to see who was going to break the silence first. Mark had started to make his cigarette, but the oldster finished before him. He stuck the old pipe into a back pocket and lit up with an air of triumph. Mark acknowledged defeat. 'Next time, so help me,' and the silence was broken.

Rolf pointed a bony finger. 'Female. Ye getting softened up at last. Wife?'

'Friend. Be polite, cobber. Samantha MacDonald has journeyed from Scotland to see you.' Mark was poker-faced.

'Ye don' say! Fame is my name. Howdy, miss.' The old prospector relaxed, but kept eyeing her suspiciously. A female friend could become a wife and his mate be damned for ever. 'Scotland, ye say? That's away apiece, by goom. 'Spect you're spitting dust. I've jest boiled cawfee, want some?'

The female had been given permission to speak at last. Big deal! Sam unearthed her sweetest smile, 'It's a long long way to Tipperary. Yes, please, I'd be pleasured.'

Mark extracted two large mugs out of his haversack and in no time they were blowing the steaming coffee. Samantha asked Mark if she could try a homey. He opened his mouth, looked hard at her, shut it again and rolled one for her. Both men watched, pan-faced, as she choked on the first draw. Sam out-stared them with watering eyes and blew a perfect smoke-ring with her third puff.

Old Rolf accepted her with sudden capitulation. 'Yon Scot is a braw lass.'

'You've just been awarded a medal, Mac.' Mark downed his empty cup. 'Pardon me, I have something to discuss with Rolf. Back in a minute.' He gestured the old man into the shack.

Sam walked a short distance and noticed huddles of cattle grazing in various parts of the valley. They were in good condition and did not have that wild-eyed look of popular conception. Old Rolf must be a good, patient cattleman to get them in this placid state. It could almost be a meadow in Scotland.

Mark joined her, haversack slung across broad shoulders and her bag containing swim-gear and towel in his hand. 'Ready for a good long walk?'

She fell into step beside him, turning only to wave to the old man who stood watching them, pipe back in the hairy

168

jungle of his face.

'Your phenomenon still safe?' Curiosity was getting the better of her.

'Rolf assures me all is well.' The aggravating man was not going to reveal anything until he saw fit. Sam compelled herself to silence and tried to keep pace as Mark strode with the ease of active muscles.

Soon they entered a belt of scrub which gradually gave way to a thick growth of wattle. Mark stopped at last on the bank of a steep-sided shallow running stream.

'It's only a trickle along here, but deepens into occasional water-holes further on. Not as dry as I expected, it will hold until the Wet. No need to worry on that score, praise be.' Mark turned from his study of the billabong and looked at his companion. His eyes approved her short, elastic-sided, rubber-soled boots.

'You're learning fast, Mac. Now listen carefully. From here on we tread softly, not a twig must crack nor be there a sign of breathing. Follow me, put your feet in my spoor, do as I do and I hope to show you one of Australia's exclusive wonders.'

Sam's voice came in an excited whisper, 'Mark, you're frightening me. I'm so clumsy ... if we make a noise will It bite or charge us?'

'No such luck, chick, but we may not be given the chance to behold It, except in captivity. You're making me say too much. Follow me.' Mark started a crouching walk and Sam followed his every move, part of his shadow. The billabong made a long curve and they followed its contour behind the screen of low bush along its bank.

Mark suddenly went down on his knees and held up a hand, whispering over his shoulder, 'Softly now, inch along with me.' Sam glimpsed deeper water through the screen of tall grasses and crept behind him, not knowing what to expect.

He stopped finally and lat flat on his stomach, patting the place beside him. Sam sidled up and did likewise, her shoulder touching his. Very carefully the tall grass was parted until they could both see the opposite bank. Roots and submerged trunks were visible under the water. Mark nudged her shoulder.

And Samantha watched as two strange little creatures

169

came sliding down the bank to land with a plop in the water. They paddled with quick short strokes, moving their heads from side to side, and then waddled up the wet mudbank to repeat the playful performance. Not unlike seals, they played and nudged and slid with endless energy. The large one, evidently the male, was a good twenty-two inches in length including his wide flat tail or flipper.

Mark turned his head and smiled at her eager face. He asked a silent question. Sam put her mouth to his ear and whispered tentatively, 'Duckbills?'

'Mmm. Our very own "living fossils",' Mark mouthed back.

For nearly twenty minutes they lay side by side and Sam thrilled to the antics of the strange creatures. The feeling extended as the warmth of a hard brown arm brushed intimately against hers.

Finally Mark backed away and Sam followed him. They settled on a stump and he offered cigarettes. Not a home rolled one this time.

'Thanks very much for bringing me, Mark, I wouldn't have missed seeing this for anything. How long have they been here?'

'Some time now. Rolf and I discovered them when we were checking the water-holes. The bank is well screened from interference so the cattle don't worry them. Their burrow, dug in the bank and lined with wet grass, isn't visible from where we were positioned. Rolf tells me they've produced a family which are kept in the burrow, being too small, naked and blind to romp. The mother feeds them by ejecting milk through pores in her abdomen. These have travelled further south than usual. They have a talent, call it a sort of inbuilt radar, for finding water when they're driven from dried river beds and can travel across dry country for astonishing distances. The female lays eggs that have a leathery shell ... studies indicate that the platypus is a true mammal.'

'And they're exclusive to Australia?'

'Yes. They haven't survived in captivity when taken to other countries. Right, nature class over. A swim first to aggravate hunger pangs, there's another smashing hole further on.' Mark settled the haversack on his shoulders and walked off with long strides, Sam tagging in the rear.

170

They came to the chosen spot and Mark relieved himself of the haversack and handed Sam her holdall. 'There's coverage behind that jut of rock. I'm wearing my trunks under my pants.'

She emerged from cover, clad in a blue one-piece, to find Mark already swimming across the pool. The water glistened on his brown body as he swung up to sit on a half-submerged root. Blue eyes travelled casually over Sam's slim figure as he called, 'Don't chicken out now, it's not very cold.'

Sam stuck a tentative toe into the water. It *was* cold. She could feel the derision starting in the eyes watching her and with a determination that stemmed from embarrassment, lifted her arms to take a perfect swallow dive. She surfaced with a gasp of sheer exhilaration close to where Mark was seated, found an underwater root with her feet and stood on it while she shook the water off her face and hair.

'I should have warned you not to dive, Mac. There are too many roots and submerged tree trunks, it can be dangerous,' Mark said, and slid off his perch to join her. They swam together and when Sam opened her eyes under water she could see the roots and branches, and understood the hazards of deep diving. She saw Mark heading for her foot and shot out of his reach; they chased and played in the water almost in imitation of the happy duckbills.

Mark was the first to leave the water. He stretched on his stomach and elbows, smoking and watching Sam as she floated dreamily on her back. Dark hair falling wetly on his forehead released crystal drops that clung to thick lashes and when she floated near she could see that his watching eyes were almost a navy blue.

Samantha felt an uprush of love for the watcher, closed her eyes to conceal the naked, revealing truth she knew was there in the green depths and swam deeply while she fought to control her emotion.

When she came out she chose a spot in the sun to towel dry her hair. Mark rolled over, sat up and pulled his pack closer. He opened a foil-covered package of cucumber and chicken sandwiches, fresh ripe tomatoes, boiled eggs and a flask of hot black tea. Strong white teeth gleamed as he reminded Sam of the last picnic they had shared. 'Do you still

171

agree with Sheila that I resemble our friends up the billa-bong?'

Samantha combed back her hair and laughter bubbled. Everything was under control again. 'Aside from the leathery face and feet, the comparison ends. They're cute, which I can't say for you, and I would love to stroke those furry backs——' She stopped in confusion, for Mark had flung back his head and deep laughter echoed across the valley.

'Oh, for a seal-like back—are you quite positive there's not sufficient fluff on my back?' He twisted his shoulder and head and squinted at the visible portion. 'No, what bad luck. As you stated so positively, a leathery face and feet, and I certainly can't be called cute by any stretch of the imagina-tion!' His laughter turned to misery.

'Never mind, Markie boy, you have your—er—good points.'

'Such as——?' Blue eyes widened expectantly while he bit largely into a sandwich.

Samantha ad-libbed hastily, 'Y-your mouth matches your big appetite, your eyes pop out alarmingly and your ego is in good health—and that's my share you're eating!' She made a grab at a sandwich, his hand shot out and imprisoned her wrist.

'. . . And your temper is showing!'

Mark held her wrist and studied her through narrowed eyes. A warm tingle started up Sam's arm.

'As you say, I have my points. Never let it be said that I don't appreciate admiration.' He released her wrist and reached for the flask. 'Tea?'

Sam nodded and stuffed her mouth with chicken and bread, choosing the safest way to stop her tongue from blurt-ing out what she truly thought of him; a back that her hand was itching to stroke, arms and shoulders that could enfold one most delightfully, long legs that were moulded of hard brown wood, eyes that could drown . . . the list was endless.

Mark looked at her curiously. 'You sure eat a lot for such a slip of a girl.' His eyes dropped to her middle. 'And it doesn't even show. Your legs must be hollow, I guess.'

Samantha buried her face in the teacup, allowing her hair to fall forward, screening her eyes. She was learning the art of camouflage, but fast!

Mark was waiting when she came from her rock cover.

They started back and he took her hand at one stage to help her over a rough decline, retaining the slim fingers in his almost absentmindedly. Sam felt sheer bliss. Coupled with that night in Adelaide this was a day she would remember for a long time. Her storage was rich and her heart must not complain.

Rolf was awaiting, as restless as the horse he held by the reins. 'I be going to the foothills, some cleanskins gotta be brang in. Them two black men I sent out er gettin' raking lazy. Any orders?' Sun-wrinkled eyes circled Sam reflectively.

Mark scrutinised the horse carefully. 'I don't give you orders, old-timer, you know what I want. Keep those abos in line. I won't be back for some time. Anything happen, use your own judgement.'

'Yeah. Where you be goin'? Alone?' Sharp eyes left Sam and rested on the lean, rangy man.

'Here and there.' Mark caught the look that wavered from himself to Sam. 'Alone, if it's any of your business. This female is spoken for, so don't get ideas in that wicked jungle that you call your head.'

Rolf swung into the saddle. 'Ye jest be careful, Mark Lane, that's all I sez.' The warning came darkly. 'Giddy up, bag o' bones!'

Mark and Sam watched him ride off. 'The old man's one fear is that I'll be clutched by some raking female and be doomed for ever.'

'Doesn't he like females?'

'Evidently not. He regards them with deep suspicion, the spoilers of man, who become as putty in their soft hands and whose minds and bodily strength deteriorates rapidly thereafter.'

'Oh, the poor poor weaklings,' Sam laughed. 'He suspects your travelling motives. Give the old chap a shock, bring back a glamorous dame and——'

'For him or myself?'

'Well, perhaps that will fix him good and proper—bring two,' she retorted.

'Yes, well ... shall we make a move?' Mark stood, hands low on his hips while Sam settled into the Land-Rover. He moved before she could close the door, put a foot on to the footplate and leaned his elbows on a raised knee.

'Samantha, what are you plans? Do you still want to marry John?'

Sam flushed deeply at the sudden, unexpected question. 'That was and is still the arrangement.'

'Do you still—desire—this marriage?'

'Still desire?' Sam managed a shaky laugh. 'Why do you think I came all this way? Now that John is fit there's n-nothing to stop us——'

'Do you, Mac?' The question was repeated implacably.

Her head was turned away from piercing eyes when she answered. 'Yes.'

A minute of thick silence followed before Mark spoke again.

'What are your arrangements? Have you and John settled the final details? I would like to know before I leave.'

His question and statement were like a blow in her solar plexus. Mark was merely expected to be advised, in order to coincide his movements and return with their arrangements.

'John and I haven't finalised the date, if that's what you mean. We haven't discussed it——' Tears threatened suddenly and Samantha bent down and fiddled in the bag at her feet.

'Rather lax and remiss of you both. Okay, don't get upset, I'll speak to John when we get back.' Mark's foot came down and he straightened up.

Sam lifted her head. 'We'll be living in Adelaide by the time you come back.'

Mark stood stock still.

'That is, there's no need for you to hurry back for the —wedding. We can surely manage without you.' Why, oh, why did she have to say all this, manage to sound so ungracious when her heart was drowning in its own tears?

Mark walked round and slid behind the wheel, resting his arms across the steering. 'Is this your idea, to live in Adelaide?'

'No! Yes, I mean . . . where John goes, I go.'

He turned an intent blue stare. 'I see. Well, that settles matters, doesn't it? You seem mighty disinclined to have me attend the nuptials, but I'll have to disappoint you. I'll be there.'

He started the motor and pulled off with a jerk that was quite unlike his usual smooth handling. Samantha gazed out

174

of her window and wondered why he should be angry; objection to the marriage came a bit late after the lapse of time. It must be her statement that she and John would move to Adelaide. Mark Lane could not understand or tolerate a preference, in any of his family, for living away from the nest. They belonged there and that was that. Sam was convinced he believed her the instigator of their move to Adelaide.

Well, let him believe it; far better than letting him discover the true reason behind her easy acceptance of John's decision.

A hand rested on her knee. 'Cheer up, Mac. Don't let this spoil our day. Look back on it as "one fine day" when we shared a secret. Will you?'

'Our day.' Part of her was consoled at the thought that he had said 'our day, our secret'. It meant something to him too and he had chosen to take her with him, to share the pleasure of watching the 'living fossils' in their natural habitat.

Her hand went out, of it's own volition, to rest on his. 'Yes, Mark, and thank you, it has been a heavenly day.'

Mark turned his hand and their palms met briefly. '*Ciao*,' he said.

An interlude to be remembered.

CHAPTER 12

RAYS of late afternoon sun made a soft halo of the girl's hair as she stood on a swell of ground near the homestead. She could see, in the far distance, a march of trees which bordered Mark Lane's home. A house which, bereft of his presence, seemed cloaked in dreamy, unreal waiting. A casual farewell after a chat with John on his, Mark's, whereabouts in case of need, and he was gone.

Samantha had plunged into chores at the homestead and tackled the garden with a ferocity that aimed at covering chaotic thoughts and tiring her to the point of deadliness. The result was a bad bout of 'flu which left her weak, listless and unduly reluctant to pull herself together. Deep down was the suspicion that she was procrastinating, thereby pushing back the day when the marriage would become inescapable.

John was quite well now. Catalogues had come with the post illustrating shimmering wedding gowns and soon he would insist on a final date. There was nothing to stop further planning. He had been good to her, anxious when she was ill, worried about her pallor and listless demeanour. And becoming aware of a lack of response to his affectionate caresses, however, Samantha tried to respond. He blamed the strain she had undergone during his time in hospital and then being ill herself.

An inner integral honesty made it difficult for Samantha to show happy response when her heart was elsewhere. She could find no solace in the emptiness left by Mark's abrupt departure. Her love was not stilled by his absence and hurt beyond endurance. Therefore she found that deceiving John into thinking she was happy about the coming union was not as easy as she had hoped.

Sam walked back towards the house and saw John and Sheila, deep in conversation, on the veranda. John looked up and saw her approaching. He came down the steps to meet her and Sam's heart glowed with gratitude, as it did every time she watched him striding on legs that were firm and strong.

He linked his arm through hers. 'Sam dear, you shouldn't walk so far and alone, you're not very strong yet.' His puzzled glance took note of her lustreless eyes. 'Come and sit down, you're overdoing things. Have a nice bracing drink; I have some exciting news to impart.'

When they were seated John spoke to Sheila. 'Sam is far too pale, don't you think so, Sheil?'

Sheila studied her with a curious intentness that made Samantha feel exposed and vulnerable so she smiled at both of them with deceiving brightness. 'John is unduly worried. There's nothing wrong, but I did walk too far. Stupid of me. Mmm, this tastes good ... tell me the exciting news, John.'

He leaned forward, brimful with enthusiasm. 'My publishers received a letter inviting me to a tour of lectures, from the University. They request urgent confirmation. Me, what do you know!'

'That's wonderful, John. I didn't realise you were such a lion! When?'

'At my earliest convenience, they say, not to delay too long if I accept.'

'If you accept? But of course you'll accept, it's just too marvellous!' Sheila's enthusiasm matched his.

'That's for Sam to decide——'

'Good heavens, what a silly thing to say! Naturally you must go, John,' Samantha expostulated.

'Have you forgotten a little matter of a wedding? It may clash with this tour and I certainly can't expect you, or myself for that matter, to spend a honeymoon on a lecture tour.'

'No, I haven't forgotten.' Sam's voice came small and she infused more spirit as she continued, 'Perhaps, if they can't wait too long, we can cut our—honeymoon short, or wait until the tour ends before we get m-married?'

John looked at her with a mixture of vexation and amusement. 'Quite the eager beaver! Which is more important, a tour or a wedding? Don't prolong the agony!' he ended on a slightly sarcastic note.

Samantha's spirit and temper came to her aid. 'You said the letter was urgent, and you said lectures and honeymoons don't mix, and I know it will be an accolade for you. I wouldn't honestly want you to miss out, so why force the onus of decision on me? Either you go on your tour and we get married when you return, or we get married, you go on tour and we have the raking honeymoon when you get back, or we get married and go away after your tour!'

'Whoops! Figure that out, Mr. John raking Lane!' Sheila exploded delightedly.

John bestowed a disgusted look on both of them before he too exploded with laughter.

Sam stood up so suddenly that her chair fell backwards. 'I don't think it's so funny. You two laughing jackasses can work it out. John is definitely going on that tour, so work around, over and under that fact. I'll be around!'

Minutes later Sheila tried the handle of Sam's bedroom door, found it locked and knocked softly. Sam did not answer.

'Please, Sam, open the door. I'm awfully sorry and want to talk to you.'

Sam buried her face in the pillow. Just this once she would be obstinate and not allow anyone to push her around. Sheila did not speak again and Sam heard her walk away.

She came to the dinner table with a look that forbade any further discussion on certain subjects. John took one look at her, nd held his peace.

Later, Sam stood on the steps and watched the moon ride high in a galaxy of stars. John stepped beside her, put an arm around her waist and led her into the garden. Well, this was it, she thought.

'Well, Sam?' John moved behind her and encircled her waist.

'John?' Stiff lips whispered his name.

He nuzzled her ear. 'Don't be mad at me, Sam. I was excited about the letter and didn't think further than my nose. Let's forget that for the time being.' With a swift movement he turned and held her close. 'Do you remember saying at the hospital that you would be ready when I am? I am and have been for a long time. Shall we name the day?'

Perspiration beaded Samantha's forehead as he tilted her face and lowered his head. He kissed her, long and gently. She willed response and his kisses became more urgent. Involuntarily she stiffened.

John lifted his head. 'Relax, darling, don't be afraid. Keep on kissing me——'

Moments passed and John dropped his arms. 'Sam, you're wet with perspiration but you're cold. Are you still ill?'

'No, John—I can't—I'm being stupid.' Agony of mind underlaid her husky stammer.

John drew her down on to the garden bench, sat beside her and fondled her shoulders. 'I'll have to teach you not to be stupid, my love.' He smoothed her shoulders and neck, running his fingers through the shining hair. Sam sat impassively, but as his hands became more possessive, shivered suddenly, uncontrollably. With a groan, the man kissed her long and hard, with grim passion, then released her and walked away—to face her again.

'It's not going to work, is it, my dear Samantha?'

Samantha sat in frozen inability to give him the comfort he sought. She had been so sure that when the time came she would overcome her reluctance. And now, at his first definite approach, her resolutions had failed miserably.

'What's happened to us, Sam? There's something missing —have I changed since this damnable accident—or have you?'

'Forgive me, John. I-I think we're just out of tune t-tonight.' She pleaded while her heart clamoured, 'Damn you,

178

Mark Lane, for spoiling John's happiness—and mine!'

'Don't force yourself, girl. You haven't answered my questions. Leave it be, you look exhausted. You're not well yet and the little contretemps we had today probably had something to do with it. We'll settle things tomorrow.' Turning on his heel, John walked deeper into the darkness.

Undrawn curtains allowed full morning sunlight into the room. Samantha opened her eyes to find Mina setting a tray of tea on her bedside table. John filled the open doorway and rapped a knuckle lightly before walking in.

''Morning, Sam. You slept so late I was becoming concerned.'

'Good morning, John, is it very late?' Her eyelids felt heavy and her heart started a dull thud as he came closer. He did not attempt to kiss her, merely put his hand on her forehead as he sat down on the side of the bed.

'I asked Mina to bring fresh tea, the other was quite cold.'

Sam struggled to a sitting position and John handed her the cup, waiting for her to drink before he spoke again. 'Last night was a bit of a fiasco, wasn't it? Forgive the dramatics and uncalled-for sarcasm, darling. I was only too ready for you to fall into my arms and it came as a shock when you didn't do so.'

He made her feel quite awful again, being so nice, apologising when he had no need to. She was the one at fault.

'John, please, I deserved it. I feel bewildered—unsure——' she trailed off lamely.

'Never mind, I believe these things happen and girls get the jitters. You've been through a strain, and having to attend me personally all these weeks takes the glamour out of any alliance. The family constantly breathing down your neck——'

Samantha silently wrestled with her conscience. This deception must come to an end. How greatly would he be hurt if she told him the true reason for her behaviour; maybe his love was not so great that it would cause untold misery? If only she could look into the future; a deep clean cut was often the wisest course. John would respect her confidences and Mark need never know. Sam drew a deep breath, on the verge of opening her heart. Courage failed and dwindled as he forestalled her.

179

'I love you dearly, Sam, but you've been strangely aloof since I left the hospital. Can you deny that?'

'Have I, John? Perhaps you're right and your explanation of strain and the family is the answer.' Sam winged a silent apology to the family for her perfidy. 'Will you be patient just a little longer?' she pleaded appealingly.

John studied her face gravely and then a rueful grin crossed his face. 'Patience is becoming a standard word in our vocabulary! Right, we'll leave matters to right themselves. I'm now going to attempt my first ride on horseback, come and view the scene.' He patted her shoulder and walked out.

While Samantha was dressing, a sudden onslaught of sheer longing and homesickness almost overwhelmed her. Oh, to put back the clock, to find herself back in the beloved cottage in Scotland, untroubled and heart-free!

And then . . . a night came when John spoke with finality in his voice and acceptance in his eyes.

'Don't look so ashamed, Sam. At least you're not pretending to a love you don't have. You've tried hard for my sake, but your integrity of soul will not permit further deception. Shall we just say—*Che sarà sarà?*'

Tears started in Samantha's eyes at his matter-of-fact acceptance. John sat down on the swing beside her and wiped her eyes. 'No tears now, love, I'll get by. Don't be so agonisingly sorry for something beyond your control. You weren't to know that what you took for love was affection, and perhaps a deep yearning for family life. Sam, stay here and let me go on this tour. That way, apart, we may gain a new perspective, and when I come back things might just—be right again.'

She simply could not let him leave without being honest. It was not fair to let him go with that flicker of hope, that things would be right again. She must make the clean break, now. With one reservation; John would never hear from her lips of the hopeless love she had for his cousin.

'—So you do see, John dear, I can't go on staying here indefinitely.' Samantha thought of Mark's eventual return. 'I've loved every minute of my stay here. The f-family, as you've rightly guessed, have filled that yearning wish of mine and I'm going to miss them and you m-most dreadfully——' She stopped as the enormity of her coming loss impacted.

She must take leave of everyone she had come to love ...
darling Mame, who had filled the breach for Mary-Gran ...
Mandy, the sister she would never have ... the others, who
had taken her to their hearts ... and John himself. She was
hurting him, but he remained loving, understanding, she
would always feel that she had tossed away with careless
hands, something of precious value. '—But I must go. I have
my little place still and there's always auxiliary work for me,
at the hospital.'

Momentary pain rasped John's voice as he took a firm
hold of Sam's hands. 'Oh, Sam, don't look so hopeless. Do
you think we're not going to miss you? But if that's your
wish, so be it. The family aren't going to let you go so easily.
You are one of us, and even if it's not in the capacity I, or
they, would have, this will always be your home. The welcome will be warm and sincere if you ever—visit—which I
feel you will, one day.' He sat back in a silence that extended
painfully, then reached certain conclusions and continued
firmly, 'I'll inform them that I'm going on tour alone, and
will see about a flat in Adelaide, which will be perfectly true
as I intend staying there anyway. We can then break the news
gradually, depending on the length of this tour. Please, Sam,
stay here; don't do anything rash, I implore you. I'll think
of a way out. Don't let this—situation—chase you away.'

Samantha put her cheek against his hand and said simply
and sincerely, 'Thank you, John Lane, for your understanding heart and everything you've said. I'll do exactly as you
say, and wait for your decision. Just one request ... p-please
don't let—Mark know.'

John smiled and brushed her cheek with his hand. 'Still
afraid of the eagle?'

'Slightly.' Samantha returned his smile.

She dismounted in the shade of the tree and waited for the
other rider who was coming up fast. Sheila drew rein and
slid off expertly.

'Phew! that was quite a gallop! Reminds me of another
day——' The dark-haired girl took off her hat and fanned
her face. 'Sam, I followed you because I want to speak to
you, and you're going to listen whether you like it or not!'

'All right, Sheila, let's sit on this stump and speak away.
You remind me of a belligerent little bantam.' Sam looked

curiously at her companion, who seemed to have joined her for a definite purpose. She was right.

'You're so elusive lately and I made up my mind to track you down today. Samantha MacDonald, why did you allow John to go away alone? Why didn't you go with him?'

'I can't see that that's any of your business——'

'I'm making it my business!' Sheila retorted, ignoring Sam's stiffening back. 'He loves you and needs you——'

'Not any more,' Sam interposed steadily.

Sheila looked at her in amazement. 'Are you crazy? Of course he does. You're his girl and your place is at his side.' She studied Sam's face and her voice dropped to a whisper. 'You're not—you don't mean——'

'I'm not his girl any more.'

Sheila's shock showed. 'But why? I don't understand. John was looking forward to the day, loving you so much. What happened?'

'He helped me find the courage to tell him I no longer loved him.'

Sheila digested this in astonishment. 'I-I can't believe it! How did he take it?'

'The only way a fine man like John would take it ... wonderfully well.' Sam dropped her eyes, to hide sudden agony in their green depths from the intent brown stare.

A hand covered hers. 'Sam, what's eating you? You've changed—would you care to talk about it? Helps, you know, sometimes.'

An intense longing to confide in someone shook the girl. Not the family, they were too close to both John and Mark. Sheila's love for John would cloud her mind to a certain extent, but she would listen objectively and Sam trusted her. No one could give her advice, there was none to give, but oh, just to spill her overflowing heart, knowing it would remain in confidence ... Samantha raised her head.

'Sheila, I've let John down most shamefully. When the time came to show my love, it wasn't there any more. I couldn't even pretend successfully, however much I intended to.' Sam took a painful breath. 'He was wonderful about everything, so understanding. I couldn't carry on with the deception. It was physically impossible when I—love someone else——'

'Mark.' The name dropped softly, not questioningly, a

182

statement of instinctive knowledge.

Samantha spoke then of the compelling attraction, her efforts to fight what she thought to be weakness and infatuation. Not sparing herself, of the day when a plane had made a forced landing and the revelation of a love that followed. Told of her resolution not to hurt John and then her body and mind's refusal to co-operate with that resolution.

And now she and John had parted in mutual agreement. He did not know about Mark, she could not let the hurt bite deeper. And her own hunger for Mark tearing at her heart . . .

'I guess my faith, my bough was not green enough . . . not for me a singing bird,' Samantha whispered painfully.

Sheila broke the long silence. 'Sam, do you really think John would be awfully hurt, if he knew about Mark?'

Samantha opened her eyes. 'How can I tell? Could I take that risk? Would you? At present his letters are cheerful and enthusiastic about his tour. I'm not going to throw another brick at his head, let it remain so.' She eased her seat. 'I'll soon be gone, then it won't matter.'

'Does Mark know of your feelings towards him?'

'The good Lord forbid!' Samantha's eyes widened. 'Can you imagine the taunting mockery—I'd rather die than court that danger!' The sheer thought made her dizzy with apprehension.

'Don't, Sam, don't look like that, it frightens me!' Sheila took a pack of cigarettes out of her pocket, lighted two and passed one to Samantha.

She smoked thoughtfully for a few minutes, then asked almost timorously, 'Sam, it won't hurt, then, if John turns to—someone else?'

'John?' Sam searched her face. 'Meaning yourself?'

'Yes, meaning myself.'

'Sheila dear, I would be sincerely happy if he could find the love he deserves. And it would lighten the load of guilt on my shoulders.'

'You really mean that?'

Sam nodded and the other girl straightened her shoulders. 'Well then, I'm going to track him down . . . he needs a secretary, doesn't he? I love him enough to go for second place—that is, if he'll have me.'

The simplicity of her statement moved Sam deeply. 'You

already have a place in his heart, my dear.'

Sheila was entranced at the prospect, but her face fell as she remarked, 'He'll come back again, and when he sees you——'

'I have every intention of going back to Scotland, and rest assured I can never go back to our former way. I can't change the way I feel. I must go, Sheila—Mark will come back.'

'Sam, I'm selfish, thinking only of John and myself.' Sheila was earnestly contrite.

'John insists that I stay longer. I can't, I can't, I've got to go!' Tears came at last and Sheila held out compassionate arms.

'—I have relinquished all thought of a future with you. It was not to be, could be the accident was fate's warning, drastic though it seems. My greatest memory will be of your wonderful faith which I believe was the mainspring of my recovery. Thank you for that. My home is yours for as long as you wish. Sheila has been a great help and godsend, in more ways than one. A rather cryptic message from her to you. I quote, "Battery very flat but working on same."??? The flat is very convenient, but may I be contrary and say, I miss you hovering over me like my good angel. Don't ever be constrained or embarrassed when and if we meet again. Remember I am also a friend. Mame is probably furious, but she will accept conditions. Don't desert her until Mark or I come home.'

Samantha raised her eyes from John's letter and found Mame watching her across the table. She too held a letter in shaking hands, obviously from the same source. They locked glances in silence and the love in the older woman's eyes reached Sam as if in warm embrace.

Repetition of John's own declaration fell softly from Mame's lips. *'Che sarà sarà.'*

'Now you know, Mame. Please believe me, I tried very hard,' Sam pleaded.

'Don't be blaming yourself, lass, it had to be. I know how you feel about Mark. Love can't be trampled upon. You're not going to leave us, Sam? John writes——'

'Mame, please! It tears at my heart, but I must go. How can I stay here, and face Mark's scorn when he hears of our—break-up? Loving him, being so close to him—no, I can't bear it. Cowardly maybe ... but let me go, darling Mame, let me go before he returns. One day I'll come back, when everything isn't so ... raw.'

'But Mark is fond of you too, Sam dear.'

'That's as maybe. I don't want him to be sorry for me, forcing me to stay simply because he'll feel, in an autocratic way, responsible. After all, let's face it, I'm not family and not exactly destitute, so there's no need for any mistaken sense of responsibility. Has he ... have you heard from him?'

'Yes, he won't be back for some time. John was supposed to let him know of your plans. I don't know now——'

'Is he well and happy?' Sam could not hide a yearning note.

'Yes, dear, I think so. Would you like to read his letter?'

'No!' Samantha lowered her voice. 'No, thanks, Mame.'

The days marched relentlessly, inexorably. Sam's booking to Scotland was confirmed. Soon she would be leaving ... leaving everything she had come to love so dearly.

A sudden, inexplicable malady struck at Mame, she took to her bed and complained bitterly of pains in her body. She was not a body who took to her bed at the slightest twitch of pain, and it happened at an awkward time, for Mandy was away visiting her children. So it was left to Sam to run the home while Allan coped with outside chores. Mame called constantly and Sam was really worried. Stephen was away as well—the family seemed to have disappeared in different directions.

Sam managed to contact Luke on the transceiver and he promised to come as soon as possible, advising her to keep the patient in bed. Sam was desperate with anxiety by the time she heard the plane in the late afternoon.

'Oh, Luke, thank goodness you've come at last! I can't understand what's the matter with Mame, she has pains which seem to travel from one limb to another. Her appetite's not too good, there's no fever——'

Mame would not allow Sam to remain in the room while Luke examined her, mumbling that it embarrassed her to have anyone watching. For all her concern Sam felt her mouth twitch at this, for she had attended the old lady constantly. Still, some elderly persons were like that when a third person looked on.

Luke came out, the slight twist to his lips cut short when he found Sam waiting outside the bedroom door, anxiety making her tense.

'Nothing radically wrong, Sam. Her heart is good, the old bones playing up a bit, a touch of 'flu——'

'But there's no fever, Luke, and her limbs move so spasmodically. You don't think it's poli——' She could not say the dreaded word.

'Samantha my dear! It's a damned shame—of course it's not that.' Luke put his arm around the shaking slender shoulders, and cursed under his breath at the devious ways of a certain old woman. 'Please don't worry, she just needs you and feels the shock of your imminent departure. Could you possibly postpone it for another week or so?'

Sam looked at him doubtfully. 'My bookings are confirmed, but if it can be arranged—I guess I can't leave right now.'

'I can arrange it for you, Sam, for a later date.'

'Thanks.' She was still puzzled. 'I'm not questioning your diagnosis, Luke, but the cases of shock plus 'flu that I've attended haven't reacted the way she does. Mame isn't one to take to her bed so easily——'

Luke spoke firmly. 'I'm a doctor, honey, rest assured everything, but everything will be all right if you'll just keep things running until Mandy comes back. I'll contact her as soon as possible. Let's hit the bottle, you and I, and we can send one in for Mame—she needs it badly.'

'No. I'm going against that order, Doctor. I feel quite sure a drink will only excite further pains.'

Luke laughed with sudden malicious glee. 'Oh, you lovely nursie you! If you say so, let her suffer a bit——' He steered Sam into the sitting-room. 'Now let's see, I know where the makings are—what will you have?'

Sam told him and added, 'How come you're on your own? Where's Tommy?'

Luke Mannering squared his shoulders. 'You see before you a man who has at last cashed in on a dream. My own plane. A fully-fledged pilot and Flying Doctor, at your service. Let's celebrate!'

Sam congratulated him, then asked, 'Have—have you seen John at all?'

Luke regarded her gravely. 'I have, my dear, and you're not to worry about him. I know everything and feel quite certain that he's facing it squarely and, given time, will get over it. Sheila spoke to me. She's a determined young woman and will succeed in her mission.'

One week later, Samantha again stood on the rise and a silent goodbye winged from her heart to the wavering outline of trees and mountain.

A dust cloud in the middle distance drew her attention—Stephen, back from his visit to Fiona's people. Soon there would be a wedding in the family, but she would not be attending. Maybe another; she thought of Sheila's letter. That girl was not wasting time; according to her it might be rebound on John's part, but he was turning to her more and more; the future looked promising.

A yearning impulse sent Samantha to the stables, to saddle Champagne and ride in the direction of hazy blue hills. Just one more painful pilgrimage to the place where gentle hands had comforted her, a voice had whispered gentle endearments. A long time ago . . .

Sam dismounted and walked slowly until she reached the stream. Yes, there was the rock where he had sat and cradled her in his arms. He had said, 'You're safe . . . Have you fallen from heaven, angel?' How well she remembered the gentle, tender voice!

Samantha sank down and her eyes burned with unshed tears.

Champagne whinnied and she looked at him affectionately. 'Darling horse, I accept your apology for spilling me . . . but what about the other things you started that day?'

The stream drew her gaze for a long time. The horse whinnied again and the loved face in the water rippled and became blurred as a shadow intruded.

'Samantha?'

Madness started this way, to hear voices, to see familiar long legs approaching relentlessly.

Mark lowered his body and rested on his heels. Blue eyes, on a level with hers, probed deeply.

'Mac, does it hurt so very much? How can I help you to bear this pain?' His deep, familiar voice was husky with tenderness.

Shock at his sudden appearance held Sam mute. She was drowning in blue, in cobalt pools of compassion, that held no mockery whatsoever.

'Why did John do this to you—why?' A smoky haze obscured the blue pools.

'Pain—hurt—John?' His meaning penetrated her senses and she spoke softly. 'You have it all wrong, Mark. John never caused hurt or pain. I did. We were—not suited.'

'Not suited? But you loved each other ... what about the misery in your eyes, right now?'

His nearness was overpowering. Sam made an effort to move away, but Mark gripped her hands and he was infinitely gentle. 'Don't run away, Mac. It's easy to mend broken heads, but hot water bottles and such can't mend broken hearts. Be truthful, trust me ... I do so want to help take that look out of your lovely eyes.'

'I am being truthful. I found the—my love was not great enough to l-live with John.' It was of extreme importance that Mark should not blame his cousin, marring the strong affection they had for each other.

'It was you, then, who put finis to your future?' Flames flared deep in the eyes watching her.

Samantha lifted her head proudly. 'It was I who started it. Call it rebellion, if you like, of body and spirit when love is absent.'

'You love—someone else?'

Desperation gave her strength and Sam stood up, her back to Mark. 'Just because I'm not in love with John it doesn't mean that I love elsewhere!'

'And you were running away before I could return. How badly have you hurt John?' The question came with relentless purpose.

'John understood and was—kind to me. Sheila is already consoling him in his not so great loss. If Mame hadn't been ill, I—I wouldn't be here now.'

Mark said drily, 'If Mame hadn't feigned illness I would have been too—late. She sent a message, that you were leaving, that your engagement to John was broken, and that was all. When I confronted her, she wouldn't speak, only to tell me where I would find you.'

Sam whirled in amazement. 'I felt there was something phoney about her illness, and Luke took it far too lightly.

Mame Lane was deliberately holding me back!'

'Oh yes, love. Just stop and think how troublesome it would have been for me, chasing across continents for a chance——'

Sam's small fists clenched. 'A chance to throw mockery and taunts at my still unwedded state? Indeed, would you travel that far?'

'—A chance to speak of my feelings. Mame has always known, that's why she delayed you. Not to mock or taunt, Samantha, you do have a low opinion of me, but to plead for a love that came to me the very day we met, right here. A love that was not to be, that was hopeless right from the start. Because you belonged to the one man I couldn't fight. You're heart-free now, so this is where I start fighting, and hope to claim what I know can be mine——'

His voice trailed, for Samantha was looking at him, and there was no longer concealment in her eyes. For long moments blue and green were locked, and certain transcending knowledge came into its own. Power was given to see, and to know. Tawny flames in green matched the flare of blue.

Mark held out his arms. 'Come here, Samantha Mac-Donald.'

Joyous welcome throbbed and echoed in her heart as she went into his arms.

'Mac of my heart . . .' Love was a husky voice.

'I love you too, now and for ever.' Happiness was her soft reply.

'I wanted to run away from you, my darling,' Sam whispered presently.

Mark looked into her eyes and caught his breath at the light in their green, sun-spotted depths. 'For that I'll surely punish you, Mac!' He lowered his head . . .

The bird above them trillingly accompanied the litany of song that rose to a sweet crescendo and the sun shone down unchanging, eternal as the flame in their hearts.

Have You Missed Any of These
Harlequin Romances?

BP 372

GOLDEN HARLEQUIN LIBRARY — $1.75 each volume

Special Introductory Offer
(First 6 volumes only $8.75)

□ **VOLUME I**
692 THE ONLY CHARITY, Sara Seale
785 THE SURGEON'S MARRIAGE
    Kathryn Blair
806 THE GOLDEN PEAKS
    Eleanor Farnes

□ **VOLUME II**
649 KATE OF OUTPATIENTS
    Elizabeth Gilzean
774 HEATHERLEIGH, Essie Summers
853 SUGAR ISLAND, Jean S. Macleod

□ **VOLUME III**
506 QUEEN'S COUNSEL, Alex Stuart
760 FAIR HORIZON, Rosalind Brett
801 DESERT NURSE, Jane Arbor

□ **VOLUME IV**
501 DO SOMETHING DANGEROUS
    Elizabeth Hoy
816 THE YOUNGEST BRIDESMAID
    Sara Seale
875 DOCTOR DAVID ADVISES
    Hilary Wilde

□ **VOLUME V**
721 SHIP'S SURGEON, Celine Conway
862 MOON OVER THE ALPS
    Essie Summers
887 LAKE OF SHADOWS, Jane Arbor

□ **VOLUME VI**
644 NEVER TO LOVE, Anne Weale
650 THE GOLDEN ROSE, Kathryn Blair
814 A LONG WAY FROM HOME
    Jane Fraser

Just Published
($1.75 per volume)

□ **VOLUME XIX**
705 THE LAST OF THE LOGANS
    Alex Stuart
740 NURSE ON HOLIDAY
    Rosalind Brett
789 COUNTRY OF THE HEART
    Catherine Airlie

□ **VOLUME XX**
594 DOCTOR SARA COMES HOME
    Elizabeth Houghton
603 ACROSS THE COUNTER
    Mary Burchell
736 THE TALL PINES, Celine Conway

□ **VOLUME XXI**
716 THE DOCTOR'S DAUGHTERS
    Anne Weale
792 GATES OF DAWN, Susan Barrie
808 THE GIRL AT SNOWY RIVER
    Joyce Dingwell

□ **VOLUME XXII**
524 QUEEN'S NURSE, Jane Arbor
725 THE SONG AND THE SEA
    Isobel Chace
791 CITY OF PALMS, Pamela Kent

□ **VOLUME XXIII**
742 COME BLOSSOM-TIME, MY LOV
    Essie Summers
778 A CASE IN THE ALPS
    Margaret Baumann
848 THE KEEPER'S HOUSE
    Jane Fraser

□ **VOLUME XXIV**
560 WINTERSBRIDE, Sara Seale
592 MARRIAGE COMPROMISE
    Margaret Malcolm
700 TAMARISK BAY, Kathryn Blair

To: Harlequin Reader Service, Dept. G.
    M.P.O. Box 707, Niagara Falls, N.Y. 14302
    Canadian address: Stratford, Ont., Canada

□ Please send me complete listing of the 24 Golden Harlequin
    Library Volumes.

□ Please send me the Golden Harlequin Library editions I
    have indicated above.

I enclose $_____ (No C.O.D.'s) To help defray postage
and handling costs, please add 50c.

Name _____

Address _____

City/Town _____

State/Province _____ Zip_____

H